THE ROGUE TO RUIN

ROGUES OF ST. JUST • BOOK ONE

CHARLOTTE HENRY

Moonshell
Books

Art by Carpe Librum Book Design. Images from Period Images, used under license.

Edited by Write Away Editorial.

The Rogue to Ruin / Charlotte Henry—1st ed.

ISBN 978-1-939087-89-8

www.charlotte-henry.com

❋ Created with Vellum

IN THIS SERIES

ROGUES OF ST. JUST

The Rogue to Ruin
The Rogue Not Taken
One for the Rogue

INTRODUCTION

THE ROGUE TO RUIN

He is a penniless baronet. She is the wealthy great-granddaughter of a tradesman. Can these childhood friends find their way back to each other when scandal strikes them both?

Sir Perran Geoffrey needs a wealthy bride to repair his family estate and to bring his sister out in Society. But what woman with money and standing will accept him as a husband—practically penniless, his title under a cloud thanks to his ne'er-do-well father, with an estate far away in Cornwall?

Alwyn Penrose and her two sisters are in London for their first Season. Imagine their surprise when they meet the heirs of the neighboring estates—gentlemen whom they are barely allowed to acknowledge. For to be seen with the Rogues of St. Just means the death of one's reputation.

Except that Alwyn is seen. More than once. And the gossip spreads all the way to the sacred portals of Almack's, which close in her face and end her hopes for a good marriage forever.

The ruin of her Season is Perran Geoffrey's fault. And when they are both forced to return to Cornwall, only one thing is clear: One good ruination deserves another.

The Rogues of St. Just. They may be the most shocking men in Mayfair, but their hearts are all too vulnerable at home.

For Bella Andre and Nancy Warren
with thanks for a walk along the Thames
and
with gratitude to those who helped bring this book into the world:
Jeff Bates
Timons Esaias
Kat Munro Glass
Troon Harrison
KC Montgomery
Leslie Peterson
Regina Scott
Sandy Sliger

THE ROGUE TO RUIN

CHAPTER 1

Cornwall, England

Alwyn Penrose's heartbeat picked up its pace as she drove her low phaeton through the main square of the village of St. Just, on the south coast of Cornwall. Her pair of ponies were good-natured and tended to plumpness, so she had determined to give them some exercise on this beautiful September day before the storm threatening on the horizon rolled in.

The left ankle of Mrs. Menabilly, their housekeeper at Morvoren Manor, was as good as any ship's barometer when it came to storms, and it had predicted a blow before nightfall.

"Good afternoon, Miss Penrose." From the doorway of her millinery shop, Mrs. Penfrey waved. The ribbons she held fluttered in the air as she knotted them on a string to attract a feminine buyer's attention.

"Good afternoon, Mrs. Penfrey," Alwyn said as she steered her equipage past her. "I hope your boy's health is improving?"

"Indeed he is. Please give Miss Rowena my thanks for the potion."

"She will be so pleased."

In the middle of the square was a bed of flowers in full bloom. The town pump lay on one end of it, and a Cornish cross stood on the other, marking the crossroads. Besides the millinery shop on the west side, one could find nearly everything one needed—the draper, the dressmaker, the butcher. The White Swan hostelry, owned by Mr. Tomgallon; the blacksmith's shop next to it, the sound of blows upon iron ringing in the air; and behind that, the cartwright.

Alwyn made the turn into Water Street, which, along with the runnel that chuckled along in its channel next to the road, included the new bookshop that had only been open since the spring.

Not far now.

Beside her, on the seat, was her portfolio of watercolor sketches—sketches into which she'd put her very best efforts and hopes. Now it only remained to be seen if they were good enough.

The ponies started and sidled to the left, jerking her attention back to the business in hand. "Oh, goodness. Not again!"

Mrs. Tomgallon's turkeys had got out of their yard, and were ranged across the road in a moving brown mass, pecking and pulling up the grass gone to seed on the verges. On the far side of the host, a wagon had been pulled up, and the farmer looked as though he wasn't sure whether to shout at them, or shoot them.

The latter must be prevented.

Alwyn knotted the reins and alighted, using her skirts as a kind of warning flag to change the birds' direction. She had plenty of practice with the hens at home—poultry was poultry, and the turkeys were the pride of Mrs. Tomgallon's heart and were not to be hurt. Since her husband—brother of the innkeeper—had passed away, and her children had both moved to Truro to find work, she treated her turkeys as tenderly as any mother.

"Shoo, my dears. Shoo! In you go."

Alwyn got them all turned around and heading back through their own gate, which was a puzzle, for it was still latched. One straggler picked her way down Water Street, but Alwyn did not have the time to round her up. After she climbed into the phaeton, the farmer set his wagon in motion, and the errant bird flew to the top of a stone wall, wittering with anxiety until it could soar down to join its flock.

Ah, so that was the trouble. The turkeys had discovered they could fly!

Smiling, Alwyn nodded to the farmer and shook the reins over the ponies' backs to continue on her way.

A few minutes later, she pulled up in front of the Royal Morvoren pottery, one of the three parts of the Morvoren China Clay Company on which, like a three-legged stool, her family's fortunes rested. She must sit for a moment, to calm herself before she went in. It would not do to be flustered and gasping from chasing turkeys.

Or from chasing dreams.

She must be calm. Gracious. Self-possessed. She must be Miss Penrose of Morvoren Manor.

When her great-grandfather August Penrose had discovered the banks of china clay near St. Austell, he had known deep in his bones that the English nobility, who until now had imported their porcelain from China and France at great expense, would be delighted to buy English porcelain at a price far less dear. And so they had. Canny Cornishman that he was, he had quietly bought up the land and established the pit that now employed hundreds of men to dig the fine white clay out of the ground, to operate the mighty steam engines that kept the pit from flooding, and to load the wagons with crates of clay for export.

Her grandfather, in his turn, had built this pottery at the end of Water Street to rival those of Mr. Wedgewood or Josiah Spode. It was housed in this elegant stone building, with a showing room in the front designed to look like the tearooms of Bath, so that a gentleman or lady might see a dinner service laid out at its best, complete with linen, cutlery, and flowers. The day the royal warrant had been bestowed upon the pottery, giving them the right to call their china Royal Morvoren, had been the proudest of her grandfather's life.

Not to be outdone, Papa had built docks in the deep Morvoren harbor, so that ships could come to them directly. He commissioned ships, too, to sail the Baltic and the Atlantic, with either raw clay or finished china safe in their holds.

And then had come the accident.

Papa had been such a horseman as the parish had never seen. But even he and his beautiful hunter Neptune had been no match for the carriage that had burst out of a lane at speed, with not so much as a shout of warning. Driven by a man from Bristol who had been viewing Trevenna—a stranger who did not know the roads and lanes and who had been inexplicably terrified into flight—the collision had been awful.

Neptune had juked—reared—and Papa had been thrown.

A broken shin bone and a chipped elbow were the result, as well as a blow to the head so severe that the doctor had shaken his own head and advised the Penrose family to prepare themselves.

But Papa was a strong man, and he had survived. Even now, though he still kept to his bed while the bones slowly healed, he left no one in doubt regarding who owned the controlling interest in the company.

Papa did not know she was here.

And she would not tell him—not until she could return home, flushed with success.

"Miss Penrose!" Mr. Enyon Lander, the manager of the pottery, appeared at the side of the phaeton to hand her down. "Why did no one tell me you were coming?"

She picked up her portfolio while he tied the ponies to the rail. "Because I did not wish to come in state. However, Mr. Lander, you are the very man I was hoping to see."

The anxious wrinkles in his forehead eased. "Please, miss, come in, and tell me how I may be of service."

In his comfortable office, with its wool carpet and rich blue draperies, he ordered tea served, "In the *Alwyn* pattern, mind, in honor of our guest." Then he invited her to sit with him at the round tea table before the fire, not in one of the chairs in front of his desk.

He was a man of middle age, his skin dark as though it had been stained with walnut juice, and an air of elegance though she knew he had come up through the ranks at the pit. It served him well here at the pottery, where a customer might arrive in a coach and four and expect a man of grave mien and infinite knowledge of porcelain. They found both in Mr. Lander.

"Have you a message for me from Mr. Penrose, miss? How fares he? Has there been any improvement?"

"His mind is clear, and he has been able to sit up to eat without the dizziness that has plagued him."

Mr. Lander's face brightened. "That is good news. When will the doctor let him up?"

Alwyn shook her head. "It is too soon for that. Doctor Harris fears that if he stirs outside the sickroom, he will catch an infectious fever. And with the injury to the head, we dare not permit him to attempt it. You may imagine how that information was received."

"Ah." Mr. Lander smiled sadly, as though he were picturing his vigorous employer reduced to such a state. "We are fortunate that Doctor Harris has seen so many broken bones, and is skilled in setting them. The war cost the country much, but in our small corner, we count our blessings to have the benefit of a naval surgeon to tend us."

"And thanks to Doctor Harris, we have every hope for my father's complete recovery." She made her tone bracing, if only to shore up her own feelings.

The tea arrived, and he invited her to pour. "Which is what has brought me here, Mr. Lander," she said, handing him a cup with its blue-gray frieze, its color mixed specifically to match her eyes. "I wish to be useful. My father has shared his correspondence with me since his accident, and allows me to act for him to some degree. I saw your letter about the departure of Mr. Cormoran for Exeter. I wonder if you might consider some of *my* designs for glazing while you seek a replacement for him."

His shock was so great that he nearly spilled his tea. "Your designs, miss!"

"Yes." She opened her portfolio and spread out her water-colors. "I understand that Egyptian decoration is still very popular in London. On this plate you can see how I have used the lotus flower and crossed flails in an alternating pattern in the border." She slid another piece of cold-pressed paper in front of him. "This one celebrates the wedding of Princess Charlotte, with a wide border—in silver and gray, of course—bringing to mind the scallops and flowers embroidered on her wedding gown. And on this one I have—"

She looked up to see the answer already written in his face, in his distressed brown eyes. "Oh, no, miss. I beg your pardon, but this would not be fitting at all."

She had known this would be his answer, and had prepared herself to run out the guns. "Why not, pray?"

"Because, if you will pardon my saying so, you are a woman!"

"Yes, I had made that observation some time since, Mr. Lander. What might that have to do with art?"

"It is not fitting that Miss Penrose of Morvoren Manor should have clay dust upon her hands."

"Mr. Lander, you know perfectly well that is nonsense. I have been coming here with Papa since I was a little girl. And painting designs for others to glaze is a far cry from digging clay in the pit."

"The designers and glazers would not take it well."

"But painting is perfectly acceptable in the drawing room, is it not? Do you not think me capable?"

"No one would ever say you were not capable, miss. These paintings are well rendered, the designs fine and original. It just isn't fitting that you should be seen in any proximity whatever to trade. Does Mr. Penrose know you are speaking to me?"

And therein lay the single tiny flaw in her plan. "No. I would not trouble him with this." In her heart of hearts she knew it would distress Papa to no end if he got wind of her forward behavior.

But goodness, someone had to address the fact that the pottery's designs must be *au courant.* Their orders could not be allowed to slow. Why should not she, the eldest daughter of the family, be that person?

"Oh, miss, he'd be as teasy as an adder if he knew you were even here, let alone what you propose. No," Mr. Lander said, shaking his head, "you must finish your tea and we will say no more about it."

"But—"

"We appreciate both your interest and your talent, Miss Penrose," he said gently. "Both do you great credit. But you must see that it is not right for Mr. Penrose's daughter to be here, aping the behavior of craftsmen, no matter how ably."

He rose and offered her his arm with great courtesy, as though that clinched the matter, and saw her out.

Alwyn drove home in something of a pet, which meant she made excellent time. The broad driving road took her over windswept hill and into sheltered, tree-filled dell, the contours of which she'd known all her life. And soon, the very hedges and slopes of her home parish of St. Just acted as a balm to her smarting spirits.

On the right, set back in trees and gardens, was Gwennel Cottage, home of the Teagues. Both father and son had served in His Majesty's navy, helping to put Boney in his place once and for all. But they no longer lived there, and the house was shut up.

Farther on, cupped in a little valley full of oaks and pines, was Minear Park, named for the *menhirs*, the standing stones the locals called the Lorn Ladies, which stood in one of its chases. It was home to the Tremayne family and empty of its young folk now. They had gone away to school and to London, and goodness knew when any of them would return. Or if they would.

In the distance, commanding a broad, windswept prospect, was the warm Georgian front of Trevenna. There were rumors that it had been sold, but no one knew who the new owners might be. Certainly not the driver of the carriage that had come tearing out of there and caused Papa's accident. The house had been closed up for years. The housekeeper was said to go in only to clean, and that under protest, because of the ghosts.

Approaching on her left was Rosevear Court, an old Tudor brick place shaped like an *E* for Elizabeth, where once a boy had lived who had swum in the sea with her. Who had kissed her—and been knocked off his feet both by an incoming wave and by her own hand, so shocked had she been.

Here were great houses of old families ... and nearly all as good as empty. How could they leave Cornwall, surely one of the most beautiful counties God had had the pleasure to make? Why did people go to places like London and Bath, and never return? But since she did not correspond with any of them, and only saw Lady Geoffrey and Miss Isolde of Rosevear at church of a Sunday, she had no answers to such questions.

She pulled up the ponies in the gravel sweep in front of

Morvoren Manor, which in her opinion was both modern and snug, with its graceful Palladian lines and warm, cream-colored stone. Her grandfather had pulled down the low farmhouse that had stood here since the days of the Plantagenets, and built the manor from the proceeds of the clay pit. He had been an ambitious man, leaving a house to his son that possessed two drawing rooms, six bedrooms, and a kitchen that had been a marvel of modernity at the time.

Alwyn loved it with all her heart.

She descended to the gravel, and after the groom had driven the equipage away to the carriage house, she went in search of a sympathetic ear. Not within the confines of the house, that was certain, for Papa would be sure to hear voices from his sickroom, which had been the small study on the ground floor before it had been commandeered for his recovery. She put off her spencer and visiting bonnet, and put on an apron hanging in the kitchen passage. A few minutes later she found Rowena in the kitchen garden, pulling weeds out of her herb beds.

"There you are," her youngest sister said, sitting back on her heels and peering up from under an enormous hat tied down by green grosgrain ribbons. "Karensa was looking for you not long ago. She is walking on the cliffs with one of her bird books, looking for a suitable subject to sculpt."

"I should take a swim in the sea if I joined her, I am in such a swivet," Alwyn confessed. "I need to be cooled down, and a sea-bathe is tempting." The kitchen garden was supposed to be her responsibility, as the eldest, but over the years Rowena had nudged her out of it and made it her own. And truly, it responded to her care as though every plant in it knew that she loved them.

"A swivet? Why? I thought you went to the village to find a new bonnet." Rowena's clear blue gaze took in her bare head. "Did nothing suit you?"

"I didn't go to the milliner. She wishes me to thank you for the potion for her boy, however. It has been effective. No, I went to the pottery, to offer some of my designs for our porcelain."

"What?" Rowena got up, dusting off her skirts, as though she needed to be standing in order to deal with her eldest sister's peculiar behavior. "Why?"

"I want to be useful. And Mr. Enyon Lander set me back on my heels in the most courteous and gentle way, and told me I could not, because I am a woman."

"He is, as usual, quite right."

"Both of you are missing the point!" Alwyn cried. "Why should I not be useful? They have lost their chief designer to an Exeter pottery, and I am perfectly capable of creating something that has not been in use for forty years."

"Because it is not your pottery, nor your business, my dearie." Rowena put an arm around Alwyn's stiff shoulders. "I applaud your courage, but you must have known that Mr. Lander would be as shocked as he likely was disapproving of such a mad plan."

"I thought it a very good plan." She sounded sulky, and felt like a child reprimanded for wanting to sit at table with the adults, instead of remaining in the nursery where she belonged. "The simple truth is that all of them think a woman incapable of producing anything useful. Except children, I suppose."

"Most women know nothing about such things as pottery designs."

"I do."

"And so does Karensa, and I, to a degree, but Alwyn, in truth you would do nothing but shame Papa, to imply to the world that his daughter must work like a craftsman. After all the family has built, after all he has been through, all he has done for our sakes, is that what you want?"

Alwyn was silent.

"Did anyone overhear this rash proposal of yours?"

Truly, Rowena would make a fine mother some day. She sounded exactly like one.

"No. We had tea in Mr. Lander's office, and the door was closed."

"That is a blessing, at least."

"Do you honestly think I am capable?" It was one thing if Rowena thought she *should* not be useful to the company. It was another thing altogether if she believed she *could* not.

"Of course." Her sister hugged her. "If we lived in a different world, perhaps you could show everyone what we two know—that if you had been a son, Papa would not only have you responsible for our designs, he would have taught you everything he knows about the oversight of the company." She laughed. "Goodness knows *I* can't tell the dries from the kilnhouses."

"It is terrible to be made to feel one is not good enough," Alwyn said, almost inaudibly.

But Rowena had sharp ears. "I'm sure Mr. Lander didn't mean to do so." She laid a gentle hand on Alwyn's shoulder. "But men have the public sphere, and women have the private sphere. Your tragedy is that you are capable in both but may exist only in one."

Alwyn gazed at her sister. "For nineteen years of age,

maidey, you are very wise. When you are not sounding like someone's mama, that is."

Rowena waved this away. "I have had nineteen years to observe the world around me. Unlike Karensa, I feel no need to remark upon its blessings and failings every minute of every day. But I do see them."

Now it was Alwyn's turn to hug her. "What would I do without you?"

"I hope you will not have cause to know. But for now, I must get these beds weeded and a syrup of elderberry made from the berries I put by last autumn. I heard that an infectious ague is making its way through our tenants, so I want to take some to the families with children. It would not do for any of them to come within coughing distance of Papa." She knelt once more in the grass. "Go and visit your hens, do. They will soothe your heated mind."

Alwyn left her to her work and wandered into the walled poultry yard. The hens welcomed her into their number with familiar soft clucks and calls, and when she sat upon an old chair that must have been used in the original farmhouse, one of them sprang into her apron-covered lap. She settled back, stroking its golden feathers and letting the sun warm her shoulders even as the hen's comfortable trust warmed her heart.

It was there that Karensa found her some time later, after the sunshine and the hens had done their good work. "I thought I might find you here. Come, sister. Papa wishes to speak to you."

"To me?" Her alarm must have communicated itself to the hen, for the bird leaped down, shook out her feathers, and took refuge with her flock. "Did he say why?"

"No." Karensa never wasted words, though she had plenty of them to dispense. "But come quickly. He is uncomfortable after exercising his arm, and you may distract him."

Inside, Alwyn tossed the apron back on its hook, washed her hands in the tin sink in the scullery, and hurried along to the small study.

"Papa, you wished to see me?" She leaned over and kissed him, pleased to see that he was sitting up.

With his mane of fading gold hair and tawny eyes, he always reminded her of an engraving of a lion she had seen in one of Karensa's books of natural history. He fidgeted a little, worrying at his sling, as she seated herself on a stool next to the bed. "I do, daughter. I have a letter here from your dear mother's sister, Lady Mainwaring."

"From London?" she asked in some surprise. "Have they welcomed their new grandchild already?"

"No indeed, though I expect the blessed event at any time." He handed her the letter on the bedside table. "Read for yourself."

The paper was of lovely quality, the handwriting upon it regular and firm.

Dear brother Alexander,

I heard with some distress of your accident and hope with all my heart that you may be recovering with all dispatch. Please let his lordship and I know if there is any way in which we may be of service to you.

In point of fact, I wish to be useful to your daughters, if you will permit me to step into the place once filled so happily by my dear sister. I wish to bring them out in Society this Season. Alwyn and Karensa are of an age to be married, and even Rowena is a year past the age when other girls are making their bows. I do not know what may be the marital prospects in St. Just, but if I may help them to good matches here, then I will feel as though Anne's dearest wishes had been fulfilled.

If you agree, I will expect them in the spring, after Easter, when I hope the roads will be suitable for travel. Do not worry overmuch about outfitting them beforehand—I will take them to the best warehouses, where we will find fabrics enough for as many balls, routs, excursions to the theater, and rides in the park as their hearts desire.

Please allow us to do this small thing for you and yours. It would make me very happy. My husband joins me in my plea for your agreement, and looks forward to having his nieces under his roof.

Your sister in law,
Celia

With a start, Alwyn realized she had quite forgotten to breathe. She straightened and inhaled deeply, feeling a little less apt to fall over from sheer astonishment.

"How—how very kind of my aunt," she said, quite unable to manage one more word.

"Kind—generous—thoughtful. Three excellent reasons for the high regard in which your dear mother held her elder sister."

"But of course it is quite out of the question." The shock had made her nearly as blunt as Karensa. "We could not possibly put her to such trouble. And all three of us at once! It is not to be thought of, Papa."

"Why not?"

Her gaze flew from the letter to his face. "Because she cannot know what she offers."

"I am certain she does. She has launched two daughters of her own, and quite successfully, too, to gentlemen of good fortune and property. Why should she not launch her nieces equally well?" Papa took a slow breath. "And if you are worried about the expense, you needn't. Leave that to me, maidey."

"But Papa, it isn't the expense. We simply cannot go to London. What good will it do us? I have no desire to make my bows to a society in which I do not live. And while Rowena would jump at attending any ball that offered, Karensa would find nothing to amuse her save Lord Elgin's marbles, perhaps, or the British Museum."

"I am quite sure London offers more than sculpture, even for Karensa," he said dryly. Then he winced, and slid down a little on his pillows.

"Papa? Oh dear, you are tiring yourself. Let me help you."

She arranged the pillows under elbow and knee until he was more comfortable, and would have called Mrs. Menabilly, their housekeeper, had he not caught her hand.

"Perhaps you do not want to go now, Alwyn, but I believe you should."

She must not allow him to agitate himself. She sat down again, both hands around his. "Papa, truly, we may speak of it when you are better."

"I may not be better."

She drew in a sharp breath, and could not control the clutch of her hands a little too tightly around his.

"Doctor Harris was looking very grave this morning about the broken rib, and I must see you settled." He spoke rapidly, as though aware his strength was seeping away. "It was your mother's dearest wish, after having married beneath her—"

"Papa!"

"—that you should marry well. Oh, do not cavil, my dear. She was a gentleman's daughter, and I was *nouveau riche*, the grandson of a pitman. Her father made his feelings plain on the subject, I remember well, but that did not signify with her. She wanted— I want you to find a man with a title as honorable as his character. If Lady Mainwaring can help you to such a man, then I will insist that you and your sisters accept her invitation."

Tears welled up in her eyes. "You will recover, Papa. I know it."

"Let us speak plainly, daughter. If you do not marry well to honor your mother and bear a son to please me, then I fear for Morvoren Manor. Though it is not entailed, and you girls are the 'heirs of the body' that Grandfather specified, there is every possibility that as 'heir male,' my grandfather's brother's great-grandson will sue for possession of this property. He is the only male remaining in that branch of the family."

If he had thrown a basin of cold water on her, it would have produced no less a chill. "You speak of Arthur Landry."

"Son and grandson of a wastrel. A drunkard. A gambler." Her father coughed, his tone roughened with pain and two generations of disdain. "He will never get his hands on what our family has built. Granted, pit, pottery, and piers may be left to whom I please according to the terms of August Penrose's will. But I will not have my daughters cast out of their home should the courts find in his favor. If you had been a boy, such a dreadful prospect would not haunt me in the long hours of the night. But you are not."

"Oh, Papa," she said brokenly. She could not help her gender, but that did not signify. There was no getting around the truth that sometimes a woman was not enough to stave off the inevitability of the laws of inheritance.

Not enough. No matter how capable, how loving, how determined that woman. Never enough.

She had known for some time now of the wretched cousin whom none of them had ever met. Alwyn had more knowledge of the company's operations in her little finger than the horrid unknown probably did in his whole body. Of the process that turned a lump of fine white clay into a cup or plate made so flawlessly it could be used without shame on the table of a duke—and was, in fact.

"I realize it may be difficult find a husband in London who loves porcelain as much as we do," Papa said, his hand taking hers once more. "But no man in his senses will refuse a woman as pretty, good-tempered, and capable as you. I must get you married so that Morvoren Manor may be safe." When she would have protested, he shook his head. "Find a good man. A titled man. I won't hope that my eldest daughter might wear a duchess's coronet, but for your sweet mother's sake, I would see you styled Lady Someone, and that right soon."

The alternative was too appalling to contemplate.

She bowed her head. A London Season was merely … a season. A length of time with a fixed ending. A few months of her life to endure in order that the place she loved would be safe.

"Very well, Papa," she said quietly. "I will write to my aunt on your behalf in the morning."

CHAPTER 2

Hyde Park, London

Sir Perran Geoffrey pulled up his horse in such surprise that the sensitive animal danced in the path. "By Jove," he exclaimed, "isn't that the Penrose sisters there, coming in at Lancaster Gate?"

Captain Griffin Teague, formerly commander of the sloop of war *Artemis*, craned his neck, causing his own horse to side-step. "Easy, boy." He patted its withers. "Where? On a fine day in London there are a thousand young ladies parading about Hyde Park—how is one to tell one lot from another?"

"There." Perran inclined his head three degrees to the northwest. "The landau drawn by the pretty matched bays. It is certainly the Penrose girls from home—bonnets or not, I recognize their mother's nose."

"There you would be mistaken, old man," said the third member of their party. Jago Tremayne had probably never mistaken a lady in his life. Or a bird, or the contents of a letter, or a hand of cards. His memory was prodigious—as was his entirely undeserved reputation as a flirt. "Mrs. Penrose died a handful of years ago. That, I suspect, is her sister, Lady Mainwaring."

"Help us." Griffin did not quite implore the skies for mercy, but he came close. "Have they come up to London for the Season?"

There was only one answer. Of course they had. "You know perfectly well we cannot renew the acquaintance." Perran spurred his horse down another path toward the Long Water. "Come!"

"Hold up—we cannot escape it now." Griffin raised a hand to stop him. "We have been spotted."

"So? Better to cut a young lady than ruin her." Impatiently, he reined in his mount.

They must be but newly arrived in Town, and their sponsor slightly out of the current, otherwise they would never have asked their aunt to stop at their approach. Never smiled so expectantly. Any sensible duenna would have averted her face and gathered her chicks to her bosom, hiding them from the sight of the Rogues of St. Just.

A ridiculous moniker, it was true. Any number of men drove their conveyances too fast, danced with too many ladies, drank and played cards with just as much enthusiasm, and yet were not labeled rogues. But it had been bestowed with a tap of the fan and an arch smile by the lovely Countess Lieven at Almack's during the previous Season, so the three of them wore it bravely, doing their best to live up to it.

For it did have its advantages.

"Cut them? We will do no such thing," Griffin told him in an undertone. "Lord Mainwaring moves in the same circles as the Admiral and my former Commodore. Though the war has been over a year and more, I would not like either of them to hear of it."

With a sigh, Perran admitted defeat. Now they were fairly in the soup, and could only extract themselves as quickly as might be.

Lady Mainwaring smiled with cautious cordiality as they trotted up, taking in the velvet facings on Perran's flawlessly cut coat, the tassels on Griffin's polished Hessians, the gleam of Jago's perfectly tilted beaver hat. Since she could not know the provenance of Perran's coat, she merely observed that they were gentlemen, added in the Penrose sisters' willingness to claim the acquaintance, and inclined her head.

Then recognition lit her eyes. "Why, Captain Teague, this is an unexpected pleasure," she said. "We have not seen you since the dinner at Vice Admiral and Mrs. Beaton's house, after peace was declared."

"Indeed, Lady Mainwaring." Griffin bowed gracefully. "I am surprised you remember one lowly captain among such a flotilla of guests."

"I do remember. I am particularly fond of a waltz, and you were the best dancer there."

Perran could have groaned at these pleasantries. They must cut the introductions as close to the wind as possible, and be off.

But no. Griffin was already smiling. "Allow me to introduce my friends, ma'am. This is Sir Perran Geoffrey, of London and Rosevear Court in Cornwall."

There was nothing for it. Perran doffed his hat and bowed. "How do you do?"

"Very well. You are an acquaintance of my nieces, I believe."

"We knew one another as children." At last, Perran turned his attention to the bouquet of young ladies, wishing at every moment he could be anywhere but here. His bow was businesslike, his tone abrupt. "Miss Penrose—Miss Karensa—Miss Rowena."

And now her eyes met his own, as stormy and blue-grey as the wind-lashed ocean below the estate he rarely visited above once a year. The image of her as a child was etched in his memory like a cameo—a little girl looking up at him over her shoulder, eyes sparkling with mischief while the hems of her shift dribbled water on the rocks. Daring him to risk his tutor's censure, strip to his smallclothes, and jump into the sea with her.

Her burnished auburn hair, once a tangle hanging loosely down her back as she dove into the waves, was now schooled into obedient curls on either side of her face, tucked deep into the lace edging of her bonnet.

He had been nine years old on that summer day he'd first seen Alwyn Penrose. Eleven when he had kissed her in the sea and been slapped for his pains. Fourteen when he had gone away to school. Nineteen when he had returned for the funeral of his late unlamented father and seen her again, bereaved of her mother. She must be twenty or thereabouts, her sisters stair-stepping down in age, a year apart.

Had all three come for the Season at once? What cataclysmic change in their fortunes would make three girls from the ends of the earth come all this way to try their luck on the London marriage mart? Heaven help them all. He must take his leave, immediately, or they would be tainted by the association.

"Sir Perran," Alwyn said, as cool and abrupt as ever he

could be, even as he tightened his hands on the reins. It was the first time she had said his name in a decade. The title that had once belonged to his father sounded strange on her tongue.

Against his will, his gaze dropped to her lips, as plump and beguiling as rose petals.

Said lips thinned at this liberty. "Will you introduce us to —" She stopped, gazing in astonishment as she belatedly recognized the third rider in their party. "It cannot be. Jago Tremayne? Is it really you?"

"Yes. Good afternoon, Miss Penrose," Jago said, literal as always. At least he could be counted upon to keep his remarks brief.

"Aunt Celia, allow me to introduce Sir Perran's friend, since he and Captain Teague are remiss in doing so. Mr. Jago Tremayne, also of St. Just. When one is from the same parish, one may count them as neighbors."

Was she deliberately baiting him?

Lady Mainwaring acknowledged Jago with a nod. "It is a pleasure to make your acquaintance, sir. My nieces are staying with us in Chesham Street. Perhaps we may see you again in our drives through the park."

"It is unlikely—"

"—that we would not look forward to such a pleasure." Griffin cut him off smoothly.

They must go. Either that, or the ladies must. Lady Mainwaring had pointedly not invited them to call, so clearly she had heard the rumors drifting about the drawing rooms of London like smoke. It would be safer for Alwyn's reputation if she were to climb up on the box, take the reins from the driver, and flee before someone saw them talking.

Jago, who normally hid his discomfort at social discourse a little better than this, kept his gaze fixed over Lady Mainwaring's shoulder. He seemed to be attempting an expression of polite civility, but only managed to achieve a kind of stony frown.

"I am afraid we must ride on," Perran said desperately. "A matter of pressing business."

He had already seen two pairs of raised eyebrows and one pointing finger among the passers-by. All these girls needed would be for one of the Lady Patronesses to catch sight of them in the Rogues' company, and they would be sunk in Society for ever. The fact that he, Griffin, and Jago all held vouchers would hold no water with the arbiters of Almack's.

He was halfway into a polite bow of departure when Lady Mainwaring said, "Will you attend the Pennington ball this evening? I have heard predictions that it will be a sad crush."

Pennington? Ball? Was she asking because she expected them to be there, or to be certain they were not?

"I doubt it very much," Jago said.

With a sinking in his stomach, Perran remembered why the name was familiar. The countess was a friend of his grandmother's, and if he did not go, there would be a flurry of letters from Rosevear Court demanding to know the reason for the slight.

Now he wished he had gone to the country. Or France. Or the moon. "Perhaps." He bowed once more. "Good afternoon, Lady Mainwaring. Ladies. Enjoy your drive."

As they rode away, the girls all began to speak at once. But he would not look back while he put as much distance between them as quickly as he could.

Even though he could swear he felt a point of heat

between his shoulder blades, where Alwyn Penrose's gaze must even now be boring into his back.

"MY GOODNESS, I never expected to see someone from home in our very first week." Rowena watched the gentlemen ride away with admiration. "Mr. Jago Tremayne has a fine seat, does he not?"

Alwyn could not say the same of his manners. Or those of any of them. Why, the brevity of the exchange among people who knew one another was positively insulting. Had she and her sisters committed some social *faux pas* in encouraging the gentlemen to speak to them? Was that why Perran Geoffrey had begun to ride away, cutting them dead before he had been recalled to his duty?

"I advise you not to say such things in company," Lady Mainwaring said in that worried tone she seemed to have developed since they had come to visit. "You will be thought fast, to be commenting upon the person of a gentleman."

"But at home, Aunt Celia, to be thought a fine rider is a great compliment."

"London likely has more fine riders than Falmouth, Truro, and Penzance combined have people," Karensa pointed out. "I have never seen so many out of doors. Do they have nothing to do but ride and walk?"

"One takes the air at this time of day so that one may be seen," Lady Mainwaring said. "It is an opportunity to greet one's friends, and cultivate connections. But old neighbors or not, I would be careful how much you cultivate those *partic-ular* connections."

Her aunt tilted her head in the direction the gentlemen had gone, and Alwyn realized she had been staring after them in some perplexity. She disciplined her gaze and turned to her aunt as the coachman shook the reins. The open landau began once more to bowl along the gravel drive with its views of the lake, the elegant swans, and the busy moorhens.

"What do you mean, Aunt?"

"While your uncle and I have been in company with Captain Teague, and found him an amiable gentleman, it is no secret that he and his two companions have been dubbed the Rogues of St. Just. You must never be alone with any of them, girls. *If* they attend the ball this evening, and *if* you are solicited for a dance for old times' sake, agree only to one. Never two. And certainly not three. Even with the most unexceptionable gentleman, three would be social disaster."

"No one is going to ask me to dance three times in the whole of our stay here, never mind in one evening," Karensa said in the practical tone she used to count linen or order another pound of clay.

"That is not true," Rowena said loyally. "You may be assured of one dance from each of our old neighbors."

Alwyn said, "Why, yes. They have been forced to acknowledge the connection and have been introduced to our aunt."

"So you noticed Sir Perran's odd behavior, too?" Karensa asked under cover of their aunt's bowing to the occupants of a passing curricle. "Never mind. Even you will allow that I am not really the dancing sort. That is Rowena's gift. And yours, to a certain extent, when you choose it."

"I have no objection to dancing, only to partners." If Sir Perran was truly so reluctant to speak to them, perhaps they would be spared his invitations to dance. "We may always stand up with each other."

"Certainly not." Rowena, sitting beside their aunt and facing forward, leaned across to speak to both of them. "What nonsense. We have not come all this way and accepted our aunt and uncle's kind hospitality to be wallflowers. We must find a husband for you, Alwyn, and bring him up to scratch without delay. To do that, you must subject yourself to the ordeal of dancing."

Alwyn had to laugh. "You should have been the eldest. You have far more skill in drawing room and ballroom than either of your unfortunate sisters."

"That is because I have had to watch you suffer, and formed a resolution that my own experience would be quite different. For instance, I was certain you would faint when we were presented at court—or at the very least trip over your hems, or laugh when the Prince Regent spoke to you."

"I very nearly did. I could hear his corset creaking with the enormity of its task!" Alwyn shook her head at the memory. She didn't know which was worse—that sound, or the faces of the lords and ladies nearby trying to ignore it.

"I wish your father's health had allowed him to see you presented," Aunt Celia said on a sigh. "Poor dear man."

Alwyn bit her lip, and Karensa turned away, pretending interest in the trees. "As do we, Aunt," Rowena said softly. "I did write him a lively account of it—though I left out the Prince's stays. Perhaps I ought not to have done. Papa enjoys a good joke as well as any of us."

"Alwyn, do smile," her aunt said to her softly. "We are about to pass Lady Blessing, and I wish to make you known to her."

Alwyn straightened and pasted up a smile nearly as sincere as Rowena's. She must remember her purpose in driving out in her aunt's landau, in her new patterned-voile round gown and blue wool pelisse cut in the latest style, her chip bonnet with its curling feathers exactly the depth that fashion dictated for a girl in her first Season. She was the very picture of an eligible match.

And the thought of it made her miserable.

CHAPTER 3

*O*h, come, Perran. It is just a ball, not a set-to with the French." Griffin leaned on the mantel in Perran's modest but comfortable lodgings, where the three of them were congregating to enjoy a bottle of fine free-trade brandy kindly supplied by Admiral Teague, Griffin's father. Like any man with connections to the West Country, the Admiral enjoyed untaxed liquor whenever he could. In exchange for a temporary place of concealment on his unused property in St. Just, a barrel or two of tribute would make its way into the cellar of the Teague town house at irregular intervals.

"I would far prefer the set-to," Perran said sourly.

"Is it because Constance Eaton is going to be there?" Jago held his snifter to the light to admire its deep tawny color before taking a sip and sighing in appreciation. "Or are you still in a pother about tainting our young neighbors by association?"

"Both." The refreshing thing about being in Jago's company is that he didn't require a man to hedge everything about in polite phrases. One could say what one thought and be done with it.

"I am sure Lady Mainwaring's good influence will mitigate any taint," Griffin told them. "You are taking this far too seriously. What is wrong with enjoying the acquaintance? They're dashed pretty girls—though I'd lay you a guinea Karensa is the bluest of bluestockings. She rather frightens me."

Since Captain Teague of His Majesty's Navy had seen action in the Adriatic and the Mediterranean too, Perran dismissed this as congenial puffery. And possibly the truly excellent brandy.

"You both know the real reasons for my wanting the connection—such as it is—to go stale," he said at last. "I must find an heiress, and that right smartly, before the chimneys at Rosevear come down on Isolde's and Grand-mère's heads."

"Not that I'm advocating one woman over another," Jago said, "but is the lovely Constance prepared to roof and repair the Court in order to have the pleasure of your company in the bonds of wedlock?"

"She's awfully fond of London," Griffin pointed out. "I can't see her posting down to Cornwall in a huge hurry to set up housekeeping, or happily handing over her fortune so that you may do so."

Neither could Perran, to own the truth. "Happily or not, as my wife, her money becomes mine. And I would make it very plain that I have need of her sharing it, both for the estate and to bring Isolde up to Town next year. She will be eighteen, and it is high time."

Jago grinned. "I would buy a ticket to see Constance acting as chaperone to anyone, let alone that hoyden of a sister of yours."

"A girl's ability to ride and shoot does not make her a hoyden," Perran said stiffly. Plain speaking had its limits. "Those are sensible skills in a county where smuggling is as accepted an industry as mining or ship-building."

Smuggling and tin, pilchards and boats—these kept the population of Cornwall in food and shelter, though each carried differing levels of risk. These were nothing like wrecking, which a man of sense and compassion could not but deplore. There were men along the southern coast to this day who saw nothing wrong with placing lanterns where they should never be placed, in hopes that a ship would mistake them for the lights of a safe harbor. Once the vessel had foundered, they murdered the crew and passengers, and pillaged the ship down to its nails.

He'd taught Isolde to ride and shoot himself, and to sail as well. She might never use the latter skills, but the former never went amiss.

It was a shame he'd had to sell the horses—both the ones his ladies rode and the carriage horses. When they went to church, the coachman harnessed the plow horses from the home farm. Perran himself rode Kit, one of Griffin's cattle. His friend never begrudged him anything. One day he would be rich enough to pay him back with the gift of a handsome chestnut or two. But in the meanwhile...

"Very well, Perran," Griffin said easily, setting his empty glass on the sideboard. "You may go to a lecture of the Horticultural Society, or whatever pleases you best, but I am off to the Pennington crush to make my bows and look over the new crop of blossoms. Coming, Jago?"

"Yes." Jago drained his glass. "I don't see what the fuss is about. We've known those girls practically since they were born. It won't do to ignore them."

"It won't do to ruin them, either," Perran said with some curtness at what had to be Jago's willful blindness. "Don't let Griffin take one into a library alone, or the conservatory. Even if he was discovered reading a passage from the Bible to her, he'd be obliged to propose marriage to the poor child on the spot."

"Why don't you try that with Constance?" Griffin teased over his shoulder as he went out of the room.

Jago eyed him. "You don't want to encourage the acquaintance because you believe there's no point. Those girls must be scraping pennies from the bottom of the paternal pocketbook to have their chance at a Season. You need more money than that. Am I right?"

Nettled, Perran gritted his teeth. "I am not so mercenary as that, to cut a woman because her purse isn't fat enough. I simply don't want to encourage a deeper acquaintance, that's all. For their sakes."

Jago waved a negligent hand. "This nonsense about our reputations—it's all hearsay. You would no more ruin an innocent girl than I would."

"Didn't you know? The *ton* thrives on hearsay. Dines out on it. Feeds on it, like greedy fish in a pond."

"Of course I know that. But to buck it is the same as taking a boat out during an incoming tide. It can be done, but you won't emerge without a soaking." Jago gazed idly over the invitations and envelopes in a pile on the mantel. "Speaking of, do you know you have a letter here from your sister?"

"I do?" Perran hadn't glanced at his correspondence. Invitations, announcements of musicales, and the increasingly frequent notices from his creditors were sometimes more of an annoyance than he cared to put up with, and he had been irritated when he'd come back from his ride in the Park.

Jago passed the letter over and he broke the seal.

Dearest brother,

Having heard nothing from you this week, I am taking the liberty of writing again so that I may tell Grand-mère in all good conscience that it is too soon to have a letter from you. We are both well and in good spirits despite the smallest of fires in the kitchen.

"Good heavens," Perran exclaimed with a sudden feeling of doom.

Do not worry. Mrs. Pollock put it out with her usual despatch and is not going to let me bake any more cakes until, as she says, I can pay attention to what is under my nose. I fear that when I am your spinster housekeeper, you will need to bid farewell to cake permanently.

How is your hunt for an heiress coming along? Is Captain Teague making certain that you are attending all the balls and routs, and making regular appearances at the theater? We have had a ball here in St. Just to welcome some relatives of Lord and Lady Tregothnan. As you may imagine, I was beside myself with excitement. Grand-mère accompanied me and allowed me to dance, so I suppose that here at least, I am officially out. The ballroom at Tregothnan was like a fairyland, with candles, music, beautiful dresses, and more food than I have seen in a year. I do hope the relatives like the neighborhood, take a house, and stay through the winter. Perhaps they might even take Trevenna. Some people are immune to ghosts.

Oh, here is some news that may interest you. You remember the Penrose sisters, of course, from Morvoren Manor? You would not be as acquainted with them as I am—you were gone away to school when I used to get into all kinds of scrapes with Rowena, the youngest. But now, things are different. You must have heard that the expansion of the family's interests in the Morvoren China Clay Company into porcelain and shipping has made them fabulously rich. Despite their father's injury in the autumn, there is talk they may build a new wing on the manor—and it is to include a ballroom and conservatory! Just think!

I do not know if you will see them in town, but perhaps you ought to make an effort, since each of them has forty thousand pounds. I can hardly credit it, but Grand-mère says it is quite true. So they—the Misses Penrose, I mean—are gone up to London to bag themselves a duke each. Mind you, that is not Grand-mère's information, but pure speculation on my part.

If you do see them, give my best regards to Miss Rowena.

Your loving sister,

Isolde

Perran was quite sure his blood had stopped flowing in his veins by the third paragraph of this missive, and by the fourth—

He met his own reflection in the mirror above the mantel, and catalogued the signs of shock: wide eyes and a face as pale as a whitewashed wall.

"Good heavens, man." Jago splashed a little brandy into Perran's glass and made him take it. "Is it bad news?"

"No. Yes." He gulped the brandy and used the empty glass as a paperweight for the letter.

"Well? Which is it?"

"Isolde has just informed me that the Penrose sisters are in town."

"Yes, we knew that. And…?"

"And due to their father's careful management of— That is to say, the unbelievable success of— In short, she tells me that those girls have forty thousand pounds apiece."

Jago's eyes widened and he drew a long breath. "I think you had better go to the Countess of Pennington's ball."

Only a fool would not. And he was all kinds of a fool.

For he had made it a point to snub a woman who might have been able to save his future. And if she were still the Alwyn he remembered, she was not likely to forget it.

Dancing was to begin at nine o'clock, and there was to be a cold collation at midnight. Alwyn was deeply thankful that her aunt had given them supper before they had departed Chesham Street. If she had not, Alwyn's choices might have been raiding the Pennington pantry, or fainting away during the quadrille.

"You look lovely, Karensa," she said to her sister as they passed through the Grecian pillars that fronted the Pennington house in Belgravia. "White suits you, while it only makes me look as though I am ill."

"Which is why you are wearing the pale rose and not I. I could not have it near me."

"I am glad the days of my wearing your hand-me-down dresses are over," Rowena said cheerfully to both of them. "This muslin is so pale and thin one can barely see it against the blue silk lining. Why, the embroidery is all that gives it any substance whatsoever. What an impractical fashion. Shall we all catch our deaths of cold, do you think?"

But Alwyn could not reply, for the majordomo was announcing their names, and they were descending the stairs, and one must smile and look as though one were not terrified at being the object of every eye. Oh dear, if only she could have worn a fichu! For her bodice was shockingly low. While it did not display great swaths of bosom like the bodices of some of the ladies present, her collarbones were exposed and a little more besides.

She felt naked. A nonentity.

Not enough—

No, no. She must lift her chin and smile, and be introduced, and curtsey as gracefully as one could with no space to move.

For the ball was certainly a crush. The Pennington ballroom itself was enormous, and lit with no fewer than six chandeliers down its length, aglow with candles and scintillating with lusters and mirrors placed to direct the light. Six sets with at least ten couple each were in the midst of a country dance—*Nonesuch*—so Aunt Celia shepherded them over to one side, where there was a single chair unoccupied.

Their aunt sank into it, fanning herself briskly. "Rumors of a crush were not exaggerated. Stay here by me, girls, until your uncle comes."

His lordship had met a group of his old navy cronies, and such was his interest that Alwyn doubted her aunt would be so fortunate as to stand up with him at all. But no, she was wrong, for here he came.

He was leading Captain Griffin Teague over to them.

"Look whom I've found, Lady Mainwaring," he said to his

wife with jovial cheer. "Admiral Teague's boy—boy no longer —captain of the sloop of war *Artemis,* by Jove. What do you think of that?"

"You are very kind, sir," Captain Teague said quietly, bowing. "Good evening, ma'am. Ladies. We are well met once again."

"How nice to see you, Captain," Aunt Celia said. Then, to her husband, "We met the captain and his friends this afternoon, while we were driving in the park."

"Capital. Then my work here is done."

"Not quite, sir." She tapped his arm with her fan. "I will have my waltz, though a hundred sloops of war lie between us."

"Yes, yes, my dear. First waltz. There is the *Magot* starting up, which has far too many figures for this old sailor to keep track of. I shall return."

Alwyn smiled at her bluff, good-natured uncle's willingness to humor his wife's love of dancing, even as he hastened away.

"If you have no objections to *Mr. Beveridge*, Miss Penrose, then perhaps you might favor me?" Captain Teague held out his gloved hand, so pristine against the navy sleeve of his dress uniform, and bowed.

She being the eldest, it was only correct that he should ask her first, but Alwyn felt a shiver of guilt as she took his hand. Rowena's toes were already tapping in their new kid slippers.

She might not have Rowena's grace, but *Mr. Beveridge's Magot* was one of her favorites, its number of figures notwithstanding. And no lady would object to Captain Teague as a partner. He had certainly become a handsome man. There was no longer a sign of the chubby boy who had once taken her fishing in his shallop. She was all curiosity to know why the gallant captain should be considered such a rogue that she might only dance with him once ... but then, perhaps she did not want to know.

They had just completed the first full set of figures, speaking cordially of mutual acquaintances at home, when she became aware of a most peculiar feeling. She turned her head during the cast-off to see Sir Perran Geoffrey standing near the door, a lady in burgundy silk and ruby earrings—far too large, in Alwyn's opinion—hanging upon his arm and speaking to him in an urgent undertone.

His gaze met hers over the lady's shoulder.

At which moment Captain Teague spoke, and she jerked her attention back to him, crossed arms, and proceeded into the promenade as though her lapse in attention had never happened. The captain never knew she had nearly missed the turn—or if he did, he said not a word.

When she looked back again, both Perran and the lady in rubies were gone.

Silly goose! After ten years of silence, his presence or absence meant nothing to her. If he had forgotten their childhood friendship, if he chose to remain as aloof as he had in the park, then nothing in the world would induce her to form an expectation of attention from him.

He was a rogue. And a rude one at that, if this afternoon was any indication. She'd do well to remember her aunt's advice.

"I see that Sir Perran has decided to attend," Captain Teague said easily as they stepped into the third set of figures. "Though from all appearances, he may wish he hadn't." Then, unaccountably, he blushed. "I apologize, Miss Penrose. I did not mean anything by that remark. As a sailor, I am used to being blunt, and sometimes it is more painful for me than for my listener."

"Do you refer to that lady in the ruby earrings?" She could be blunt, too. "Do they have an understanding, and have consequently quarreled?"

His eyebrows went up and she could see he was trying not to smile. "No indeed. But Miss Penrose, a poor opinion you must have of an understanding between a lady and a gentleman. They do not *all* involve quarrels."

"I would not know," she admitted. "But in my small sphere I have seen great emotion and passion produce results not pleasant to those around them."

The day Papa had found out that one of the foremen had been skimming the wages of the pitmen, for instance. She and Karensa had sat at the top of the stairs as quiet and wide-eyed as owls, listening for all they were worth as Papa's bellowing penetrated wainscoting and plaster both.

"No, that lady is the Dowager Countess Eaton," he said when the figure brought them together again. "She has just left off wearing mourning for her husband."

Unbidden, Alwyn's mind did the arithmetic. One wealthy widow plus one rogue equaled—

Now it was her turn to blush.

Thankfully, *Mr. Beveridge* came to an end, and by the time Captain Teague had escorted her back to her aunt, the flush had faded. She would simply not think of Perran Geoffrey any more. She would get on with the business of smiling, and fluttering her fan, and blushing at the gallantries of the next several partners who were introduced and were promised their dances in succession.

Even Karensa had been invited to dance, in her storklike, smileless fashion. And it turned out Rowena had been lower down in another set for *Mr. Beveridge*—she could be trusted not to waste a moment where dancing was concerned. But they, unlike she, did not feel the urgency of Papa's desire for her Season. With the help of her aunt and uncle, she must do her best to seek out a flock of titled quarry, charm them, and bag one of them without delay.

The very thought of such behavior sickened her, but there was nothing for it. Even though Papa was healing nicely, according to Dr. Harris, anything could happen. It was still up to her to see that all he had built did not go the way of the ruined chapel on the point near Morvoren Manor, slowly sliding into the sea for lack of use and care.

CHAPTER 4

*P*erran berated himself for the loss of self-control that had caused him to stare like a schoolboy at Alwyn Penrose as she danced with Griffin, to say nothing of losing the drift of what Constance Eaton had been telling him.

His impressions of Alwyn were undergoing a rapid transformation. A girl in the sea—a demure young lady in a bonnet—an arresting woman in a silk ballgown that, as the mamas were wont to say, showed her figure to advantage. Even without her money, he was not certain his heart could take too much more evidence that little Alwyn was a woman grown, and ripe for the plucking by some overbred sprig with a quizzing glass.

"Perran, are you listening?" Constance hissed, clinging to his arm. "Shall I save you the waltz so that we may continue this discussion?"

What had they had been talking about? He remembered nothing after he'd greeted his hostess and turned to walk straight into Constance's trap.

"Certainly," he said vaguely. "Pray excuse me."

The country dance was ending as he circled the ballroom, nodding to his acquaintance and making young ladies blush quite without meaning to. Griffin escorted Alwyn off the floor and Perran excused himself to two matrons as he slid between them to bow to Lady Mainwaring.

"Sir Perran, how dashing you look." Despite what she must know of him, she smiled with real feeling, the way a mother would at the sight of a son. At least, he assumed so. It had been many years since his mother had passed away, and he hadn't realized until now that it was possible to miss that look of gentle welcome.

Though why Lady Mainwaring would be glad to welcome someone with his reputation was beyond him.

Alwyn was looking pensive as Griffin took himself off, so he took the opportunity to move into his place. "Miss Penrose."

"Sir Perran," she said, coming to herself with a blink. "How do you do?"

"As well as I did this afternoon in the Park, thank you. Is your first waltz spoken for?"

She actually had to take a moment to think, though it was about to begin. "Why, no."

"Then I will not be cutting anyone out if I ask you to dance without further ceremony?"

She laid her gloved hand upon his with a slightly stunned expression as the orchestra struck the opening notes. They did each other their courtesies, and then she stepped into his arms.

"The waltz has reached the dancing masters of Cornwall, I see," he said, casting about a little awkwardly for a topic of conversation. Which was most unlike him. "I wonder if Isolde has learned it yet."

"Is your sister well? I confess I do not number her among my correspondents since we have come here. And it is some weeks, of course, since I last saw her and Lady Geoffrey at church."

"She is very well, thank you. Both she and my grandmother enjoy good health, according to her latest letter."

"Your grandmother dined at Morvoren Manor when my mother was alive, but of course with my father still recovering we do not entertain. Do you see Lady Geoffrey and your sister often?"

Once a year, whether he could afford the visit or not. Hence their lively correspondence. "As often as I can. Isolde wishes to come to London, but—"

What a fool. Did he really mean this girl with forty thousand pounds to know that he hadn't a feather to fly with? That taking a house in town for his family was utterly out of his power? That he was having his father's and grandfather's clothes from the previous century made over by a close-mouthed tailor because he could not afford new?

"There is much in London to entertain a girl of that age," Alwyn said. "Rowena adores it here, but I am afraid that Karensa and I will be just as happy to travel home again once I—"

Once she what? Secured the affections of Lord Somebody's overbred heir?

"Once the Season is concluded," she finished.

Perran frowned, and to cover it, turned them both into the main stream of dancers rather than hugging the middle as the more timid might do.

It was no wonder the Lady Patronesses had resisted the waltz for so long. He could feel the heat of Alwyn's body through the fine stuff of her dress—and though he held her the requisite distance from himself, her thighs brushed his in the turns. She was not the conventional golden-haired beauty about whom the fops sighed and wrote reams of verse. Her sister Rowena would likely come in for her share of dreadful stanzas, however. Alwyn's coloring was as russet as an autumn day, with her auburn hair and rosy cheeks. Her mouth was generous, her lips full, her chin a warning that she had a mind of her own.

He really must stop looking at her lips.

And before the thought could result in action, she had caught him at it.

Again.

"What are your plans for the Season?" he inquired hastily. "I understand that Kemble is playing Hamlet, and Madame Orozny will be singing for the Duke of York at Rutland's house next month."

"I might aspire to the first, but hardly to the second," she said after a moment. "We are not the sort of family to receive invitations from such exalted circles."

"I could secure you one," were the astounding words that came out of his mouth. He closed his jaw with a snap.

"I have no doubt that you could, but for my part, I must decline the honor. I would much rather attend a concert by Schubert, or a lecture on china glazing."

"China glazing." In his surprise, he nearly steered her into a gentleman who turned out to be Lord Mainwaring. Lady Mainwaring gave him a sunny smile from within the circle of her husband's arms, and they spun away.

"Perhaps your sister does not include news of the neighborhood in her correspondence," Alwyn said. "The Morvoren China Clay Company was awarded a royal warrant some years ago. Papa and the other investors have improved the pit operations enormously, and the pottery, and Papa has built docks in the harbor for the ships that take our china and clay to France and America."

So thoroughly had he detached himself from the distressing state of his home in Cornwall that he'd had no idea. So this was the reason for the rise in the family's fortunes. Now he understood why all three sisters were able to come up to Town to pick and choose among the noble prospects. Any one of them could crook her finger at any gentleman in the room and have him calling the next day with a nosegay of flowers and the offer of his heart.

"How is your father?" he said, his mind whirling.

"You are aware of the nature of his accident?"

"I am … but I regret to say I have had no recent news." He would have to encourage Isolde to be more specific. Alwyn would think him impossibly unfeeling.

She told him of her father's state of health, succinctly, but in the slight tremor of her mouth he could see what it cost her to do so. He had no business looking at her mouth when she was speaking of people she loved.

"How dreadful," he said at last, meaning it. "Miss Penrose, you and your father have my utter sympathy. I am sorry to have caused you to speak of it in company."

"No—" She gulped, clearly wishing to be anywhere but in the public eye.

Here was a chance to redeem himself and make up in some small way for his behavior so far today. "You should step outside for a moment to compose yourself."

"No, I am perfectly—"

Her throat closed altogether, and he danced her gracefully over to the French windows that opened on the terrace. It was not a terribly large terrace, for the house took up nearly all the space on its land, but it would do.

He saw her over to a cluster of hyacinths blooming in a porcelain urn glazed in blue and white, and bowed. "I will leave you here, and fetch your aunt."

"Leave me?"

"Miss Penrose, I have but seconds before every tongue in the ballroom begins to wag, to the detriment of your reputation." He bowed again, turned on his heel, and entered the ballroom once more.

He waited for Lady Mainwaring to be escorted from the floor, and whispered in her ear that she was wanted out on the terrace.

"Goodness. Is Alwyn not well?" And without waiting for a reply, she hastened along the draperies to the French doors.

In any other circumstance no one would bat an eye at a couple taking the air. In any other city, perhaps, he and Alwyn could have remained outside for ten minutes together, talking of whatever they pleased. Perhaps indulging in a touch of the hand, or a caress of the cheek. But this was London, and his were no ordinary circumstances.

He took refuge in the card room, where he made himself visible to a number of his acquaintances and drained a glass of brandy. Then it was time to return to the ballroom.

With a sigh, he saw the splendid figure of Constance Eaton bearing down upon him for the waltz. The second waltz. Very much too late, he realized she had been expecting him for the first, and he would have to make it up to her. He manufactured the smile that the scandal sheets had said was responsible for many a lost reputation, and went to meet her.

Perran was nothing if not a realist. He avoided the fresh-faced girls in their virginal white dresses because he had nothing but his title to recommend him. The income from Rosevear Court did not stretch to support a wife and children in Town. It barely stretched to keep his ladies in bread and meat. But he had no objection to ladies with fewer expectations, where one might enjoy oneself socially without being dragged into church by one's ear. He had become Constance's favorite only a month after the old earl died. He had ignored the shocked whispers of the *ton* at their indecent haste in being seen together in public while she was still in black.

Constance looked ravishing in black.

Theirs was an arrangement that suited them both. But an arrangement was not designed to last forever. It was not the same as a commitment. It was time to put himself into harness and do something respectable with his life. Constance had been left with an enormous jointure, a house in town, and a carriage and four, and required nothing more in a second husband than a handsome ability in both ballroom and bedroom.

If he ever hoped to put a new roof on Rosevear Court, and make the tenant cottages livable enough to actually retain a tenant for more than one harvest, he could do worse than the dowager countess. There was something to be said for a marriage of mutual benefit. And really, did he ever plan to live in Cornwall again? His person, such as it was, was a fair exchange for funds to make his grandmother's golden years comfortable and give Isolde decent prospects for the future.

Love, in this day and age, was simply too much to ask.

So why, then, was he still looking for a coronet of autumn curls tied up in pink ribbon over the head of the woman he held in his arms?

"HE HAS DANCED three times with Lady Eaton," Karensa informed Alwyn as they enjoyed ices at midnight. "Am I supposed to be shocked, or ought I to have expected it?"

Just that thought—*ices at midnight*—felt so decadent. Something so utterly foreign to their life in Cornwall and taken so much for granted here that some of the other young ladies had turned up their noses because the flavors on offer were not their favorites. Alwyn had never tasted a lemon ice before this evening. It was sublime.

"Who has danced three times?" she said as her teeth recovered from the chill.

"Sir Perran, of course."

"Careful," she warned her sister after she had swallowed the last delicious mouthful. "Perhaps your reputation will be soiled merely by watching him."

"Perhaps the two are already engaged," Karensa said, apparently not much bothered by this prospect.

This had not occurred to Alwyn before, and after the initial jolt to the stomach, she found herself becoming cross. "Then he has no business asking us to dance, does he?"

"Better ask Rowena. If anyone knows the etiquette of the ballroom, it is she."

"Rowena has not been off the floor since we arrived,"

Alwyn told her. "She is quite the belle, and we will have to take care that her head does not swell."

"Do not take to composing rhymes, maidey," Karensa teased.

"Certainly not. I will stick to clay and watercolors. And one day perhaps I shall be able to combine the two."

Alwyn was saved from Karensa's reply by the orchestra tuning up after the collation and a young man from … where was it? Oh yes, Kent … coming to claim the country dance, which turned out to be *Black Nag*. What an odd choice for just after the midnight luncheon, with its vigorous *galops* down the set. But Alwyn was exhilarated as, afterward, he bowed her back to her sister, and then it was Monsieur Comborn for *Jamaica*. This was much slower, and allowed more conversation than the occasional gasp permitted by *Black Nag*. And according to Aunt Celia, one must certainly converse with the son of a French *vicomte* whose property and chateau had somehow survived the Terror intact.

"I understand you are new to Town, Miss Penrose," he said in his delightfully accented English during the first figure. "Are you enjoying its delights?"

"I have enjoyed those I have experienced," she said shyly. She had never danced with a viscount's heir before. "We drove in Hyde Park this afternoon, and yesterday attended a watercolor exhibition."

"The Summer Exhibition at the Royal Academy?"

"No, I believe it was at a large gallery, but I could not say where."

"Ah, the one near St. Paul's. I was there myself, though not yesterday. Are you fond of *les aquarelles*?"

They had reached the bottom of the set and were obliged

to wait out one figure. Though she did not speak French, she gathered from the *aqua* in the word that water was involved, and he must be referring to the watercolors. "I am," she said. "Though my sister Karensa is the true artist in the family. She is a sculptor in clay."

"That seems rather—er, I mean to say, is it not an art form usually pursued by a man?"

This was not the first time Alwyn had heard such a question. Clay did not know the sex of the hands that shaped it, only their firmness and skill and respect. "They are not large sculptures, monsieur," she said. "She makes porcelain figurines. Of birds, mainly, and animals. Sometimes a bust, if a human subject is willing to sit for her."

He nodded the tempo and they joined hands and rejoined the set. "If you enjoy art, perhaps the estimable Lady Mainwaring would permit me to accompany you to the Summer Exhibition? Everyone must go at least once, I am told."

Goodness, what was she to say? He must be a man of good character, or her aunt would never have permitted the introduction. And there was his father the *vicomte*. And the chateau. "Monsieur, I feel quite certain that it is too soon for me to be driving with you unchaperoned."

"Of course we will include your sister in the party. Did I not say? A sculptress she might be, but it is likely she would appreciate other forms of art as well."

Aunt Celia would set him to rights if it were not proper for one or both of them to drive with him after so short an acquaintance. "Perhaps you might call in Chesham Street?"

"*Bon.* I shall look forward to it very much."

But she did not know if he meant escorting her to the exhibition, or calling in Chesham Street. Oh, dear.

The music came to a close with a flourish, and he bowed and escorted her from the floor. To her relief, her aunt had returned from visiting with her hostess, and had resumed her chair.

"Lady Mainwaring," she said breathlessly, indicating her partner, "Monsieur Comborn would like to escort Karensa and I to an art exhibition tomorrow."

Karensa straightened with interest, and left off being a wallflower for a moment.

"Would he?" Their aunt rose, and he bowed.

"With your kind permission, of course," he said, and smiled at Karensa to include her in the conversation. "I understand that Mademoiselle Karensa is an artist herself."

Lady Mainwaring gazed at him, his father's title clearly holding no weight with her. "Perhaps you might call first, and save the exhibition for another day."

"But Miss Penrose has already—"

"Miss Penrose, naturally, is anxious to see the sights of London, while I and her uncle are more anxious that she and her sisters make better acquaintances of those who would accompany her."

"Miss Karensa—"

"I may be old-fashioned, monsieur, but the proprieties never go out of style," Aunt Celia said in a tone she might have used in a field general's tent. "Do you not agree?"

The young man visibly wilted. "Yes, of course, Lady Mainwaring. I do beg your pardon. I look forward to seeing you all, then, tomorrow afternoon, when you are at home."

He bowed once more and vanished into the crowd.

"Have I made a misstep, Aunt?" Alwyn asked anxiously.

"Should I not have accepted his invitation on so short an acquaintance?"

"It would likely have been perfectly acceptable, dear," said her aunt, making herself comfortable on the striped chair once more. "But one does not want to make it too easy for these young men. It has been some years since I brought your cousins out, but that, I dare say, has not changed. Certain proprieties must be observed."

Over the next two dances, the older guests began to take their leave, and with the thinning of the crowd, it seemed the gentlemen had thrown off some forms of restraint. Or perhaps it was simply a matter of greater visibility.

After only two country dances, Karensa was invited to waltz for the first time that evening.

Alwyn fielded two more invitations—one to ride in the park, and one to walk in the gardens of some lord or other's house, which were said to be the finest in London. She told both young men that they would have to apply to her aunt for permission to call.

She was sitting out the quadrille at two in the morning when Rowena collapsed beside her, breathing as though she had run through two of the hay fields at home. "You will never guess what I overheard just now," she said, holding her side as though she had a stitch in it.

Alwyn handed her the cup of punch she held. "Drink this. What did you hear?" If it was anything to do with how many times Sir Perran Geoffrey had danced with any lady present, she would walk away, having offered to fill the cup again.

"Say nothing to our aunt, but I thought it most peculiar. Fancy a man boasting of taking Karensa for a drive!"

Alwyn glanced at Karensa, who was actually dancing with

an individual as tall and angular as she. It was like watching two hairpins galloping about the room together.

"Our sister is quite a catch, you will remember," she told Rowena on a laugh. "We all are."

"Yes, but Karensa is far too good for her name to be bandied about in public. You, too. Apparently you were one of the party. Have you been making conquests and keeping them from me?"

A tiny stitch appeared between Alwyn's brows. "Was it Monsieur Comborn? He invited us both to see an exhibition of watercolors tomorrow, but our aunt insisted he call and become better acquainted first."

Rowena shook her head. "I do not know who it was, but his companions thought him a great success for his coup."

"Dear me." Was this what it meant to be the talk of the town? As though one were the prize heifer in a market auction? Suddenly the lights seemed too bright in the ballroom, the heat overpowering, the punch too sweet.

Lady Mainwaring's posture was beginning to wilt. Alwyn took her aunt's hand and said to Rowena, "Our aunt is tired. I believe we ought to take our leave of our hostess and call for the carriage."

CHAPTER 5

From across the breakfast table, Constance smiled at him as languidly as a cat in the warmth of the morning sun falling through the dining room windows. Perran had arrived before ten of the clock, which, had the *ton* known of it, would have shocked them all into twitters. They frequently took a late breakfast together, as Constance preferred a lazy morning after the exertions of a ball the night before.

She lifted the pot and when he nodded, poured him a second cup of tea.

"It is still hot." He sipped the Indian blend, which went down as smoothly as a skein of silk, and had the secondary effect of waking one up properly.

"It should be. My staff know my habits well. I should never serve lukewarm tea—though they cannot say the same at Almack's."

She was brave enough to appear downstairs and sit in the sunlight at this hour. Her skin was smooth and unlined. She was only five or six years older than he—and had been at least thirty years younger than her late husband.

"Perhaps we might take advantage of the sunshine?" She peeped at him hopefully. "I should like to ride in the Park this morning."

He smiled at her. "Such a greedy girl. You have ridden every day since you got your hands on that lovely bay mare."

"I always was, you know," she said with no shame whatever, and bit into a scone slathered in marmalade. "Eaton deplored it in me, but you see how well off he has left me in spite of it."

"I wonder that you are satisfied with the company of an impoverished baronet. I saw the Duke of Elleswood dancing with you more than once last night."

"Pfft." She waved the scone in a negligent hand. "He is the kind of dancer who *displays* his partners, like an angler showing off his catch. Horrible man. I know his kind. No, Perran." She slid her foot from her slipper and gently pressed the toe of his boot under the table. "He is impoverished in ways that you are not. But were you jealous, even for a moment?"

"One may as well be jealous of a butterfly for leaving one's garden for that of a neighbor."

She pouted. "I've no interest in other gardens, as you well know. One dances for form's sake, and for exercise, and to pick up the latest *on dits*. I should like to know, though … when you plan to make an honest woman of me."

His brows rose in spite of himself, and his interest in what her foot had been doing went a little flat.

"I did not realize our relationship was progressing in that

direction," he said at last, changing position so that her foot slid away.

He'd had rather more than an inkling. Only a blind man would not. Her taking possession of him last night at the ball had been only the latest of several similar acts in public. He had allowed it because for one, it kept the shine on his reputation with no effort on his part, and for another, he honestly liked her. She was good company, well read, and could ride and drive nearly as well as he.

But how long would it be before she tired of him and moved on to someone with a decent house in the country where she could entertain as lavishly as she liked? Someone with a string of horses and two more carriages? With a set of family jewels locked away that would outshine those she already possessed?

"Of course you have realized it." She filled her empty teacup, leaving it black. He preferred his with milk. "I have made my preference plain, have I not?"

"Only until a better landscaped garden beckons to my lovely butterfly." She flinched, and too late he realized he had hurt her. "Constance—"

She set the teacup on the table with a clink. "That was cruel."

"I did not mean to be."

"Is it so difficult to believe a woman might be in love with you?"

It is difficult to believe you *might be.* But that would wound her even further, and he could not say it. "Yes, frankly."

He had surprised her … and himself.

So much that instead of storming out of the room, she

reached across the glossy table to touch his fingers. "You cannot mean it."

"But I do. What do I have to offer you but a minor title, a ruin of a house, and a bad reputation?"

She straightened when he did not take her hand, and took a sip of her tea. "I have a title of my own, a lovely house or two right here, and I don't give a fig about your reputation, since I am the cause of much of it."

He smiled to be obliging, because she wanted to make him feel better. But if she desired marriage, then there were a few points on which he wanted clarification.

"What about Rosevear Court?"

"What about it?" She gazed at him over the rim of the cup with interest.

"You know I want to bring it back to life. To make it fit to live in. More than that, even—to make it a welcoming home once again."

"Are you telling me your grandmother and sister are housed in a place unfit for them to live? That does not sound like you, Perran."

"They are living in a constant state of fear that they love me too much to show. The Court is in dire need of repair."

"And you need funds for those repairs."

"In a word, yes." Or, like Admiral Teague, he would have to give serious thought to augmenting his income by taking part in Cornwall's most profitable industry. Which was *not* tin mining.

"So you do plan to live in Cornwall, at least part of the time. If you were to go to the trouble of making these repairs."

"Does that not please you?" He could hear in her voice that it didn't. "St. Just is my home. My roots are there. Mine, and

Griffin's, and Jago's." And those of the Penrose sisters, but now was not the time to add them to the list.

"Really?" she said lightly, her attention flickering to the sideboard, where sausages and eggs waited. "I had no idea that your roots were anywhere but here. Now who is the one looking over the wall to another garden?"

They were talking of different gardens, and he knew she knew it. "There is another matter—my sister, Isolde. She will be eighteen soon, and ready to be presented."

A sidelong glance of merriment. "Do not say that anyone in this room is to be her sponsor, chaperoning her about. Sitting on the sidelines in a turban and feathers. Doling out dances on the girl's behalf like a miser."

"Is it so onerous a task? A sponsor may accept a few dances. Look at Lady Mainwaring last night—she had her fair share, and she was chaperoning three."

"That estimable lady is at least fifteen years older than I, and should be well past dancing." Her gaze narrowed in on his like a hawk stooping upon a mouse. "But I believe we are come to the real subject of this entertaining conversation."

He stared at her. "I do not follow."

"Until yesterday, if left up to you, I would have made an entry in the betting book at White's saying that we would be churched by Christmas."

"How do you know about the betting book at White's?" he asked in some astonishment.

"Do not change the subject. But now, contrary to all appearances, my fine stallion is balking at the hedge, suddenly unwilling to jump. I wonder why that might be?"

"I am not balking," he said crossly. "I am simply bringing

up subjects that must be brought up if we are to go on in harness together."

So much for her metaphor, but it was all he could think of under duress.

She blinked at him, drawing in her chin in surprise. "Did you just ask me to marry you?"

"If I were ever to do that, my dear, you would know it without a doubt. No, I was simply saying that one ought not to jump a hedge unless one knows what is on the other side."

"It depends on the hedge. Sometimes it is more exciting to jump first and see where one lands."

"I believe I sketched the dimensions of my hedge rather clearly," he said. "The question is, are you willing for what lies on the other side?"

She left the table to inspect the sideboard. "What a tiresome metaphor. I prefer reality. Shall we ride together in the Park or not? I can have Griggs saddle my grey if you would like the bay mare this time."

By which he gathered that their conversation was at an end. He didn't know whether to be annoyed … or relieved.

ALWYN WOULD NEVER HAVE BELIEVED that so many flowers could fit into one sitting room … and still they kept coming. Forced roses from the hothouse, freesia, lilies. A basket of fruit. Even a book of the gothic sort, bound in black and silver, which to Karensa's dismay, Aunt Celia dispatched back to its sender as being utterly unsuitable. Some of the nosegays were delivered by a flower-seller, and bore cards. Some came in the gloved hands of young men, some of whom were obliged to leave their cards when it became apparent that only a certain number might be seated in the room at one time.

"This is so very entertaining," Rowena exulted on the fourth day. "I have never received so many callers in my life."

"I don't even remember half these people." Karensa turned over an engraved card as though there might be a reminder of her meeting with its sender scribbled on the back. "Has every eligible man who danced with us sent something?"

"Never fear, Aunt Celia is keeping a ledger, I am quite certain." Alwyn put on another of her bonnets and tied its *eau de Nil* ribbons to one side, as was fashionable, rather than under her chin as she might have at home. "I am glad that Monsieur Comborn passed muster and she is allowing us to go to the Summer Exhibition with him."

"Or rather, that he is going with us," Karensa corrected her. "Our aunt is a vigilant chaperone and will not be left behind. We will be three on the facing seat, so pray do not bring umbrellas."

Monsieur Comborn's carriage was waiting, and he held its door for them, much to the chagrin of two hopefuls on the pavement. Alwyn and Karensa accepted their nosegays with a pretty show of thanks, which had to be enough for the forlorn pair as the party of five bowled away in the open carriage.

"I thought this vehicle the better choice today," he said, patting the hinge of the hood. "It may rain later."

Imagine having a choice of carriages, depending on the weather. Alwyn supposed that Papa could spend money on such things now. They had had a good report of his walking in the garden from Mrs. Menabilly this week, so she dared to think of the future with optimism.

"Perhaps we might persuade Papa to buy something like

this glossy equipage, just for us to travel about in," she said to Karensa. "I do like this cream and black finish."

"Were Papa able to go to Truro to choose a carriage, I would be so grateful," Karensa said.

"I shall be happy when he is able to walk the length of the drive without a cane," Alwyn said.

"I would be honored to assist in the former effort," Monsieur Comborn said eagerly. "Nothing would give me greater pleasure than to help you choose a carriage."

Would a gentleman not inquire after the health of their father, rather than offering to help them spend their own money? Alwyn had no way to know. This was not home, where everyone they met asked after his progress and spirits, and expressed their hopes that he would be walking and driving again soon.

The Summer Exhibition was enormous. The watercolors had their own room, filled with light from tall windows. "Oh, how lovely," Karensa said, standing entranced before a landscape that might have been Italy. Their aunt and Rowena joined her, leaving Alwyn to stroll from one picture to another with Monsieur Comborn.

"Allow me to share this one with you," he said, indicating a painting of a sunlit statue in a garden. "It was painted by a friend of mine."

"It is lovely. Does he live in London?"

"No. Sadly, he was killed in the war. This is only one of half a dozen of his paintings that survive him."

"I am so sorry. Will you buy it, then, in memory of him?"

"No, I can't—I mean to say, I believe it is spoken for already." He flushed, and turned to speak to someone of his acquaintance.

Had he meant to say *can't afford?* He could not afford a watercolor painted by a man he had known—and yet they had come in his landau? Perhaps she had been in error to assume that the carriage belonged to him. It had never occurred to her until now that such might not be the case.

"Which do you prefer, sir—the still life, the portrait, or the landscape?" she asked as he turned his attention back to her and they walked on.

"Each has its beauties, but if pressed, I must admit to preferring the portrait. A still life shows us a stage. A landscape shows us a memory. But a portrait can show us the inner man—his thoughts, his attitudes. Do you not agree?"

"It can also show the world exactly what the sitter wishes it to see," Alwyn pointed out dryly. On the one occasion she had attempted Karensa's portrait, she had been both amused and frustrated by her sister's insistence on "setting a proper mileu." It had included wet clay and a stained overall, which had not made the prettiest picture, though Papa had been delighted with it.

"Do you mean to say that this woman—" He indicated a portrait of a matron in blue silk seated in front of a drape, a book in her hands. "—may be acting?"

"I believe she is showing the viewer what she wants him to see. She may not enjoy reading at all, but she wishes to be thought educated, even literary."

Monsieur Comborn laughed. "How can you say such a thing?"

Alwyn smiled back. "I am simply taking the opposite point of view for the sake of argument."

"What a singular young lady you are. One might never

know your thoughts, then, if you are in the habit of speaking for the sake of argument."

"Perhaps I do not wish anyone to know them."

"Then am I to labor fruitlessly, never permitted to know what you think of me?"

Now it was her turn to laugh. "Monsieur Comborn, I have hardly had a chance to form an opinion of you yet."

He opened his mouth to speak, but was greeted from behind by a trio of young men who came in, their voices bouncing off the plaster walls and polished floor. As it turned out, they were the source of two of the bouquets in the drawing room, and the third reminded her with a bow that he had been her partner for the last waltz two nights before, and that his card was no doubt in the tray in Chesham Street at that very moment. They had come to the Royal Academy directly upon learning where the Penrose sisters had gone.

They made a merry group, and the tall one who had left the card managed to impress Alwyn with his knowledge of atmospheric perspective. As they parted on the pavement with promises to call again, Alwyn heard the tall one, who was walking behind with Monsieur Comborn, say to him gaily, "Take good care of my landau, Raoul. I shall want it tomorrow to take Miss Karensa for a drive along the Long Water. She wishes to see the swans." His reply was lost among the general raillery and good humor.

So, Alwyn thought. Son of a viscount or no, Monsieur Comborn owned neither the landau nor the horses that drew it. He called a painter his friend, but could not afford his work. But he possessed in spades the ability to cause one to think he did. Or at least not to question the appearance of it. Not that she could blame a man for setting his cap at a way to change his situation. But did she want to attach herself to a man who began his acquaintance with a host of small deceits?

"Monsieur Comborn," she said when they were seated in the landau and were bowling along the busy streets once again, "where did you come by the flowers you sent? The lilies have a lovely scent—enough to perfume the whole room."

"I don't know how you could tell which was Monsieur Comborn's bouquet, sister," Rowena pointed out gaily. "So many nosegays came this morning."

"I am glad that mine stood out in some way." Monsieur Comborn's eyes twinkled as he smiled with pleasure. "But to own the truth, I am fortunate in my friends. Danforth, the shorter of the three whom you met just now, lives with his sister and her husband. Their conservatory is a wonderland, and she does not mind my pruning a stem or two when it is absolutely vital that I do so."

Alwyn returned his smile, and lowered her gaze so that he would not see in it the conclusions she had drawn.

Later, when they were removing gloves and bonnets in the vestibule at home, Aunt Celia spoke in a low voice. "I have had a change of mind, Alwyn. I hope you will not encourage that young man—the French boy. He is a gentleman, and one cannot fault the chateau in his future, but—"

"But he has no money," Alwyn said into the delicate pause. "And the chateau is so very far away."

"Quite so. His purpose in his attentions to you is quite clear."

"Do any of the gentlemen we saw today possess a competency, or are they all penniless?"

"I believe Mr. Danforth has six thousand a year, but I have also heard that he is on the point of proposing to the Montgomery girl. You remember—the heiress from Stoke in the pale blue silk at the Pennington ball."

Alwyn did not remember, but she was very glad that Aunt Celia had. "I will take your advice, Aunt."

"Good girl." Aunt Celia patted her arm and bustled away to see what was keeping the tea tray.

Alwyn followed Karensa up to their room, and sat upon the bed with a defeated bounce.

"I know exactly what you are thinking." Karensa watched the maid put their bonnets in their boxes and return them to the shelf. The girl bobbed a curtsey and departed to perform the same service for Rowena. "Is there a man to be found in London who would like us for ourselves rather than our forty thousand pounds?"

"I could not have said it better." Alwyn regarded her pretty half boots with less pleasure than usual. "Ask also whether there are any we are permitted to like, without regard for their pocketbooks."

"I should not think so."

Unbidden, a memory flashed into Alwyn's mind of Perran Geoffrey as a child, solemn and hesitant, clinging to the cliff while she urged him to jump in and take a swim with her. To his credit, he had plucked up his courage and dived clumsily into the heaving water between the rocks. They had explored as far as they dared that day. Swum until they were nearly blue with cold.

Or the day he had taught her to drive her pony cart. He had insisted that she, and not the hovering groom, should know how to harness and hitch the pony. Even as a child, he had paid her the compliment of assuming her capable of doing such a thing.

She had thought they were friends.

As they went downstairs for tea, Alwyn reflected upon the things that she had believed as a child. That friendship lasted for more than a season. That parents would live forever. That a woman could do whatever she set her mind to.

Learning the truth about the world was turning out to be one of the most painful parts of growing up in it.

CHAPTER 6

In the days that followed, Alwyn was to hear rather more of the Rogues of St. Just than she cared to. If it had not been clear to her at this ball and that rout that a young lady's reputation could indeed be tainted by association with such men, whether they had been friends in childhood or not, it was certainly clear now.

But that did not mean she had to accept it meekly when it was just too annoying.

"Really, it is too bad of them to have put themselves beyond the pale," she told Karensa in the ladies' dressing room at Lady Blessing's card party. "They are practically the only gentlemen we know in Town, and we ought not to speak lest some busybody see it and spread gossip."

"Do you want to speak?" Karensa patted her own hair in a way that made one think she meant to soothe it. *There, there. It will be all right.*

"They are our neighbors. I would speak to them if we were in company at home."

"Goodness, Alwyn." Rowena pinched color into her

cheeks, leaning into the mirror. "There are any number of other gentlemen who would be delighted to speak to you. Be happy with the birds in your hand, and stop fretting about the ones up in the boughs."

It was good advice. But the situation still galled her.

It was more galling still when they descended the stairs to see Jago Tremayne walk into the study, laughing with Lord Blessing and several other men.

"What is he doing here?" Rowena whispered as they seated themselves at a table with Mr. Danforth and the young lady rumored to be the object of his affections. Once again she was wearing pale blue. Perhaps she knew that the color looked well with her eyes.

But Danforth overheard her as he was dealing the cards. "Whom do you mean, Miss Rowena?"

"Mr. Tremayne," she said, flushed at having been caught speaking out of turn. "I had understood he was not fit for good company."

Danforth laughed, and the girl in blue laughed with him. "Do not say so in my brother-in-law's hearing," he said. "He and Blessing have been friends since they were at Oxford together, and he is a frequent guest here. My sister says he is refreshing."

"So his reputation as a rogue is not justified, then?"

The girl in blue still looked amused. "Oh, I daresay it is. But one likes him all the same, even with all his peculiarities. After all, if he and his two friends have vouchers for Almack's, they cannot be all bad, can they?"

"So says the lady for whom he once set his cap," Danforth teased her. "Ought I to be anxious?"

She turned over a card and waggled the queen of hearts at

him. This seemed to satisfy him, and the game began in high good humor.

"I think there are degrees of danger to a lady in the company of men like the Rogues of St. Just," his partner in blue mused aloud as she laid down a card. "Perhaps for a young lady recently come to town for her first Season, they do pose quite a risk. Such a person may not know how to behave, or may be inadequately chaperoned."

"But to someone who lives here, who is regularly in company, and has danced with one or all under the noses of the Patronesses, perhaps the risk is not so great," said Danforth. "Is that a fair assessment, Miss Montgomery?"

She nodded, and took the card he had just laid down. "And for someone like the Dowager Countess Eaton, why ..." She allowed her words to trail away suggestively.

Alwyn could contain herself no longer. "She is in no danger at all, and may keep company with whom she pleases?"

Danforth chuckled. "The Dowager Countess occupies such a place in society that no one can afford to cut her, even if they wished to. While there might be whispers, no door remains closed to her. She is received in all the best circles."

"As is Sir Perran Geoffrey, her most frequent escort," Miss Montgomery said. "Goodness, listen to us gossiping. Quite awful. Let us talk of something else. Miss Penrose, I so enjoyed the ball Lord and Lady Mainwaring gave for you and your sisters after you were presented. Will they be giving another?"

Alwyn had been staring at her cards, seeing not the hearts and clubs but the countess on Perran's arm. *Her most frequent escort.*

"Are Lady Eaton and Sir Perran Geoffrey engaged, Miss Montgomery?"

The blue eyes widened. "I beg your pardon?"

Too late, Alwyn realized she had not only been rude in ignoring the young lady's question, she had displayed a deplorable interest in returning to the subject of gossip.

"Not that we have heard," Mr. Danforth said into the pause. "There has certainly been no announcement in the papers. Do you have a particular interest, Miss Penrose?"

Under the card table, Rowena's foot pressed gently on Alwyn's toes.

"No, indeed," her youngest sister said smoothly. "It is only that we are acquainted with the gentleman's family in Cornwall. His grandmother, Lady Geoffrey, dined with us frequently before our mother died, and we see her and Sir Perran's sister at church. We have known them since we were all children together."

"Have you?" Danforth exchanged a glance with the insufferable Miss Montgomery that Alwyn could not read. "I understand your interest, then. Is Mr. Tremayne also a childhood friend?"

"My sister was too young to have known much of him at home," Alwyn said as calmly as though she had not narrowly missed disgracing herself by pressing near strangers for details about someone else's love affair. "But yes, both he and Captain Teague are known to us. You may not be aware that my uncle is great friends with Admiral Teague, who once served as lieutenant under Admiral Nelson himself?"

"I did not know that." Miss Montgomery smiled, all good humor restored. "I see now why their reputations in town are a matter of concern to you. As they should be. I am very much afraid, Miss Penrose, that your childhood friends have changed irrevocably."

"So I observe," Alwyn said. "But surely it is possible for us to speak, in a house such as this, in respectable company?"

Miss Montgomery smiled at her with the kind of condescension that a lady of society gives an inexperienced schoolgirl. It made Alwyn want to upend the young woman's neat stack of cards into her lap. "Perhaps you ought to ask Lady Mainwaring these questions. I am certainly no chaperone." Her laughter tinkled, and she and Danforth proceeded to win the trick.

"Have a care, Alwyn," Rowena said to her as they made their way to the refreshments table some time later, having received a sound drubbing by Danforth and his partner in blue. "You are asking too many questions about those gentlemen."

"I know, but—"

"Your interest in Sir Perran as an old friend is understandable. But he is changed. They all are. We must simply put them out of our minds and find new friends elsewhere." Her sister glanced at her as she selected a *petit four* and a piece of fruit. "Unless there is something you are not telling me."

"Certainly not."

"Then why do you pursue the subject?"

Alwyn felt her throat close, and she swallowed. "I suppose it is because … that summer before he went away to school, we got on so well. Perran and I. We were inseparable."

"You were children. That is no reason to make people talk about you now."

"Can I not miss what once was? Can I not wish that I might find my friend again?"

Rowena gazed at her. "You may as well wish the old king would regain his sanity, or that Papa had never gone driving that day."

"You sound like Jago Tremayne," Alwyn said crossly. "Telling the truth with no regard for the pain or inconvenience it inflicts."

Rowena tossed her head, and her golden curls bounced upon her cheeks. "I do not. As Mama would certainly remind us if she were still here, people who live truthfully are never hurt by it."

Alwyn could only wish that were so. But when Jago Tremayne entered the room in search of refreshments a few minutes later, she and Rowena departed it in favor of the music room, and did not engage him in conversation.

"Dash it all, Griff, I had much rather go to the club," Perran grumbled as Griffin practically dragged him up the steps of the Blessing house.

"I don't doubt it, but Blessing and Danforth are good company, and her ladyship has a crowd in this evening. Jago is probably already here. You know Lady Blessing is always good for an excellent spread."

"Were we invited?"

"Jago was."

Which meant that they all were. Perran resigned himself with as good a grace as he could muster. It lasted for exactly as long as it took to follow the footman and the sound of "Robin Adair" up the stairs, where Rowena was seated at the pianoforte. While she played and sang, Alwyn turned the pages for her.

Had he known the Penrose sisters were going to be here, he would have told Griff to jump in the Thames and taken himself off to his club alone. Reluctantly, he took up a station along the side wall with Jago and one or two others, and permitted himself the pleasure of watching Alwyn only because it would have seemed strange if his attention were fixed elsewhere.

She leaned close to Rowena, not enough to impede her sister's skill upon the keys, but as though she were unaware of her own protectiveness. Her cheeks were flushed, no doubt at being the object of every eye, but her timing as she turned the pages was perfect. Rowena did not miss a note.

There was an art to turning pages, as he had learned when his grandmother or Isolde had played the pianoforte and that task had fallen to him. He sighed at the memory. They had had to sell the beloved instrument along with the harp some time ago, and he did not think his grandmother had forgiven him yet.

Tonight Alwyn wore a muslin dress the color of cream, with short puffed sleeves, its skirts embroidered in cream thread in a pattern of flowers and leaves curling up from the hem. Her hair was caught up in a thin gauze scarf. All she needed to complete the Grecian effect was an urn upon her shoulder, and possibly a lamb at her feet.

He could not imagine which would be softer, her skin or the lamb's—

Griffin nudged him. "I did not know Miss Rowena played the pianoforte."

"Nor did I."

"She plays very well." Jago's gaze had not left the winsome pair, either.

The young buck on Perran's other side leaned in to whisper, "Are you acquainted with them? Any chance you might put in a good word for me with the fair musician?"

Perran mastered the urge to insert the puppy headfirst into the nearest potted palm. "Good evening, Bettisham. Have you been introduced?"

"Yes, but the young lady is always surrounded. I had hoped to find a way to make her notice me."

"She likes to dance," Griffin said helpfully. "Perhaps they will be at Almack's on Wednesday."

The boy brightened and slouched away to find a better view of Rowena.

A gathering thunderstorm, however, had a happier aspect than Jago. "You are not helping," the latter growled.

Griffin and Perran both glanced at him in surprise. "Are you acting the part of elder brother and attempting to winnow the field?" Griffin asked with some interest.

"Certainly not. But sending the puppies crying after her? Was that necessary?"

"Nothing wrong with being thought a belle," Perran pointed out, more to stick a burr under Jago's saddle than because he really thought so. "Doesn't every young lady wish to conquer London and be sought after by lovelorn swains?"

The selection came to an end, and Jago was forced to beat his hands together in applause rather than reply. Griffin's lips were pressed tight. He seemed to be stifling the urge to laugh.

"I think we must find out whether our erstwhile neighbors and their chaperone have tickets for Wednesday next," Perran went on mercilessly so that Jago could hear. "If they have not yet made their obeisances at the temple of the *ton*, that is."

"I quite agree," Griffin said.

This was too much for Jago. He pushed past them, no doubt heading for Blessing's study and the decanters on the sideboard. Rowena and Alwyn took their seats while the Montgomery heiress took her place at the pianoforte. She did not appear to need sheet music, but rather executed a tarantella with all the sensitivity and emotion of a mantel clock …. or a purebred racehorse in a headlong gallop to the coda.

Danforth thought her a diamond of the first water. The sooner he proposed, the less likely the rest of them would be forced to endure exhibitions of such skill.

It was only after the other young ladies had played and sung that the audience broke up to enjoy sherry and conversation in the spacious rooms. Several men who were card players took themselves off to Blessing's study to make up hands for a second round. Perran, who had learned his lesson early on about the flirtatious habits of Lady Fortune, declined.

And while his attention was distracted, he lost track of Alwyn's whereabouts. It was not until he entered the library for a bit of peace that he realized he was not the only one who had come seeking it.

"Excuse me." His stomach did a somersault at the sight of her slender form in the delicate gown, contrasted against the dark leather spines of the books. "I did not realize this room was occupied."

Alwyn turned, a book in one hand. "Sir Perran. Pray do not run away. I will not bite."

He felt the heat rise in his face and willed it down as he

leaned casually on the door frame. "Perhaps not, but gossip will."

Her fine dark brows knit, then smoothed out. "I understand that in a house such as this, I may at least converse with you without being compromised. Though in that quarter, I hardly think I am in any danger."

No? He begged to differ. For as she stood in the soft glow of the candelabra on Blessing's oak desk, it became starkly clear that only good manners and Constance put her in the right. Otherwise he might have lost his head and touched her. Stroked her bare arm between glove and sleeve with his fingers, just to see if her skin was as soft as it looked. Cupped her jaw to feel its fine bones. Lowered his mouth to taste the soft invitation of her lips.

He pushed off the door frame and wandered over to the shelves to distract himself. "What have you found to interest you?"

She glanced at the volume in her hand as though she had forgotten it. "Lord Byron's new book. I hadn't seen it before. Listen—

> She walks in beauty, like the night
> Of cloudless climes and starry skies;
> And all that's best of dark and bright
> Meet in her aspect and her eyes;
> Thus mellowed to that tender light
> Which heaven to gaudy day denies."

Every thought fled Perran's mind. Every ounce of his being seemed caught up in her voice, in the words that could have been describing the very woman who stood there in the tender light of the candles' glow.

Lord Byron had not met Alwyn Penrose before he decamped to the Continent. But he had captured her perfectly.

She walks in beauty.

Beauty he had just been touching, tasting in his imagination. Beauty that was as unreachable as the very stars. Beauty that he had best flee if he knew what was good for him. And her.

"I leave you to your reading, then," he choked out, and left the room before he did something he would regret.

CHAPTER 7

The next afternoon was an exhausting round of calls orchestrated by Aunt Celia, the only advantage of which was that Alwyn and her sisters were not at home to callers themselves. At least, that was Alwyn's private opinion.

"What if Lord Tallboys calls and I am not there?" Rowena fretted while Aunt Celia was occupied with several of her large acquaintance in Lady Woodbury's parlor. "I do not want him to think I am avoiding him."

"The butler will tell him you are out paying calls," Karensa said patiently. "He cannot blame you, since he is calling himself. What a nonsensical custom this is. A quarter of an hour, whether you like the people or not. Why does Aunt Celia do this?"

"Because it is the done thing," Rowena said.

"That is circular reasoning, and most unlike you."

"Because Aunt Celia likes people," Alwyn corrected them both. "She does this for the same reason you call on the vicar's wife and Lady Tregothnan, Karensa. Because you like them. If you did not go, you would not receive the invitations you do."

"*And* you hope to slip away long enough to see Lady Tregothnan's figurine collection every time you visit," Rowena put in slyly.

Karensa sighed. "Sadly, no one whom we have visited here possesses a collection of anything nearly so interesting, or I might be more inclined to return. Birds' nests and rocks from Egypt hold no charms for me."

Alwyn's definition of *interesting* did not resemble that of her sister. The other night at the Blessings', for instance, had been *interesting* in the last degree, though she would not repeat such a thing for the world. What did it say about her company that Perran Geoffrey had practically bolted from the room after exchanging only a few sentences? Had her reading of Byron's poem been so poor?

Not good enough.

Their forty thousand pounds apiece ought to make them good enough. But it did not, in his eyes at least. So, following that logic, his reasons must be more personal.

He did not like her as a woman grown, and that was that.

Not that she wanted to be liked by a rogue such as he. She wanted to know if that boy who had taught her to drive, who had kissed her in the sea, still had any regard for her. Except they were the same person. Which was very vexing.

"Miss Penrose," their hostess said to Alwyn, "are you enjoying your Season?"

"I am indeed, Lady Woodbury." Alwyn smiled to cover up the fact that she had been woolgathering and not attending to the conversation. "But I must say I am looking forward most to visiting Almack's on Wednesday."

Her hostess waved a hand to dismiss this notion. "High sticklers, bad food, and watery lemonade, my dear. No matter their status or title, the Patronesses' guests are treated to day-old bread and indifferent cheese. You would be better served going to the Darlings' ball. I hear young Comborn will be there."

"He may go where he pleases," Aunt Celia said crisply, "but I have gone to some effort to get tickets for the girls. We must make a good impression, after which even more doors will be open to them."

"I suppose that is the point," Lady Woodbury sighed. "What a tiresome business the Season is!"

Another lady leaned in. "I think a good Season is exciting. This one looks as though it might be shaping up well—I hear that an engagement is on the point of being announced, and it is only May."

"Danforth and the Montgomery girl?" Aunt Celia nodded once, decidedly. "I should hope so. They are far too familiar with one another in company for Lady Blessing to let this go on much longer."

"They were merely partners at cards last night, Aunt Celia," Rowena protested. "And Alwyn and I were partners opposite. They trounced us. My sister wasn't paying attention."

"Partners at cards, two and three dances together at balls, seats so close at the theaters that they can converse openly…" The second lady shook her head. "But it is not they of whom I speak. I understand that soon a certain young dowager countess may be relinquishing her late husband's name."

A rivulet of icy crystals seemed to cascade down Alwyn's back.

"Is that so?" Lady Woodbury did not wait for a reply. "The pair of them are a scandal."

"The Dowager Countess Eaton and Sir Perran Geoffrey?"

Alwyn could have kissed her aunt for clarifying the matter. She was certainly not about to ask.

"Who else? She has money, and he has a great need of it. To say nothing of an abundance of charm and good looks on both sides. I have it from Lady Pennington that his house in Cornwall is going to blow down in the next wind—and his sister and grandmother still in residence."

"One must never blame a man for marrying well," Aunt Celia said comfortably. "He has a respectable title, and she a respectable fortune."

"But neither of them are respectable, are they?" Lady Woodbury glanced at Alwyn and her sisters, cleared her throat, and subsided.

"He has been a perfect gentleman when he has spoken to us." Good heavens, where had that come from? Horrified, Alwyn wished she could snatch back the words.

But it was too late. Lady Woodbury's gaze became glacial at being thus contradicted.

"You must remember, dear Lady Woodbury, that my late sister's family and that of Sir Perran are known to one another in Cornwall." Aunt Celia hastened to correct Alwyn's misstep. "It is difficult for me to forget that my dear sister often visited Rosevear Court—though it was not in any danger of blowing down, then—and received Sir Perran herself at Morvoren Manor."

"He was a boy." This seemed to clinch the matter.

"Is there no hope for them?" Karensa asked. "The Rogues of St. Just are doomed to be rogues forever, with no prospect of redemption?"

"A good marriage covers a multitude of sins, it would

seem," Aunt Celia said when it appeared Lady Woodbury could or would not answer. "Constance Eaton is no fool, despite her willingness to put off her black gloves so soon. She'll have him in the traces and pulling his weight in no time, you'll see."

To Alwyn's mind, this did not sound like something to look forward to.

"It often happens that even a rogue may redeem himself in Society by attaching himself to a young lady of good fortune and good character," agreed the lady whose name Alwyn couldn't recall. "I would not recommend it for present company, however."

"Why not, Mrs. Hemphill?" Rowena asked. "May we not redeem a man as well as anyone?"

Hemphill. That was her name. Rowena was much better at remembering who was who than Alwyn could ever hope to be.

But Mrs. Hemphill merely colored, sniffed, and sided with Lady Woodbury on the subject of the Rogues. Which meant an uncomfortable silence until Aunt Celia was driven to remark upon the weather.

How soon would an engagement be announced, Alwyn wondered, and the boy she had once known lost to her forever? With his woman of good fortune—the kind of fortune, indeed, that made up for certain deficiencies of reputation.

She should take her sister's excellent advice and think of him no more. For what could she do? Aside from forcing him into a compromising situation and thereby delivering her own character into disrepute—nothing.

And besides, who wanted a husband who had to be forced

to the altar when there were so many other prospects willing to be led?

THERE WAS a purpose to paying calls, and Aunt Celia laid out her strategy with the military precision of any colonel. If their Season was to be a success, it would be entirely down to her social connections, to say nothing of her pleasant conversation and amiable way of making everyone in the room feel comfortable and included.

Alwyn could only hope that she would be such a hostess some day, even if she could not fully appreciate her aunt's efforts at every moment.

Today's entertainment was to be singular, though. Alwyn would gladly have paid a dozen calls if it meant being able to see a balloon lift off in St. James's Park.

"They are to take people up in it!" Rowena practically bounced on the seat of the landau in excitement, making its springs creak. "How I should love to fly, too."

"That you will not," their uncle said firmly. Since he was as interested as they, he was their escort today while their aunt stayed at home to receive callers. Someone had to deal with the bouquets. Much as Alwyn adored flowers, she had resolved she would not be the one to stay behind.

"But Uncle, I am sure it is safe," Rowena protested. "Why, the papers say the Pettyfer brothers have sailed nearly all the way to Bath without incident."

"I do not doubt they have, these brave men. But no niece of mine will risk her neck in such an entertainment. Your necks are worth a pretty sum, my dears. I'll not have you tumbling out of baskets today."

The balloonists had drawn quite a crowd—several hundred—despite the fact that the day was grey and they had to put up the hoods of the landau in case it rained. They had been fortunate in several days of sunny weather, but as Karensa had said as she pulled an umbrella out of the stand next to the door, "The month of May cannot be trusted. Darling buds must come from somewhere."

Alwyn gasped with awe as they caught sight of the balloon, tied to stakes driven into the grass. It was striped in red and buff, and around its circumference was a festive garland of bunting in the colors of the nation's flag.

"Such a sight to be seen!" their uncle said happily. "I have not viewed an ascension since Sadler, during the celebrations in 1814."

As they made their way through the crowd, a man handed a woman in a brown velvet pelisse into the basket. Another man who was clearly in charge gave them some instructions, and then the fire roared, the ropes were cast off, and the balloon rose gracefully into the sky.

The crowd gasped in wonder. Alwyn held her shako hat with one hand so that it would not tip off altogether as she craned her neck back to watch. In a moment, it seemed, the balloon and its fortunate occupants were safely above the trees and sailing in the direction of Buckingham Palace.

"Imagine being able to look down upon the Prince Regent," she said to Karensa.

Her sister did not reply, which was odd. She had an opinion about everything—and Prinny in particular.

Alwyn brought her attention back to earth with a bump to see that neither of her sisters was anywhere near her, and the crowd was moving and surging like the ocean itself, some currents carrying people toward the man selling tickets, and some carrying them in the direction of the palace, perhaps to see whether or not the balloon would bump into the royal chimney pots.

A crack of thunder sent another current of people scurrying for the trees and shelter. Where on earth were her sisters and uncle? Alwyn cast about, and caught a glimpse of the yellow plumes of Rowena's hat. But when she caught up to the lady, she found it was not Rowena at all.

"Well, goodness me," she said to no one in particular, looking anxiously into one face after another.

And now it began to rain in earnest. Sadly, a number of people besides Karensa had brought umbrellas, so instead of being able to pick her sisters out, she was worse off than before, for she could see neither faces nor clothing.

And they were dry, and she was not. Oh, her poor hat, to be treated so on its first excursion out of doors!

There was nothing for it—she would have to return to the landau and horses and wait. Perhaps they were inside it already, warm and dry, while her brave hat with its tassels and gold braid would be altogether ruined. But when she got to the pavement where she could have sworn the landau had been waiting, she could not see it. Other carriages there were in abundance, and people climbing into them seeking shelter from the downpour, but not the glossy yellow and black equipage belonging to Uncle Edward.

Bother! She had got turned around. They must be on the other side of the park. She must go at once.

"For heaven's sake, Miss Penrose, get in."

She looked up in some astonishment at the sound of the

familiar baritone, clipped with irritation. "Sir Perran," she said rather blankly. "What are you doing here?"

"Fishing you out of a deluge, obviously. Get in before you are soaked further."

Another crash of thunder acted like a blast of steam from the beam engine at the pit, and she practically leaped up into the sleek little two-seater he was driving. He hauled her in beside him and shook the reins over the two greys' backs.

"Where is your family?" he asked. "What are you doing in all this crowd alone?"

"I am not alone, of course. Or I was not until a moment ago." She pulled a slightly damp handkerchief from her reticule and dabbed at her face where water had run off the brim of her hat. "We came to see the ascension, but the rain has scattered everyone. I thought my uncle had left the landau here, but I do not see it. Where are we going?"

"I am taking you home."

"But my uncle—"

"We cannot very well drive around and around the park looking for them, not in all this traffic. The wretched balloonists ought to have gone to Primrose Hill, where at least there is space."

"Then their passengers would not have been able to say they flew over the Prince, like the cow jumping over the moon."

His mouth twitched, then settled into a firm line, as though he had been going to smile and thought better of it.

"You are a very good driver," she said presently, as he took them away from the park at a rapid clip. Lesser equipages moved out of the way as the authoritative sound of his greys' hooves gave them advance warning.

"Thank you. I have had plenty of experience, and this little phaeton is easy to handle."

"May I take the reins?"

"Certainly not." He glanced at her with a frown. "This is not exactly a pony and trap."

So he did remember!

"I haven't driven a pony and trap since I was sixteen," she informed him down her nose. "Papa gave me a phaeton and pair when I turned eighteen, so that I could pay calls and go to the pit."

"Go to the pit? Do you mean the clay pit? Whatever would you do that for?"

This did not even deserve the dignity of a reply. "I need only a little practice in the traffic," she said instead. "The horses seem to be used to it."

"They are. But I ask again, why go to the pit? That is no place for a lady."

"I have been going my whole life," she said, since he would pursue it. "And to the piers, and to the pottery. Mostly the pottery. While I may not know as much as Papa or Enyon Lander, the manager there, I do know a great deal."

He stared at her, before his attention was jerked back to the road in front of him by a high flyer coming out of a side street. He hauled on the reins and the other vehicle careened past them, practically on two wheels. The driver grinned like a madman and touched the brim of his hat with his whip in thanks.

"Crazy fool," Perran growled.

"Do you know him?"

"Not to speak to, only by sight. Landry, I believe. Foolish puppy."

She could no longer see the vehicle, for the flap in the hood behind her was closed. "He will see someone killed if he does not slow down. As I was saying—"

"Indeed. But allow me to advise you, Miss Penrose. Even if you were expert in all matters concerning your family's interests in St. Austell, you'd best not let it get out, or you will be accused of dabbling in trade."

"Nonsense." Should she ask him what had happened between them the other evening? Would he think her a fool—or indelicate? Oh, bother. If one did not ask, one did not learn. "I hear you dabble in things far worse, and you are still received."

"What on earth do you mean?"

He could not possibly be unaware of his own reputation. "In Cornwall a young lady may go to the pit, but here she may not even speak of it—or of much worse things," she said primly. "And yet a gentleman may behave in ways he never could in Cornwall."

This time she did surprise a laugh out of him. "You minx. I hope you have perceived that the reason I am driving these poor cattle at such a pace is so I can get you home before anyone realizes who it is you are with."

"Heavens, no. I had thought rather that you enjoyed the speed of it. I was about to protest for the horses' sake."

To her gratification, he did slow them, though not to a walk. They were nearly to Chesham Place, though, and if she was to discover what she wanted to know, she must screw her courage to the sticking point and be quick about it.

"But I must know, Sir Perran … why did you leave the Blessings' library in such a hurry the other night?"

The smile faded from his lips. "I did no such thing."

"Indeed you did. If you were a pilchard and I a sea gull, you could not have quitted it faster. Had I offended you? Or do you simply dislike Lord Byron's lines that much?"

"A pilchard?"

"Yes, the fish that—"

"I know what a pilchard is. I have just never been compared to one, that is all."

"They are utterly necessary to a large part of the population of Cornwall. I am sure you are quite as necessary to your sister and grandmother. So you see, the metaphor is apt."

He shook his head. "I see I had best keep my wits about me, or next I shall be accused of being a grunion. Or possibly a crab. There was nothing in your behavior that was unseemly, unlike the author of your choice of reading material. I simply judged it time to leave you in solitude, before some curious matron appeared in the doorway."

"Must you be so solicitous of my reputation?"

He made the turn into Chesham Place. "It is too late for my own, so I must be careful of yours. Believe me, you do not want it otherwise. It is the only currency you possess in Society."

"I will thank you to leave what I want to me."

"Is that wise, Miss Penrose?" He drew up before the door of the Mainwaring house. "Young ladies are notorious for not knowing what they want."

Her gaze dropped from his eyes, long-lashed and hazel and full of false gravity, to his mouth, just as his lips formed the shape of a kiss on the word *want*.

Her breathing stopped. The world went silent.

She dragged her gaze from his lips, tracing his straight

nose, his eyes, the line of his brows under their fashionable tumble of dark curls.

His eyes. Which had not moved from her face—as though he, too, could hear the word *want* still echoing between them.

"Miss Penrose?" said a different voice. The moment snapped with an almost audible sound, and Alwyn turned to find the footman next to her on the pavement. Wordlessly, she put her hand in his and allowed him to assist her to the ground.

She turned to thank Perran for conveying her home, but the horses lurched into motion and his phaeton rolled away down the street.

Neither of them had thought to say good-bye.

Perran returned Constance's phaeton and greys to the mews, and to his surprise, found her upstairs at her desk in the sitting room. She was finishing up a note in her quick, decisive way.

"I did not expect to see you here." He bowed, and she lifted her hand for his kiss. She was dressed to go out, her hat—a dashing affair much like the one worn by Alwyn Penrose—on the table beside her.

"I did not expect to be here, but I found I must send one or two notes, including one to dear Silence."

Since he did not care overmuch for Lady Jersey, he did not press her about the subject of such a note. Her correspondence was none of his business.

"Did you see the ascension?" She folded the note, sealed it, and collected her gloves and hat.

"I did. The Pettyfers are offering flights at a guinea a couple. Would you like to visit someone in Bath, or Kent, and arrive by balloon?"

"I would not." She pulled on the gloves—the green ones he had given her. "What a question."

"Imagine if a balloon landed in the field at Rosevear Court. My grandmother would expire of the shock, and my sister would run out to ask if she might come up in it."

"Mm."

Seeing that she was not about to accompany him even on a flight of fancy, he said, "Are you going to the shops? Would you like me to escort you? "

Now she stopped, a wrinkle forming between those fine brows. "Perran, my goodness. Do stop pressing me."

Pressing her? He was merely being polite. "I was not aware I was."

"Well, you are. Why are you here? Where are you going? Next you will ask me who I am going with, and I will lose my patience."

She was not in the habit of speaking to him like this. He removed himself to the fire, which she had likely had lit because of the gloomy day that was more like November than May. Leaning on the mantel, he affected a study of the bristling flock of her invitations. "I would not dream of asking any such thing."

"Good, for I find such behavior tiresome. Are you here for dinner?"

After this, he was tempted to go to the club and see if Jago or Griffin were there. "Only if you want me to be."

She sighed. "The only thing worse than a hoverer is a martyr."

Stung, he kept his voice level. "I had planned to go to my club."

"Very well. Do that. Perhaps I will see you tomorrow."

Tomorrow. He watched her leave the room, the leather heels of her black half-boots tapping on the parquet floor, the fine wool of her hunter green pelisse swinging about her ankles. *Tomorrow* meant that she had no objection to his visiting her at breakfast. Was he really such a lapdog? Would he allow her to treat him like this?

Not he, by George.

Perhaps he would stay abed tomorrow, and appreciate the freedom of having no obligations to fulfill. Or go out to improve his boxing, or fencing. He could do any number of things with a free morning.

He found Jago at the club, buried in the scandal sheets with a glass of wine at his elbow. Perran settled into the leather chair beside him, ordered the same from the steward, and relieved his friend of several of the sheets, purchased on a number of different street corners.

The sheet crinkled as Jago looked over it. "Didn't expect to see you here."

"That seems to be a common theme today."

Jago looked pained. "Do I want to know?"

Perran half expected him to duck back behind the rampart of the news. "A tiny upset in the domestic teapot. Constance accused me of hovering, and so I have come here to prove I am doing no such thing."

"You? Unlikely. Unless Isolde is ill. On those occasions I have seen you hover."

"A polite interest in someone's activities is not hovering."

"Certainly not. Perhaps she does not wish you to know of her activities."

"I do not need to know them. She may do as she pleases, and so may I."

"Which is why you are here."

"Precisely."

"Supper?"

"Of course."

Jago returned to the sheet, and Perran glanced at the topmost of the ones he held. Tickets were advertised for Almack's for the upcoming month. For the price of them, he could glaze half the windows at Rosevear Court. Perhaps he would, and annoy Constance to no end when she found out.

He snorted as his eye fell on an announcement. "Danforth has put his hand to the plow, it seems."

"I beg your pardon?" Jago folded the paper down again. One of his more peculiar traits was that he could not hear when he was reading.

"Danforth's engagement to the Montgomery girl has merited two full inches."

"For this you dragged me out of an account of the boxing?" Jago complained, and returned to it.

Perran turned the page over. The gossip column purportedly written by An Observant Gentleman was hardly worth a serious man's attention, but everybody read it. Half the *ton* were convinced it was written by a woman—Lady Cowper had the lead in the betting books. The other half believed the Prince Regent himself was responsible. But that was ludicrous —for leaving off the difficulty of his going about unseen in company, when had Prinny bestirred himself to read anything, let alone write it?

It was our pleasure to observe this week that young Monsieur C— is squiring about town the lovely Miss P— and her £40,000. We wish him good fortune! Heaven knows that chateaux are expensive to keep up. Just like appearances.

Speaking of the Misses P—, we were delighted to observe that the youngest is an accomplished dancer. Perhaps she ought to make herself known at a certain temple of the ton? But not too much known. There is nothing more disgusting to the arbiters of taste than a young lady who is too forward. Why, anything could happen. Look at Lady C— E —. She bagged an earl between the lemonade and The Punchbowl.

Speaking of that lady, when will a certain desirable event take place, we wonder? Come, come, Sir P— G—. If you don't saddle that purebred mare, someone else is sure to! Then again, without a stable it's difficult to house any creature of a delicate constitution. Best to fill the manger left by its previous owner and be done.

Perran put down the sheet, a cold tingle of rage and certainty running down his spine. Could this scurrilous and disrespectful bit of spite be the reason for Constance's temper this afternoon? Surely she hadn't taken it seriously. They were both perfectly content with the progress of his courtship.

Weren't they?

A new arrival in town has caused quite a flutter among feminine hearts. A certain Mr. L— was recently spotted at the opera in the company of young Lady S— D— and her redoubtable mother. A little bird whispered that he may be a relation of Miss P— mentioned above. If so, perhaps one might wonder if young Lady S — has chosen her china pattern yet? One hears that the Gilded Lily *pattern can be had for the asking!*

Perran folded the sheet and dropped it under his chair. He

had been the target of An Observant Gentleman's acid pen many a time, as had all the Rogues. But this column seemed particularly pointed. Particularly eager to point out the flaws of its victims, most of whom were enjoying their first Season and were thus especially vulnerable.

He had been right to be cautious in his acquaintance with the Penrose sisters. From the looks of this column, Alwyn had had a narrow escape. If anyone had seen the two of them in the Blessing library or driving home in the rain today, her reputation would be on such precarious footing that all it would take would be one more whisper, one flicker of an eyelash, and the whole edifice would fall.

The antidote to rumors of being in company with another young lady was to put himself at the disposal of the one society believed to be his object. He had best make it up with Constance. And perhaps they had better have a more serious conversation about the future.

He believed their expectations to be similar, but despite their conversations, he still did not know with certainty. It was all too easy to take an enjoyable situation for granted and not wish to change it.

Jago put down the sporting columns. "Anything interesting?"

"An Observant Gentleman has made a few too many impertinent remarks."

"I said *interesting*."

Perran retrieved the sheet from the floor, folded it so the column was uppermost, and handed it to him. "He is making rather free with the young ladies from home."

Jago read, his frown deepening as he got to the foot of the column. Then he, too, tossed the sheet on the floor. "Dashed cheek. I'd like to call the wretch out and stuff his words down his throat."

"I would be your second without hesitation."

"He has no business making such remarks about our young friends' behavior, which is above reproach."

"Almost."

Jago's startled gaze swung to his. "What do you mean? Has Rowena—"

"No, not she. I was alone in the library with Alwyn for two minutes at the Blessings'."

"Stupid, but not irredeemable."

Little did he know. Nor was Perran about to inform him. "And I conveyed her home in Constance's phaeton this afternoon. She became separated from her party at the balloon ascension in St. James's Park."

Jago blinked. "Great Caesar's ghost. What were you thinking? Were you seen?"

"Only by Landry, who is getting a raking-over of his own, as you just observed. And what I was *thinking* was to get a girl out of the rain so she did not have to walk a mile in the wet."

But this did not seem to hold any water with Jago. "You know Landry? Can he be trusted to keep his trap shut? Is he actually related to the family?"

"No—I don't know—I have no idea." Perran knew Jago would insist on his questions being answered in order. "Heaven only knows where the Gentleman gets his information. Alwyn did not seem to recognize Landry, so perhaps the Gentleman is merely stirring the soup hoping something will float up from the bottom of the pot."

Jago sat back, a finger along his upper lip. The burgundy leather cushions creaked softly as they adjusted to the shift in his weight. "I highly recommend that you do not allow yourself to be alone in her company again, to say nothing of taking her up in Constance's phaeton. What if that lady should hear of it?"

He had not thought of it that way until this moment. "Let us hope she does not. Though I would probably tell her exactly what I have just told you."

"If she gave you the chance and did not throw a piece of china at your head."

With Constance, one was as likely as the other. Possibly simultaneously.

The bell rang for dinner, much to his relief. In the dining room, he and Jago seated themselves at a table set for three in case Griffin should turn up. They were just being served the soup when he did.

Wordlessly, the steward vanished and returned in a moment with a third basin of soup.

"Thank you, Fielding," Griff said. "You take good care of me."

"It is my pleasure, Captain," the steward said. Then, "Sir Perran, a note has come for you. Would you like me to bring it in now, or after dinner?"

"After dinner, if you don't mind, Fielding." Whatever it was could take second place to the club's excellent food; he was hungry.

"Very good, sir."

By the time the roast arrived with a boat of horseradish and roast vegetables, Perran was himself again. "Griffin, have you seen The Observant Gentleman's column today?"

"I have." Griffin tucked into his beef with gusto. "Can't say I appreciate his sporting with our young friends' names."

"My sentiments exactly," Jago growled. "Cheeky wretch." He then proceeded to regale Griffin with an orderly list of Perran's lapses in judgement where the young ladies were concerned.

Griffin shook his head. "What's got into you, my friend? Never known you to have a taste for white dresses before. Too dangerous."

"The innocent ingenue may be tender, but to me she is bland and tasteless, as well you know," Perran retorted. "I must say, it is dashed inconvenient that they are here. One can hardly cut them, yet speaking with them—"

"Or, heaven forbid, dancing with them," Jago put in.

"—is fraught with dangers."

"For them," Griffin said.

"Precisely," Perran agreed.

"And yet somehow there is the library, and the ballroom, and the phaeton," Jago mused, helping himself to another slice of roast. "To be quite blunt, old man, Miss Penrose is an excellent prospect for you. Forty thousand pounds, houses in the same parish, families acquainted. And there's something to be said for knowing somewhat of one's bride before the wedding. Don't care for the thought of taking a pig in a poke, myself."

As one, Griffin and Perran put down their cutlery and stared.

Jago looked up at the *clink* from either side of him. "Why are you gaping at me like a pair of pilchards?"

Pilchards again!

"Did you just recommend to our friend that he propose to Alwyn Penrose?" Griffin's voice was a little high, as though laughter were strangling him under his perfectly knotted linen.

"Are you mad?" Perran managed. Instead of igniting his own urge to bellow with laughter, Griffin's hilarity irritated him past bearing. Must everyone bat the poor girl's name about like a shuttlecock today?

"Not at all. Quite sensible, really. Except for the Countess. Bit of a high hedge there, I grant you."

Perran scrubbed at his mouth with his napkin. Flung it down. Rose and pushed back his chair. "I'll not listen to such nonsense from people who purport to be my friends. Excuse me. I'll see about that note Fielding mentioned."

He stalked from the dining room in high dudgeon, perfectly conscious that his behavior was making Griffin laugh even harder. He nodded to the gentlemen he knew as he passed their tables, and found Fielding in the corridor.

"I was just coming in with it, Sir Perran."

"Fielding, you are a treasure."

He took the note into one of the studies, which was empty during the dinner service.

Perran,

I am taking a few days to visit Brighton with the Duchess of Barminster. I find London tiresome just at the moment, and good-byes can be so taxing.

Feel free to use the mews as if they were your own. I have the carriage and greys, but Atlas and Henriette will need to be exercised. I know I can trust you, at least, not to haul upon a horse's mouth.

I expect to return on Tuesday, so if you like, we can enjoy dinner together the day following, and attend Almack's.

Your own

Constance

Blankly, he reread the note. Send a note or two, she had said. She had written this right in front of him! Why could she not have told him to his face she was going to Brighton? Why the subterfuge?

It was no secret that Constance adored the machinations of society, of maneuvering people to do what she wanted so winningly that they hardly minded. He had been one of the pawns on her chessboard a time or two, but since there was no real harm in it, he had allowed her the pleasure.

Now he resented her obvious attempt to make him feel … what? Guilt for allowing their names to be coupled in a gossip column when he had not proposed? Was she simply giving him the opportunity to miss her? Or was she testing her charm, to see if he would chase her to Brighton like a hound baying after a fox?

He was no hound.

Nor was he a lapdog.

He tossed the note in the fire and returned to his dinner, where he engaged Jago in a rousing debate over the merits of the latest star of Gentleman Jackson's boxing establishment.

The names of the Penrose sisters did not come up again.

CHAPTER 9

On Sunday after church, Lord and Lady Mainwaring welcomed their son and his wife and children to Chesham Place for lunch. They were all armed with umbrellas, but the fractious spring weather had decided to improve while they were still singing the final hymn, and presented them with flirtatious sunshine in which to ride home.

After lunch, Alwyn suggested to the children that they make paper boats to sail in the park. But unaccountably, the sheets and newspapers were missing from her uncle's study, and none of the staff could seem to locate them. Which was a shame, for she hadn't yet had a chance to read the gossip columns, and they were so very diverting.

Never mind. The children made do with laurel leaves, which were sturdy enough for toothpick masts, with bits of paper for sails. By the time the Penrose girls returned with them in high spirits, it was time for tea.

"Here you are, miss," the butler said, handing over several of the scandal sheets. "We found them at last."

"Oh, good. Where?"

"Her ladyship's room, miss."

"I hope she will not miss them, Pickering."

"No indeed, miss. They were under the bed."

It was too late to use the paper for boats, but at least Alwyn could take the smallest peep at the gossip columns before she joined the company in the drawing room. She sat in the cushioned window seat in her bedroom and immediately found today's column by The Observant Gentleman. Granted, his remarks this week about Monsieur Comborn still stung, to say nothing of his speculations about Mr. Landry, but imagine being noticed by such a personage as the Gentleman! Who could he be? Why, he might have been standing next to her, gazing at the pictures in the Summer Exhibition, and none of them the wiser.

We are overcome with desolation at the news that the lovely Lady E — has decamped to Brighton in august company. One wishes her ladyship a delightful time and cannot help but wonder if His Royal Highness is planning to follow to inspect this week's improvements to the Pavilion.

Or perhaps there are darker forces at work. A force colored a rather bilious green, perhaps, a most unflattering shade. For one hears that a certain Miss P— was taken up in a conveyance driven by Sir P— G—. A conveyance seating two. A conveyance, moreover, belonging to the aforesaid Lady E—. One hardly dares speculate, but cannot help but wonder if the two events are connected.

We beg that someone take pity on poor Miss P— and educate her as to the unsuitability of her transportation. She may find herself overturned in the mud and that would never do.

Alwyn could not breathe.

How in the name of heaven had the Gentleman found out? The driver of the barely controlled high flyer—Landry—it could not be their cousin, that was ridiculous—did not know her. Had some passer-by spotted them and sent a salacious note? The scandal sheet slid from her lap as she jumped to her feet, pacing to the bed and back while the very blood ran cold in her veins.

You did nothing wrong. Perran was merely being kind.

Perran's name was linked with that of the countess, and she'd had no business accepting a ride from him. No business looking at his mouth, either.

It is not as though he belongs to her. Not a man like Perran Geoffrey.

And now she was quibbling with herself.

Alwyn pressed both hands to her burning cheeks. No wonder Aunt Celia had flung the wretched sheets under the bed. Alwyn wished her aunt had burned them. She clearly had not believed a word, or she would have rung such a peal over Alwyn's head as would have deafened her for days.

She must conceal her new, unwelcome knowledge. She must walk more circumspectly in future. Perran had warned her, hadn't he? And she had not listened. She, a newcomer, had believed herself above gossip, and now she was the subject of it. Public, printed gossip!

Alwyn shuddered in horror.

She would not confide even in Karensa, though in all likelihood someone would remark upon it before the week was out. And they were to attend Almack's on Wednesday! What shame might her behavior bring upon her sisters? Had she spoiled their chances, too?

Well, she had learned her lesson. Never again would she

allow Perran Geoffrey to bully her into his phaeton, though she were caught in a deluge of biblical proportions.

Lady Eaton's phaeton.

Alwyn blushed all over again, as though she had been caught red handed in the other woman's closet, trying on her dresses.

There was a tap upon the door and Karensa poked her head in. "Are you coming down, Alwyn? A new guest has arrived and our aunt is asking for you." She paused. "You look flushed. Are you quite well?"

"Yes." Alwyn gathered about her the scattered shreds of her self-control. "Yes, quite well. I will be down directly."

Not before she caught up the handful of scandal sheets and stuffed them into the fire. But even as the Observant Gentleman's words blackened and curled away into ash, she saw in her mind's eye hundreds, maybe thousands, of such sheets all over London—sold on street corners, lying out on tables, being shaken into order in clubs, waiting on desks in studies. And in every one, her behavior laid open to the censure of all.

No, she must not think such things. She would drive herself mad. Her aunt and uncle's guests were waiting; she must go down.

The children had been taken home by their nanny, leaving Mr. and Mrs. Mainwaring to stay for a simple dinner *en famille*. "And look who is but newly arrived in Town, Alwyn," her aunt said, leading her over to a young man who was deep in conversation with Lord Mainwaring. "It is your cousin Arthur Landry. Are you acquainted?"

Arthur Landry!

The young man turned around with a smile. Two facts tumbled into her mind at once, like a pair of dice tossed on a table. The first was that she recognized him: he was indeed the driver of the high flyer that had nearly collided with Perran's—Lady Eaton's—phaeton.

The second was his name—a name so reviled at Morvoren Manor that her father no longer allowed it to cross their lips. For Arthur Landry was the dreadful spectre—the 'heir male' spectre—who might sue for the inheritance of the Manor, if Alwyn did not find herself a gentleman to make a Lady and a mother of her.

In all their minds, Arthur Landry was a wastrel, a drunkard, an idle, slovenly pig who would inherit a property on which he had never lifted a hand, from a family he had never met. All because he was a man and she, Karensa, and Rowena were merely women, and in the event of Papa's death, alone and unprotected.

And yet—and yet—

He did not *look* like a spectre. And from his turnout, he was far from a slovenly pig.

A wolf in sheep's clothing, perhaps?

"Miss Penrose," he said in a voice that held music in it, "I am delighted to make your acquaintance at last. Our great-grandfathers were brothers, and it has always been a source of distress to me that their, shall we say, *rancorous* relationship has precluded my knowing your family."

His relations held such sway over his life that he could not have made the effort to become acquainted? But then, her own father, in loyalty to his late papa and the grandfather who had founded the family business, would no more have received the younger Landry than leaped from the cliffs into the sea.

Mr. Landry's eyes were the same clear blue as Rowena's,

and his straight dark hair was brushed forward a la Titus. His collar points were starched to a wonderful stiffness, his cravat a purposeful contrast, tied in the softer waterfall style.

When she offered him her hand with a soft, "How do you do?" his was firm and warm. The handshake of a friend well met.

"Mr. Landry was introduced to me at my club," her uncle said. "When I discovered that he was related by marriage to Lady Mainwaring, it was a matter of a moment to secure his acceptance to my invitation to dinner." To Mr. Landry, he said, "As you see, we are a small family party."

"The very best kind," Mr. Landry said with the firmness of conviction. "My mother does not entertain since my father's passing. I have two sisters, but they do not go out much in company. So you see, a family party with all new faces is a source of great delight to me." He twinkled at Alwyn in a way that would have been forward if he had not been a relative. "And some faces, I see now, are delightful all in themselves."

"I see you are a flatterer, sir," she said, uncertain whether or not to disapprove.

"Oh, no." The twinkle became an expression of gravity. "I merely observe and report, like a man of science." He excused himself to Lord and Lady Mainwaring, and invited her to walk with him over to the fire.

"And are you indeed a man of science?" she asked. Her father's raised voice on the subject of this gentleman banged so in her head that she hardly knew what to say. "What is your profession?"

"I had a year at Oxford before my father died," he said. "There it was my pleasure to study the classics—Latin and

Greek, with a particular focus on the travel epics." At her inquiring look, he explained, *"The Odyssey* is a good example."

His father must have been comfortably settled, then, to have afforded such an education for his son, even for only a year. Could Papa have been wrong? "Did you expect to find such tales useful in your own travels?"

"Alas, any hope of following in the footsteps of the ancient heroes was dashed when Papa was taken ill. He died of a putrid throat, I am sorry to say."

"My sincere condolences, sir." One of the porcelain glazers had died of the same, and though both Dr. Harris and Rowena had administered every tincture and potion they knew, they had not been successful and the poor man's pain before he died had been dreadful.

"You are most kind," he said quietly. "But time has been a great healer. Even my mother can now speak her husband's name with fond recollection rather than grief."

Fond recollection. That would mean, surely, that Mr. Landry's father had not shared his father's and grandfather's defects of character.

Rowena joined them, a little hesitantly. After a glance at Alwyn to see which way the wind blew, she relaxed and said, "Mr. Landry, do you stay long in London?"

"My plans are unsettled at present." He made room for her, generously seeing that she was warm enough without blocking the heat for the others in the room. "I find London to be infinitely interesting. One could spend years here without coming to the end of its diversions."

"One certainly could," Rowena agreed with a smile. "Though one hopes one will not have to."

"What do you mean, Miss Rowena?" He was already smiling, too, as though anticipating a pert answer.

"Why, simply that one hopes for an offer by the end of the Season," said Karensa with her usual blunt honesty as she joined them, and again Mr. Landry moved to the side so that she had the benefit of the warm hearth and he did not. "There are those in their fifth or sixth Season who see the young ladies becoming progressively younger. In my view, the prospects of interesting, well-read young women ought to depend upon their own abilities, not upon the whims of dance partners."

"Only too true," Alwyn agreed. "Instead, as you say, they must stand about in ballrooms, looking as though their life's ambition is to be asked to dance by some ridiculous dandy."

Mr. Landry looked rather as though he had swallowed his tongue. Rowena was quite used to her sisters' speeches, but Alwyn supposed that to a new acquaintance, they must come as rather a shock.

"I am certain that you will not meet with such a fate, Cousin Karensa," he said at last. "Nor you, Cousin Alwyn."

"On what do you base such a certainty?" Karensa asked with some interest. "We have only just met, and to be truthful, we expected nothing like—"

"What my sister means is that we did not expect to be so happily agreed," Rowena interposed smoothly. "It is such a shame that our families have been estranged. Perhaps it falls to the young to build where the elder would not. Do you plan to visit St. Just?"

"In the absence of Greece or Rome," Alwyn put in, "it has many beauties, including some ancient history that might interest you. While we have not the Roman ruins that some other areas of England boast, we do have a number of *menhirs* —that is, standing stones set in circles."

"To say nothing of barrows," Karensa agreed, having apparently taken the hint that her conversation ought to be less personal. "And old forts on practically every other hilltop."

It would never do for this attractive, amiable young man to know what they had been taught to think of him. Rowena was quite right. They ought to form their own opinions of his behavior, and not be influenced by old quarrels long past. Besides, Lord Mainwaring would not have introduced them, nor even invited Mr. Landry into his home, had he not been convinced he was a gentleman of good family and reputation.

"You make an appealing case for an historian," Mr. Landry said now with a chuckle. "Perhaps I ought to be managing a dig and writing learned books about your barrows before others decide it is an excellent idea, and steal a march on me."

At this interesting juncture, dinner was announced, and their host and hostess led the way into the dining room. Alwyn found herself seated between Mr. Landry and Mrs. Mainwaring, her cousin's wife. The latter was a gentle conversationalist, given to stories of her newborn son and the prospects of her garden now that early summer had arrived.

When the game course was served and the table turned, Alwyn felt a sense of anticipation at being able to speak to Mr. Landry of subjects that ranged a little farther afield.

"Have you had many invitations to balls and other gatherings, Mr. Landry?"

"Oh, do call me Cousin Arthur," he begged. "We may only be cousins once removed, but that does not signify." His gaze fell to his plate, puzzled. "Or is it twice removed? Second cousins?"

"Second cousins, I believe," she said. "Or possibly third. Where is your home? Do you live in Cornwall also?"

"No, I am sorry to say," he said. "While I have lodgings here at present, my mother and sisters live in a village far to the north, near York. She was the granddaughter of the aforesaid brother of your great-grandfather."

"I think I shall have to begin drawing a family tree," Alwyn said with a laugh. "Entire branches have been concealed from us, and they are becoming quite long."

If his great-grandfather had had no sons, and hers only one—Papa's father—then truly Arthur was the next male heir. How extraordinary that in all the population of London, they had come to meet!

"I feel the same way," he assured her. He handled fork and knife like a gentleman.

"My great-grandfather founded the Morvoren China Clay Company," she said. "Have you heard of it?"

"Only in passing," he replied, addressing himself to his excellent venison and vegetables. "My father knew nothing of it, and my grandmother had only secondhand information from her father."

"So you know nothing of the china clay industry?"

"Indeed not. My late father was a churchman with two livings. The closest he came to working with his hands was turning the pages of books, or pottering about in the garden, which he enjoyed very much."

And he had sent his son to Oxford? She could not very well ask Mr. Landry if he knew he might lay claim to such an inheritance, but surely he must know. If Papa knew his name, then surely their cousin would have been informed of the existence of the Morvoren estate.

How she wished Papa were here! Then he could see for himself that Cousin Arthur was no dreadful spectre, but simply an amiable man, the son of a clergyman. Someone not likely to steal anybody's property—who, in point of fact, seemed to have his own pleasures and plans for his life.

In Papa's absence, she would consult with Aunt Celia. Perhaps she and their uncle might make deeper inquiries into their cousin's family and prospects.

For it was not lost upon her that her relatives had been exceedingly hospitable to a virtual stranger. Alwyn was no fool; she could see through a grindstone when there was a hole in it. For if Cousin Arthur had come to London in search of a bride, what better choice could he make than one of his cousins? Could that truly be his aim? And had her aunt and uncle provided their tacit agreement?

He might very well propose to Alwyn.

And then Sir Perran Geoffrey could take himself to—to perdition in his lady's fancy phaeton, and cease plaguing her in the darkness of her dreams.

CHAPTER 10

I don't know why we come to these occasions," Jago complained as the three of them, dressed in black coats and pantaloons and dazzling white shirts as required, paused in the doorway to the receiving room upstairs at Almack's.

"We come to dance," Griffin said, for which unbelievable chaffing Jago quite reasonably implored patience from heaven.

"We come tonight, as you know very well, because the Penrose sisters are expected." Perran kept his voice low. "Try to behave. Ask none of them to dance, on pain of a beating with a flat blade next time we visit the piste at Angelo's."

"Oh, very well, Madame la Chaperone." Griffin elbowed him. "Fortunately, the field is alive with delightful pheasant this evening."

Obeisances to the Lady Patronesses duly made, the three proceeded into the ballroom. Had Lady Mainwaring and her charges already come? Had they been safely admitted into Society? Could he at last take a breath free of the fear that his own reputation might have done at least one of them harm? It was nearly ten o'clock, and at eleven the doors would be firmly closed. Not even the Lord High Admiral himself would be admitted in the unlikely event he were to take it into his head to attend.

There was no sign of the party he sought in the crowded ballroom, though Perran observed that Constance was dancing with Lord Haverstock, who was sporting a toe with the best of them. The ladies adored him because, as Constance put it, "he is a divine dancer, and loves fashion and gossip as much as I. As much as you love driving and that horrible beating about that men do with fists." Since Perran had not seen her since she had left for Brighton so unexpectedly, and had declined her invitation to dinner this evening, he allowed himself a moment to watch her and Haverstock together. They made a very pretty couple, to be sure.

It was also clear that the dance would not be over for some time yet, and he would not interrupt any pleasure of hers for the world. Nodding to his acquaintance, stopping now and again for a word of conversation, he stalked back into the receiving room, where he made the cardinal error of accidentally catching Countess Lieven's sparkling dark eye.

With her fan, she beckoned him over.

He bent to her hand like a European courtier, which he knew she loved. *"Comtesse,"* he said in French. "You are looking lovely tonight. An empress wreathed in gold tissue."

She tapped him on the arm with her fan. "Little do you know, my Rogue."

He probably didn't want to know. It was an open secret that the countess's fearsome intelligence made her a political force to be reckoned with. Tall and slender, with princes and cabinet ministers in her intimate circle, this woman had probably changed history twice since breakfast.

"We did not expect the Rogues this evening," she said, her accent charming, her French fluent. Had it not been for Grand-mère's tutelage, his own would not have been up to the task. He had had many an occasion to thank the stars that Lady Geoffrey had cared enough to tutor him herself in pure Parisian French.

"We would not wish to be thought predictable." He smiled at her. "Would you have missed me had I not come?"

"You? Pah," she said. "The captain, the divine dancer? Ah, now that is a different matter." The twinkle faded from her eyes. "I have been hearing something of you."

"Is that unusual?"

"In some circles, no. In respectable ones, *certainement*. Tell me, is it true that you and *ma chère* Constance are at odds because of a certain young lady making her bows this Season?"

"At odds?" He gazed at her in astonishment. "Not that I am aware of. Constance is in the other room at this moment, dancing with Haverstock."

"I do not care about her partner. But I did notice that she came alone. And now here you are."

"I had another engagement." He smiled into her eyes in just the way she liked. "Constance and I have not quarreled. As for Miss Penrose—"

"Ah."

He saw his error at once. "I did not mistake your meaning, *Comtesse*. Our families are long acquainted. It would be rude in the extreme for either side to deny it."

"Perhaps it would have been better for her if you had."

"You of all people would never judge someone by the opinions of … an observant gentleman, for instance."

"*Certainement pas.* I have sources much more reliable, if less entertaining. But I will be frank … you have done this young lady no service by your attentions to her." She was no longer teasing.

Perran felt the first stirrings of unease. "My attentions? There have been none, *Comtesse*, of that I assure you."

"So you say. But even if there have been, you can do better. A young lady's fortune may be as attractive as her form, my Rogue, but the dust of the clay sticking to both are not worthy of you."

Only with the greatest self-control did he prevent his jaw from dropping at a snobbery she did not usually display in conversation with him. A moment too late, he realized what she was going to do. *"Comtesse,* I implore you—"

But she inclined her head with a smile of dismissal, and turned to greet the Duke of Somerset. Their conversation was over.

Perran bowed with deep respect and returned to the ballroom, where the wretched country dance still had not concluded. Sickened, he stood in thought while both Jago and Griffin took advantage of the endless repetitions of figures to ask two ladies to stand up with them.

He could not bring himself to do the same. Plans and solutions flew through his mind, discarded just as quickly. Could he descend to the street, and prevent Alwyn's party from entering? No, for there was not time to explain. Could he cause some kind of distraction? But what? He heard Countess Lieven's voice over and over, reproving him while at the same time as much as telling him that a decision had already been made over which he had no control.

Surely they would not—he could not possibly allow them to—but how was he to—

The clock struck the quarter hour and two events occurred simultaneously.

Constance looked across the room and saw him.

And there was a stir at the outer door.

"Lady Mainwaring," announced the majordomo into the murmuring silence. "Miss Alwyn Penrose, Miss Karensa Penrose, and Miss Rowena Penrose."

The room seemed to stand a-tiptoe. Over half of them had read that wretched gossip column and were waiting to see if the Patronesses might have, too—and whether they would choose to smile at the girls in white, or frown.

ALWYN COULD HARDLY BREATHE, so anxious was she—so important was this moment. To be presented to the Prince Regent was merely the penultimate step on the ladder to social seventh heaven. To be accepted at Almack's was to be handed the keys to the otherwise unassailable gates of the *ton*. Lady Mainwaring had instructed them carefully in the precedence of their curtseys to the Patronesses, how much to smile, and how to behave once they had safely passed the sacred portals.

Like her sisters, and no matter how little it became her, Alwyn was dressed in white, with the most delicate of scrollwork and embroidery at hems and sleeves. A mist of gauze trimmed her *décolletage,* a pouf of the same resting in her curls. She wore no jewelry, as befit a young lady in her first Season, save for the delicate gold cross at her throat. Under her long kid gloves, her hands were cold. She was quite certain that if she had to pick up a glass of punch, she would drop it, her hands were shaking so.

She dared not look to the right or left, or even at her sisters for moral support. She kept her gaze on the embroidered border of her aunt's blue silk train as they moved forward.

Lady Mainwaring advanced to the dais where the Olympians of Pall Mall sat. Tonight there were only three—Lady Jersey, the Countess Lieven, and Lady Sefton. Lady Mainwaring sank into a curtsey as deep as though the dais contained Princess Charlotte herself. Alwyn, Karensa, and Rowena did the same.

When Alwyn saw her aunt rise, she did so also, praying that her knees would not crack, and finally dared to look up.

Three chins rose. The corners of three sets of lips fell.

Should she smile? Should she look at the floor? Why was it so quiet? Even the music had stopped.

"Lady Mainwaring," the Countess Lieven said in a tone one might use at a funeral service. "We have not seen much of you of late."

"We have been much occupied," Aunt Celia responded in her gentle way. "It is my nieces' first Season—you may remember their mother, my late sister Anne? May they be introduced?"

The silence engulfed Alwyn, compressing her lungs with trepidation. Why did the Lady Patronesses look so forbidding? Why did they not reply?

"I think not, dear Lady Mainwaring," the Countess said at

last. A ripple went through the room, a sigh like the outgoing tide on the golden sands at home. "It is not fitting for such young ladies making their bows for the very first time to attract such attention as they have of late. Such very *public* attention."

"Countess," said Lady Mainwaring, turning very pale, "Pray forgive me—but I do not—attention?"

"I wish you every pleasure that the Season may afford," the Countess said, "and hope to see you at one of our little assemblies another time. You and your nieces may withdraw."

"Withdraw?" Lady Mainwaring whispered, and in that sound Alwyn heard the deafening crash of all her hopes—her future—and those of her sisters. Of Morvoren Manor, and everything she loved at home.

But there was nothing for it. They had been judged, and found wanting. There was no appeal, and no mercy. They had only one course open to them.

Aunt Celia gave another deep curtsey. Like marionettes, Alwyn and her sisters did the same. They turned. The crowd parted, making a clear path to the door … and outer darkness.

Alwyn's heart was thundering so loudly that she could not hear anything but the tide of murmurs that flowed across the floor in their wake. She held her head high, blinking rapidly so that the tears of humiliation would not escape her welling eyes.

No one should see her cry. She would not give a single snobbish personage in this room the satisfaction.

Somewhere in the crowd, a male voice said, "My lady —wait—"

She knew that voice.

Dear heaven. Had Sir Perran Geoffrey been witness to the

doom of all her hopes? Was he actually coming over to speak to them?

The sheer horror of it propelled her out of the door, down the steps, and into the cool evening air and the bustle of King Street. If she could, she would have broken into a run, putting miles between herself and this place.

If she could, she would have screamed at the mocking ninnies at the windows who were certainly making free with her name and those of her sisters at this very moment.

If she could, she would have struck Perran Geoffrey—the author and finisher of her destruction— across the cheek.

But she did not.

Ruined as surely as though she had really been discovered with him in a passionate embrace in the Blessings' library, Alwyn climbed into the waiting carriage with her silent companions and was driven away into the whispering night.

CHAPTER 11

St. Just, Cornwall

It was quite possible that Papa was never going to forgive her.

Aunt Celia and Uncle Edward had abandoned the delights of their own Season among their many friends—and with their voucher for Almack's still in their possession—to travel down to Cornwall with Alwyn and her sisters. Never had Alwyn been so thankful for her aunt's loving nature, to whom it was unthinkable that young ladies should be consigned to the stage, or heaven forbid, the post, for the many days of the journey.

Not with their lives in such disarray.

Instead, they traveled in the relative comfort of the Mainwaring carriage with its coat of arms on the doors, attended at every inn with the greatest respect and given every attention they could desire.

Which only served to keep Alwyn's spirits out of a howling abyss of despair. Just barely.

Rowena was convinced that Alwyn had done something terrible, for otherwise, how could society object to young ladies of otherwise unsullied reputation and forty thousand pounds apiece? Rowena had not addressed one word to her all the way down from London, which had made the journey, in all other ways so pleasant, trying in the extreme.

Alwyn added Rowena to the list of the unforgiving, along with Papa.

Just outside the French doors of the second drawing room that the family called the "sea parlor," Papa paced slowly back and forth on the terrace, supported by his cane. His leg was healing well, his elbow, while permanently bent, no longer needed a sling, and he no longer used his crutch. After Christmas Dr. Harris had prescribed a course of exercises to remind the muscles of their duty following their long rest. The arm might never be able to straighten properly, but Papa had adapted to a more limited reach on that side.

The flagged terrace on which they walked overlooked the lawns that sloped down to the cliffs, where sheep grazed contentedly in the sunshine. Beyond, the sea sparkled and heaved, its breathing undisturbed by the catastrophes of men. Or women.

The sea parlor had been Mama's favorite room, with its blue silk hangings and comfortable sofas. This afternoon, Aunt Celia was reading aloud from *Emma*, the new novel by the author of *Pride and Prejudice*, which she had procured at the bookshop in St. Just.

Karensa was entranced, her embroidery fallen to her lap, as she listened to the dreadful parson propose marriage to Emma in the coach. Rowena stabbed her muslin with her needle as though it or the parson had personally offended her. But Alwyn could not concentrate, either on embroidery or on fictional young ladies who received proposals whether they wanted them or not.

Not when a similar proposal now seemed a complete impossibility.

The day before they had departed London, a note had come for her from Perran Geoffrey. An apology? An explanation? No matter who was at fault, no matter who had attempted to keep the acquaintance at arm's length, the damage was done and there was no repairing it. She now had to live with the knowledge that her behavior and his had damaged her sisters' hopes, too. She could bear no more. Alwyn had thrown the letter into the fire unopened and gone back upstairs to continue packing. Her lovely dresses now seemed too fine for Cornwall, likely to attract more censure than admiration. It must never be said that the Penrose family were above their company.

She supposed she ought to be grateful that gossip, like smoke, had not drifted so far to the west before it dissipated. Here, the families with whom they dined were unaware of what had happened, and would likely wonder what all the fuss was about if they learned of it. They were happy to receive them and hear news of their travels, though most had had the delicacy not to remark on the fact that the Penrose girls had come back as unattached as they had been when they left, and rather sooner than expected.

Emma Woodhouse got rid of the insufferable parson, and Aunt Celia closed the book. "Shall I ring for tea?"

"I'll tell Mrs. Menabilly." Rowena jumped up, tossing aside her hoop, and was out the door in a twinkling. Not a moment later she returned, a young man in a workman's clothes trailing in her wake, crushing his hat in his hands.

"Begging your pardon, milady—young ladies—but I'm sent from Rosevear Court to speak to Mr. Penrose on a matter of urgency."

Alwyn fetched him from outside, and he stood with dignity, though he gripped the back of the wing chair to ease the weight on his left side. "All right, young Tregarrow," he said in some surprise. "I'll have your message. Is aught amiss with Lady Geoffrey?"

"You could say so, sir. For what we feared most has come to pass, what with the storm we had two days ago. The great oak on the west side fell against the house last night and broke through the roof. There are birds roosting in the bare rafters of Rosevear Court at this moment, sir."

"Good gracious," Lord Mainwaring exclaimed. "Rosevear Court? Is that young Geoffrey's family, he who is so great a friend of the Teague boy?"

"The very one, dear," his wife said. "Mr. Tregarrow, how may we help?"

"I'm sent to ask if Lady Geoffrey and her maid, and Miss Isolde, and her two cousins presently staying, might find a refuge here until the tree is cut away and the upper floor is repaired. For I'm much afeared that the weight of the tree will take down another floor before my father can get the saws to it."

"Goodness me!" Alwyn could hardly imagine how large the tree must have been to wreak such destruction.

"Disgraceful," Papa said. "What is that young man thinking of, to leave her ladyship in such straits while he gallivants about London like the Prince himself?"

"To be fair, Papa, he lives modestly and is doing his best to marry money." Karensa laid a conciliatory hand upon their father's. "We expect the announcement of his engagement to a countess any day. General repairs will likely be contingent upon the marriage contract—but what is to be done in the immediate future?"

Papa snorted with the disdain of a man who was capable of looking after his dependents himself. "Yes, Mr. Tregarrow, of course they may come to us as soon as they please. The late Mrs. Penrose's room will do for her ladyship, and I imagine Rowena will not object to Isolde's company, will you?" He turned to his youngest daughter.

"Of course not, Papa." Rowena smiled at him. "We do not know her cousins, but I am sure they are delightful—and there is the mermaid's room, you know, that has two beds."

The *morvoren* for whom the manor was named was a carving upon the aged mantel in that room. The only original part of the farmhouse that had been on this spot since the fourteen hundreds, the mermaid held court in the room on the ground floor typically used by elderly relatives who came to visit and could not manage the staircases.

"That's done, then." He turned back to the messenger. "They ought to come to dinner this evening, and stay as long as may be."

"Thank you, sir," young Tregarrow said with some relief. "If you weren't able to accommodate them, my next stop was to appeal to the housekeeper at the Teague place—or try Trevenna."

"Dear me, no," Rowena said. "It's been shut up for ages and haunted, to boot. Even the housekeeper lives in the gatehouse instead of in the manor itself."

"More absentee landlords," grumbled Papa. "I'd lay a wager on her ladyship against any haunt, but it's glad I am that she is not to reduce her circumstances so."

Alwyn hastened off to the kitchen to tell Mrs. Carrow, the cook, that they were to have four extra for dinner. Which naturally sent that good lady into a flap, and when she chased Alwyn out so that she could get on with her preparations, Alwyn hastened upstairs to find the housekeeper already stripping the bed and changing the linens in Mama's room.

"Thank you, Mrs. Menabilly," she said with relief. "I am sorry to disturb your work so unexpectedly."

"Never you worry, miss," she said comfortably, snapping out a clean sheet to float obediently to the mattress. "I keep this room aired and dusted, both out of respect to your late mother's memory, rest her soul, and because I want the Manor ready to receive guests at a moment's notice."

"We are of one mind there, Mrs. Menabilly," Alwyn said with a smile. "Her ladyship's maid can sleep on a cot in the dressing room. Set out Mama's silver comb and mirror, if you would, and I will go into the garden and cut some flowers."

"One thing about this household," the housekeeper said as she tucked in the sheets, "there is no shortage of pretty vases."

There were several, it was true, produced by Royal Morvoren and decorated in the manner that had been popular in the mad king's time. Oh, if only she could have convinced Mr. Lander to allow her to design and paint some new patterns for the pottery! But as her conversation with him in the autumn had proved, even this relatively feminine accomplishment was denied her.

Worst of all, Mr. Lander had told Papa of her visit.

"I'll not have you dirtying your hands with the clay, even

to that extent, maidey," Papa had said when he'd called her to his bedside. "A lady doesn't make her china, she orders it made. And besides, painting flowers and landscapes in your little book is no kind of training for glazing. That kind of work takes a good eye, a steady hand, and years of experience. No room for mistakes, not if your platter is being carried in holding a roasted haunch for a duke."

Not good enough.

Once again Alwyn had bitten back her frustration, schooled herself to obedience, and contented herself with her own imagination. With vibrant colors, with flowers and the whorls of shells that brought to mind the waves of the sea, she painted china in her sketchbook as she wished to see it, and locked it away.

The sun was just touching the ocean, laying a path of glimmering gold across the waves, when an ancient, boxy carriage drawn by a pair of plow horses came creaking up the drive. Alwyn and her sisters spilled out of the front door into the softness of the early evening, while a coachman nearly as old as his coach folded down the steps and assisted its occupants to alight.

"Lady Geoffrey." As her father's hostess, Alwyn dipped a curtsey and said, "Our father apologizes that he finds the steps difficult, but he has sherry poured and waiting in the drawing room."

"And glad I am to hear it." Ghislaine, Lady Geoffrey, had been accounted a great beauty in her day. Even now her long-lashed blue eyes missed no detail of Alwyn's hair and dress, her back was as straight as a fireplace poker, and her cheekbones and chin were sculpted as finely as those of any of

Karensa's Greek goddesses. "Isolde, give your courtesy to our hosts, for they deserve our gratitude."

"Of course, Grand-mère." They exchanged curtsies, and then Rowena hugged the younger girl in greeting.

"I am so glad you have come to us," she said in her impulsive way. "I have always wished to be better friends—and now we will share a room."

"You may regret it," said Isolde with a laugh. "I have brought barely enough clothes to stand up in. Everything I could lay hands on is in this basket."

"Then you shall have your pick of the dresses in my wardrobe," Rowena said firmly. "Our coloring is similar, so everything will look well on you." Isolde was certainly as slender as Rowena, if a little taller.

If Alwyn felt any uneasiness about playing hostess to Sir Perran Geoffrey's family, she pushed it down where it could not be examined. These were simply people in need who had appealed to their neighbors for help. Only a beast would refuse such help on grounds that another member of the family had caused certain of them embarrassment and disgrace.

"Miss Penrose, may I introduce my late daughter's children, Mr. Pasco and Miss Lamorna Truscott," Lady Geoffrey said. "They had the misfortune to be visiting us on their way from their grandparents' house in Bath to their father's home in Penzance. What tales they will have to tell of our hospitality, I cannot imagine."

The young gentleman, who was about Alwyn's age, laughed as he bowed. "It is not every day that the ceiling practically comes down upon one's head. I thought it was the end of the world—quite the exciting night. I am only glad that the stones held firm until we could all take refuge on the ground floor."

"Was it so bad as that?" Karensa said on a gasp.

"Every bit, and more," Lamorna Truscott told her. "We cannot say how grateful we are that there is room here for us, as well. We will not trespass long upon your hospitality—perhaps only a night or two, until a conveyance can be sent for us."

"Come in, come in, do," Alwyn said, hastily recalling herself to her duties. She had not realized the cousins were a lady and a gentleman, and thus could not share the mermaid's room. She would have to change her arrangements. "Lady Geoffrey, if you will follow me—"

"I know the way, Miss Penrose," her ladyship said, sailing up the steps and into the spacious hall unaided by either cane or courteous arm. "I helped your mother choose the paint for the walls in the sea parlor long before you were born."

While Perry the footman looked after the luggage tied to the roof of the carriage, Alwyn directed their guests. Mr. Pasco could still sleep in the mermaid's room, and Karensa was already leading Miss Lamorna to her room as though that had been the plan all along.

"We keep country hours," Karensa told the girl as they climbed the staircase, "so dinner will be at seven. Feel free to come down earlier, for Papa is anxiously waiting to hear how it all happened."

When Alwyn had seen to the arrangements for dinner, and made sure the flowers in the drawing room would stand up to Lady Geoffrey's inspection, she stole a few moments for herself upon the landing with its beautiful view to the sea.

Perran's family. Here in her home. As Rowena was often

wont to say outside her father's hearing, didn't that just cap the globe?

Dearest Perran,

You will see by the return direction that we are not at home—nor are we likely to be for quite some time. There was a dreadful storm two nights ago and the old oak has come down upon the house. Such a scene of destruction you never saw in all your life. If I had not gone to pieces in the middle of the night when it happened, I certainly did in the morning when I had my first look at both dying giant and damaged home.

Oh dear brother, how is it all to be set right? I implore you to come to St. Just with all speed. We are encamped for the time being at Morvoren Manor, where we have been welcomed with open arms and treated quite like family. Mr. Penrose has told us that we must stay as long as we like—which could be months. Years, even, if we cannot find the funds to make repairs.

Can you not carry off your countess to the altar immediately? I have no pride—I am quite happy for you to tell her that your grandmother and sister are living upon breadcrumbs and charity until the Court is rebuilt.

Actually, we are not living on breadcrumbs. The table at Morvoren Manor is every bit as generous as one could wish, with such silver and china that one feels like an elegant lady simply by handling them! Grand-mère is in her element, and restrains herself with difficulty from giving orders to the staff. Miss Alwyn Penrose is the lady of the manor here, though she gives precedence at every opportunity to her aunt Lady Mainwaring, who is also visiting, along with his lordship.

On second thought, never mind your countess, brother mine. You ought to marry Alwyn, and solve two problems at once. Cousin Lamorna tells me that she heard something dreadful happened to Alwyn in London. No one seems to know quite what, but you know as well as I that even Napoleon did not have as fine a spy network as our grandmother. I am sure she will ferret out the details sooner rather than later.

Which does not signify one jot. Alwyn is perfectly lovely, and her forty thousand pounds would restore the poor old Court to its former glory and more. We might even plant more oak trees ... a little farther from the house.

Please write soonest and let us know when we might expect you. There is no more room here until Pasco and Lamorna depart for Penzance, but I am sure the Tremaynes would welcome you at Minear Park. The Teague house is shut up, as far as I know, and Trevenna, of course has been empty for years except for the ghosts.

I am crossing my lines now, so must close. I will watch the road daily until I see you.

With all love,

Isolde

CHAPTER 12

Belgrave Square, London

Perran let out an exclamation so abrupt and hoarse that Constance raised her fine dark brows in alarm from where she sat upon the sofa.

"Good heavens, Perran." She laid down down some silly publication that made its money telling females what to wear from month to month. "What has happened?"

He threw Isolde's letter in the fire, where it flared up and curled into ash, castigating himself anew for bringing it with him to enjoy before tea. Not for worlds would he risk Constance's seeing those final paragraphs.

"I do not wish to speak of it," he ground out. He had to think. Had to come up with some sort of plan. But he had been thinking and trying to plan for weeks without coming to any workable conclusion—and now Neptune, god of sea and storm, had forced his hand.

"Very well," she said, and picked up her magazine once more.

He had offended her, and now must make amends.

"I am sorry, Constance." He turned from the fire to face her. "The news from home is bad, and I am cudgeling my brain to think what is best to do."

"Come. Sit here, and tell me." She patted the sofa beside her, and relegated the magazine to a table at her elbow. "Two heads are always better than one."

So he unburdened himself—not entirely, for it would not do for her to know the depths of his perpetual, unending humiliation thanks to his father's lack of self-control. His self-hatred at not being able to provide for his family. His uncertainty and despair at having to flush a bride out of the hedges under these circumstances.

But enough. He told her of the storm, of the damage to the house, of the disposition of his family, now living upon the grace and favor of their neighbors.

"Morvoren Manor?" she repeated in astonishment. "Not the home of those girls who were turned away from Almack's last month?"

"The very one."

"Why on earth would they go there?"

"Because, as I've said, our families have known one another since before I was born."

Her face drew up as though controlled by strings. "How distressing to think of Lady Geoffrey hobnobbing with people covered in clay dust."

Countess Lieven had said practically the same thing, and it had gained no delicacy on Constance's lips. "The property has been in their family since the fifteenth century," he said with an effort at patience. "They are not precisely *nouveaux riches*—the present gentleman's grandfather acquired the clay pits, and made the family's fortune. The latest generations—the young ladies and their father—may still call themselves gentlefolk without a blush. The family have a controlling interest in the company, and enjoy a certain involvement in shipping and pottery, but do not actively manage it."

"I should hope not." She shuddered delicately.

"Isolde begs me to go down at once." He returned to the matter at hand.

"To Cornwall? Why must you?" She gazed at him, her dark eyes limpid with sympathy. "You could have no reason for such a journey, surely. Your estate agent will see to the repairs, and your neighbors' generosity will see to your family. Unless I have misapprehended something?"

She couldn't be serious. She couldn't believe him to be so cold as to ignore Isolde's plea. "I cannot leave them homeless, Constance. I am responsible for their security, if not their comfort. If I have to saw oak branches out of the rafters myself, I must see to the Court for their sakes."

"How noble of you." Her smile turned to a frown as another thought occurred to her. "And how inconvenient. His Royal Highness is said to be attending the Dorchesters' ball on Saturday. I had hoped we might go together. The most exalted circles of the *ton* will be there … and if you are with me, that includes you." She smiled at him again, with tenderness—as though they shared common goals and ambitions in that regard.

He clamped his molars together so that he would not shout his true opinion of such feather-headed nonsense at a time like this. For Constance was not a featherhead. Far from it.

"We have discussed my situation before, my dear. Funds

for the repairs are scarce upon the ground. The tenants' properties and fields have long needed repairs and amendment, and my purse has not been able even for that. My grandmother's legacy from my grandfather keeps food on their table, but is not up to replacing walls and roof. I see no option but to give up my lodgings in Town and go home. Perhaps brute labor added to those few pounds saved in rent will at least make a beginning."

"You could always move into my house, you know."

He gazed at her, more scandalized for her sake than his own. "Are you proposing to me, Constance?"

"Certainly not. I did not mean this house. I meant the one in Chelsea. It has been cut up into six flats. I could give you a very good reduction in rent … as a dear friend." She batted her lashes in a way that made him laugh.

"You are eternally generous." He took a deep breath and leaped from the cliff—or at least, slid from the sofa and knelt at her feet, taking her hand. "But why don't we make it a less distant and more permanent arrangement? Constance … dear Constance … despite all you know of me, will you do me the honor of becoming my wife?"

For a moment, all he could hear was his thundering heart. All he could feel was his rolling stomach, as though he stood on the deck of a ship in an uncertain sea. And all he could see was her face, draining of blood until it became as pale as translucent porcelain.

"Are you … in earnest, Perran?"

"I would not be down here on the rug if I were not."

"Oh, do get up."

He did, and resumed his seat upon the sofa beside her, but he did not relinquish her hand.

"I will ask you a question in return," she said slowly, "and I require that you remain calm while you answer it."

"Of course." If she wanted a closer accounting of his sorry circumstances, she should have it, though goodness knew she was now more familiar with the general outlines than anyone but Griffin and Jago.

"I married the first time for money. I wish to marry the second time for love. Are you asking me to marry you because you love me, or because you are desperate to bring Rosevear Court back to its former glory?"

For a moment her bluntness took his breath away.

And in that dreadful pause, while he scrambled for an acceptable reply, she removed her hand from his. "I see."

"Constance, you know the latter is not the sum total of my reasons for making you an offer." He felt rather as though he was wasting his breath, but he had to make up for that pause. "We get on well together, we share a similar taste in pursuits, and while you outrank me, I do not think that either you or the *ton* will hold that against me."

"Certainly not."

"Well, then?"

"Well, then," she mocked his tone, "do you love me?"

"As much as you love me," he said, with an honesty equalling her own. "I believe we would enter the marriage state with more knowledge of each other than many do."

"And would you expect me to live in your beloved pile, if it were to be repaired and made as new again?"

"I … well …" He collected himself. "Not if you did not wish to, of course. But I would like to visit my family at least twice a year. At planting and harvest."

"Why?"

He smiled at her. "Country traditions aside, I do enjoy seeing my sister and grandmother. I have not been able to go down as often as I would like."

Restlessly, she rose. "Planting coincides with the beginning of the Season, and the reconvening of Parliament. That would mean my going without your escort for a certain number of weeks at the most important time of the year."

So, she did not plan to make these excursions with him. "This is a small consideration, is it not? Besides, it is so unfashionable to always be on the arm of one's husband."

At the hearth, she turned, clearly not appreciating his attempt at humor. "My social circle and its pursuits may be a small matter to you. But they are life itself to me. We are less compatible than you think, Perran, but I seem to be the only one who has looked at it clearly since our last discussion of the subject. I know how restless you are here—why you find an outlet in driving and fencing instead of dancing and theater. The simple fact is that you belong at Rosevear Court. The only reason you have been here for three Seasons, wasting time and building up your bad reputation, is because you have not been able to bring yourself up to scratch for any of the prospects. And despite what I hinted at before, I confess I am weary of being the means to help you avoid them."

Her insight burst in on him like a thunderclap accompanied by flickering forks of lightning.

"That is not it at all," he blurted. "Not one of your *prospects* wants a man for himself. Only for his title and estates. And in my case the former is worthless and the latter a liability. What woman in her right mind would accept me?"

She gazed at him silently, brows raised, until he realized what he had just said.

"I am sorry, Constance—my proposal was sincere—I did not mean—"

"I know what you meant," she said. "And I suggest you take yourself down to Cornwall to find the answer to that question. Because clearly you are not going to find it here."

"Am I not?" Then, more gently, "Are you certain?"

Her eyes were full of regret. "Yes, Perran. I do more than dance and attend the theatre, you know. Occasionally I have interludes of thought. And they have made me quite certain. If it makes a difference, I am sorry for it."

He let out a long breath, one that seemed to come from the depths of his soul. "I am, too." Sorry that she had to be the one to force him to see himself with even more merciless clarity. Sorry that she would not attempt, even in a small way, to enter into his life and the things he loved. Sorry that for her, he came up short.

When he departed shortly afterward, he felt as though a door in his life had closed, and there was an empty road before him, containing nothing.

Nothing save a deeply welling fear that in making one choice over another, the road before him led straight to his own ruin.

THE FOLLOWING DAY, Perran wasted no time in informing his club and his landlady of his imminent departure. He sent his portmanteau and trunk away with a bearer to the coaching inn from which the stage would depart. And when his London life was at last tidied away, he called at Admiral Teague's town house to make his farewells.

He found Jago there also, comfortably ensconced in the

study with the Admiral and Griffin, old and young awash in newspapers, coffee, and contentment. Of all the pleasures that London afforded, Perran would miss the company of these friends the most.

"Perran, old boy!" Griffin exclaimed, fighting his way off the ancient sofa that the Admiral would not allow anyone to remove, for it had come with his late wife as a bride forty years before. "What brings you here in a greatcoat? We are in the midst of summer."

Perran shook hands with the Admiral and shrugged out of the coat. They might be in the midst of summer, but as he had reason to know, the West Country weather was always fractious and often downright dangerous. "I am going straight to the George after I leave here. The stage departs for the West Country in two hours, and I plan to be on it."

Both his friends stared. "You're never going home," Griffin finally managed through his astonishment. "Why, it is the height of the Season."

"That matters not a whit in comparison to what has happened." Perran sank into a leather-covered chair with a sigh and gratefully accepted the Admiral's offer of brandy. He toasted his companions—and the absent smugglers. "The old oak has fallen on the house, and knocked part of it in. Isolde wrote to beg me to come home at once."

Consternation and questions reigned in the comfortable room until the Admiral was able to make himself heard. "But Lady Geoffrey, Sir Perran. What of her?"

"She is well, and unharmed, sir. Both she and Isolde, as well as my cousins Pasco and Lamorna Truscott, are staying at Morvoren Manor until repairs can be made."

"You don't say," Jago said. "That's very handsome of the Penrose family."

"Handsome, nothing," Admiral Teague said gruffly. "It's what any good neighbor would do, including your parents, Jago. Was their assistance solicited?"

"Morvoren Manor is larger, sir," Griffin put in, "so I expect they would have applied there first. But I say, Perran, you can't be going down all alone. What do you plan to do?"

"I imagine the sawing of limbs and clearing of rubble will be completed by the time I arrive, but I have two hands, a clear head, and a knowledge of my responsibility in the matter," he replied. "In the absence of money, I will contribute my labor. I must also risk embarrassment at the bank and ask for a loan. Then I will see how we get on."

"It will get on so slowly the ladies will be back in the house in time for Christmas of 1820," Jago told him. "I'm coming with you."

"And I!" Griffin exclaimed. "Admiral, will you send my trunk down after me? If Perran is to be on this afternoon's stage, there won't be time for me to pack."

"And you were a sailor," his father chided him, "once used to carrying all you owned over your shoulder. But never mind this stage coach nonsense. I find I have tired of the city and want some employment. I will send a message down at once so they may get Gwennel Cottage out from under holland covers."

It always made Perran smile to hear the name of the Admiral's country residence. It was not often than four bedrooms, stables for six, and a staff of four living on fifty acres of property constituted a cottage. Still, the swallows for which it was named still nested in the barn, as snug and safe as the place itself. The Admiral's late wife had brought the property with her, and in time Griffin would inherit both it and this house in town.

"You will all come with me in my carriage," the Admiral went on with firmness, "and together we will ease the burden for Mr. Penrose. Your cousins, at least, may stay with us, Sir Perran. Or even your sister and Lady Geoffrey, if it pleases her." He looked a little self-conscious at this offer, as though one of them might chide him for some impropriety in it.

Griffin looked so astonished that he could hardly get words out. "Go down to St. Just with us, sir! Surely you will be more comfortable here, among your friends and congenial circle?"

"They will be waiting for me when I return in the autumn," his father informed him. "Since when has comfort mattered when there is a job to be done? There are people in need here, sir—neighbors in need. And no time to cavil about it!"

Abashed, Griffin clapped his father on the shoulder. "Forgive me, sir. You are altogether in the right. Well then, if we are to travel in the coach, I will pack my trunk this very day."

Perran, overcome at such generosity, finally found his voice. "Admiral—Jago—Griffin—truly, this is not what I expected when I came. Surely you must consider—think of your friends, your engagements!"

"Bah," Jago said with his usual elegance. "All my friends are in this room. I'd much rather help you than spend one more insipid evening squiring ladies to the opera. I don't even *like* opera."

"But you like ladies. What of them?" Perran demanded. "How are you going to explain this to Miss Heatherington, after she risked her immortal soul by dancing two with you the other night?"

Jago's brows drew together in a frown. "I owe no one explanations. The girl doesn't care for my conversation anyhow. She will be on to her next partner with embarrassing speed, you may depend upon it. And I like the thought of having something useful to do. I used to be rather handy with a saw and hammer—until my tutor caught me in the barn building a rabbit hutch with the carpenter's boy and put an end to it."

Perran had never laid hands to a hammer and saw in his life, and to his knowledge, neither had Griffin. But when it came right down to it, he would learn if he had to. They all would.

"Then that is settled," the Admiral said, slapping both hands upon the arms of his chair and rising. "Have your things brought here and stay the night, Sir Perran. We will depart for St. Just immediately after breakfast."

CHAPTER 13

St Just, Cornwall

lwyn heard the sound of galloping hooves coming up the gravel drive only moments before Isolde cried, "Perran is come!" and dashed out of the sea parlor.

"La, girl." Lady Geoffrey laid down her sewing, though she did not rise. "Have all my years of teaching her manners been for nothing?"

"Pray excuse me, ma'am," Alwyn said, already on her way out. "It is more likely to be a messenger from Rosevear Court. I will send him in to you."

She reached the front steps in time to realize that not one but three horsemen were trotting up, and were far too well dressed to be workmen. The rider in front barely had time to swing down from the saddle before Isolde flung herself into his arms, and he gave her a hug in which his whole body expressed relief that she was safe and well.

Alwyn's knees went weak with shock.

Sir Perran Geoffrey. Here, in Cornwall.

Not where she had thought him to be, days away in London squiring rich, titled ladies from crush to crush. But here, at Morvoren Manor, her own home!

The two other riders dismounted, and as the grooms led the horses away, she saw that Captain Griffin Teague and Mr. Jago Tremayne looked ridiculously fit and happy, both equally far from the sphere in which they ought to have stayed.

The Rogues of St. Just, real as life.

Alwyn would have given anything to take to her heels—to dodge between the rhododendron bushes, around the side of the house, and out over the lawns to the cliff path. But no. She was the lady of the manor, and must not shirk her duty.

No matter what it cost her.

She advanced to drop a curtsey to their callers, and receive bows in return. "Sir Perran," she said with as much civility as she could muster. The effort made her voice a little husky. "This is unexpected."

"Not to me." Happily, Isolde seized his arm and wrapped both hands around it. "I wrote the moment we arrived, and have been watching the roads and cliffs for the past three days at least. You have made very good time," she said to her brother. "This horse must surely be of the bloodline of Pegasus."

"He may be, but my friends are certainly of the bloodline of Apollo," he told her fondly. "Admiral Teague himself has come down in his carriage, which seemed to go as swiftly as any sun chariot. I, Captain Teague, and Mr. Tremayne rode the captain's horses beside him." To Alwyn, he said, "The Admiral has opened Gwennel Cottage with a view to placing it at Lady Geoffrey's disposal, if it pleases her, and asks that I let my cousins know they are welcome, too."

"How very kind of the Admiral," she said, sounding a little more like herself. "Your grandmother is inside, in the sea parlor. I hope you will tell her so yourself."

"Pasco and Lamorna left the day before yesterday," Rowena told Sir Perran. "They will be sorry to learn they have missed you, but we could not prevail upon them to stay a moment longer."

"So the mermaid's room is free now, Perran," Isolde said eagerly, "if you wished to stay here with Grand-mère and me."

His gaze flashed up to Alwyn's own and away again so quickly she almost missed it. In that moment, could he see her feelings written plainly on her face? *Oh no, no, not in my house.* "Of course you are welcome at Morvoren Manor," she said as graciously as she could, while her mind screamed, *So close! It must not be!*

"While Miss Penrose might indulge your wish to invite the entire countryside to stay," he said affectionately to his sister, "I would not think of it. We are very comfortable with Admiral Teague, and in fact, would not feel easy if we were to leave him alone in the place, after all his kindness."

"Perran, are you certain?" Captain Teague asked. "Jago has gone to his family. There is no reason you should be separated from yours."

No. Please do not accept. Please.

He had been the instrument of her undoing, and even this moment, every one of her senses was far too aware of him for their own good. His long legs in their riding breeches ... the trimness of his waist ... the breadth of his shoulders under his coat with its dashing silver buttons. And his eyes, long-lashed and hazel ... eyes that had spent as much time gazing at her mouth as she had spent in gazing at his.

Oh dear oh dear ...

"I must stand firm," Perran said on a laugh. "At least I will not be obliged to bivouac under the dining room table at Rosevear Court, which was my other option."

Alwyn nearly collapsed from relief. But instead, she gestured that they should go into the house, and led the way inside.

She was quite sure, from the prickling up her spine, that she could feel Perran's gaze upon her back.

Isolde clung to her brother's arm as they crossed the hall. "Grand-mère and Lady Mainwaring will be wondering what is keeping us all."

"The Mainwarings are still here?" Captain Teague asked Karensa in some surprise. "I did not realize that."

"How could you, if you have only just arrived?" she remarked in her no-nonsense way. "They were kind enough to bring us down in their carriage, after—"

"Lady Geoffrey," Alwyn announced a little more loudly than strictly necessary as she preceded the group into the sea parlor. "Isolde was right. See who has come."

As he passed her, his coat sleeve brushed her bare arm, and gooseflesh rose upon it. Her intake of breath had been only a whisper of sound, but he glanced down at her sharply, as though to see what was the matter.

Again, their gazes met. And clung.

"Why, Perran." Lady Geoffrey's surprise could hardly be greater, and Perran's gaze swung abruptly to the party near the windows. "I expected young Tregarrow, with news that they have finished cutting up the oak."

"Then allow me to bring you that news." As though nothing had just happened, Perran bowed to his grandmother and to Lady Mainwaring, and then kissed the cheek of the former. "Mrs. Tregarrow will have wood enough for the kitchen fire for three years and more, she tells me. We only arrived last night, Grand-mère. We left the Admiral issuing orders to his household troops, and rode to Rosevear this morning. I had a report from Tregarrow on the progress thus far, and here I am."

"It is a heartbreaking business, Perran. I am glad you are home."

Alwyn realized that a certain strain, a certain tightness in the older lady's face, had relaxed in the presence of her grandson.

"That it is, Grand-mère. And I am glad to see the old place again, too, despite its recent blow."

Griffin turned from the window, where he had been taking in the view. "At least it is not a hopeless case."

To hear him speak, you would think Griffin had never met a cloud without a silver lining. Alwyn very much suspected he was gulling them. The damage must be much worse than they thought.

With all their company, she had not had an hour to drive the phaeton over to Rosevear Court to see for herself, but from Isolde's account, it had indeed seemed heartbreaking—if not actually hopeless. To hear Isolde tell it, the upper floors could not be lived in, and only a few hardy servants remained on the ground floor.

Their father, who had come in from the terrace without assistance, now crossed the room, leaning on a cane but beaming at the sight of his company.

"Sir Perran—Captain Teague—Mr. Tremayne," he said with delight. "The sight of you does me more good than all the potions Rowena tries to dose me with." He turned the smile on his youngest daughter, who shook her head severely at him. "What's this I heard—that the Admiral has brought you all down?"

"We have all three come to help with the repairs, sir," Jago told him respectfully.

"What—all of you?" Lady Geoffrey looked scandalized. "Are you laborers, to lift a hammer in your shirt sleeves?"

"We are cheap," Jago said bluntly, which made Papa bark with laughter. "As long as Mrs. Tregarrow feeds us, there will be two men fewer whom Sir Perran here will be obliged to hire."

Alwyn had almost forgotten that Jago was nearly as tactless as Karensa. And Papa, the rascal, was enjoying it as much as ever he had done when they were children.

"You must take me for a simpleton to believe you will do any such thing," Lady Geoffrey said with a shake of her silvery head.

Before Jago could protest that he was telling the absolute truth—Alwyn knew he must want to, for as a child he always told the truth even when he ought not—she said to her ladyship, "Admiral Teague has issued an invitation for you and Isolde to stay at the cottage, ma'am. Is that not generous of him?"

"Very generous," Lady Geoffrey said. "I wonder what he means by it, for the house has been shut up for a year and more."

"Not any longer, ma'am," Griffin said. "My father has had it opened, and plans to stay for the summer."

"Does he indeed? Well, he is most kind, but my granddaughter and I are settled comfortably here, and can only hope that Mr. Penrose and his family will continue to forbear with us until the house is repaired."

"Nonsense, ma'am," Papa said robustly. "There is no forbearance in the case. We are your neighbors, and can do nothing less. Sir Perran, will you stay as well?"

Alwyn had another bad moment, for a chance existed that Perran might have changed his mind between the front door and the sea parlor. What if he should accept this second invitation? What if he should allow himself to be pressed?

"I thank you for your kindness, Mr. Penrose, but I cannot relieve my household burdens at the expense of yours. No, the Admiral has made Captain Teague and I very comfortable at Gwennel Cottage."

Papa looked disappointed, for he loved company. "Very well, as you like. Mr. Tremayne, how are you set up? Are you staying with the Admiral, too?"

"He is at Minear Park, much to his parents' delight," Griffin offered.

"My twin brothers are down from Oxford for the summer," Jago said, "and my sister is at home, of course. My mother is quite transported to have us all back again. Though none of them know as yet that I will have the twins with hammer in hand before the week is out, see if I don't."

"Do they know anything of carpentry?" Mr. Penrose asked with some amusement, since Lady Geoffrey's horror had rendered her speechless.

"They are scholars, sir," Jago said. "If they cannot learn the difference between a hammer and a saw, I do not hold out any hope for their academic careers."

Alwyn saw her opportunity to excuse herself and, instead of ringing for tea, found Mrs. Menabilly and ordered cheese and cakes to go with it. Then, seeking a moment to compose herself, she went along the garden passage into the mermaid's room. If anyone asked her, she would say she was making certain that Pasco Truscott had not left anything behind that might need to be sent on to him.

In the squares of sunlight from the mullioned windows, she allowed herself a moment to breathe. To be grateful for the narrowness of her escape. The thought of Perran Geoffrey in the house—of chance meetings upon the stairs—of dinners *en famille*—was overwhelming. Appalling. Not to be thought of. Thank heaven for the Admiral and sensible arrangements already made!

She must be more sensible, too. She must remember that this fascination with him was foolish in the extreme. He had brought her only disaster, and she could not forget it.

No more would she react to his presence as she had at the door just now. For he was such a man as knew the effect he had upon a woman. He noticed everything. She would be cool, and ladylike, and civil. No more.

She was not certain what brought her out of her thoughtful study of the mermaid carving. A breath? A whisper of fabric? But when she turned, there he was, leaning upon the door frame and gazing at her, just as he had in the Blessings' library.

Her heart gave a great thump, and she drew in a breath.

And now she knew the true root of her relief that he would not be staying. For her first instinct in that moment was anything but cool, ladylike, and civil.

He is a rogue, and probably has this effect on every woman under sixty. You are right to be relieved that he is not staying.

He looked as a man might who was asking permission to

cross the threshold. To be alone with her. His curls fell over one eyebrow, as though he had just raked a hand through them, and his hazel gaze held hers as though commanding her to come to him.

I will not. I am not one of your society playthings. I am Miss Penrose of Morvoren Manor, and you are the next thing to a stranger here.

"Is there something you wished, Sir Perran?" she asked coolly, as though her throat and mouth had stiffened, too, along with the rest of her.

"I wish for many things." He stood easily, with a casualness that belied the tension in his jaw. "Forgive me for disturbing you. Your estimable Mrs. Menabilly told me where you were. I do not wish to put you to any more trouble. Admiral Teague's invitation was sincere. Despite what Grand-mère says, if I desire her to remove to Gwennel Cottage, she will yield."

"Certainly not." She was in the frying pan of his presence now, and pride alone prevented her from leaping out of it and fleeing the room. "She is very comfortable in my mother's room, and Isolde with Rowena. Our sisters are becoming fast friends."

His gaze did not release her, nor did he veer off into a discussion of family. "I am sure you know my real reason for choosing to go to the cottage rather than accepting your father's kind invitation. I saw it in Lady Mainwaring's face just now—and in yours."

His bluntness took her breath away even as it confirmed what she had been thinking. Or perhaps it was merely that he had levered himself off the door frame and was walking toward her. It was all she could do to stand her ground and not put one of the beds between them. "I do not know what you mean, sir."

"And that is a Banbury tale if ever I heard one."

Ooh, if he could take off the gloves, as the saying went, then so could she. "What would you have me say? That I wish the man who ruined me at the bottom of the ocean—and in the absence of that, in someone else's house?"

Instead of rearing back in offense, he smiled, as though appreciating her ability to rise to his challenge. "I cannot blame you, for of course that scene at Almack's has been much on my mind."

"Has it really, sir?" she said in mock surprise. "I had thought that your conscience would have had considerable experience in lifting similar burdens."

"So one would think," he agreed mildly. "But in this case, the only thing that might do so is your acceptance of my most sincere apology."

She had not thought that bluntness would lead to this. A quarrel, perhaps. One of them slamming out of the room, to keep their distance for several days.

But an apology? That he might offer one had never once occurred to her.

Suddenly, she found her lips trembling and her eyes pricking with tears.

As she struggled silently for control, he said, "I had been speaking with Countess Lieven immediately before you were presented. In that moment I realized the consequences of my behavior, but it was already too late. For I am the first to agree with you—it is I who brought you to the notice of our friend the Observant Gentleman. Had I not done so, you would still be in London, fighting off the attentions of the heirs to any number of estates."

"The ruination was not only mine," she said past the tightness in her throat. "It was my sisters' also. While Karensa and I may resign ourselves to our losses in time, I do not think Rowena ever will. She has barely spoken to me, and we have been home nearly a month."

"Would it help if I approached her?"

"It would help if you brought one of those heirs you spoke of and presented him to her, tied up in a bow," she said bitterly.

"Jago wouldn't like that," he muttered.

She could not have heard him correctly. "I beg your pardon?"

"Nothing," he said. He indicated the fireplace mantel. "Is that the mermaid for whom this room is named?"

Jago? Jago had a *tendre* for Rowena? La, as if this could be any worse! She must do everything in her power to prevent Rowena's suspecting any such thing. Jago Tremayne! He was the last man on earth with whom Rowena would find anything in common. Why, they were chalk and cheese!

"Miss Penrose?"

"I'm sorry?" She came out of her surprise with an effort. "Yes. Family legend says the mermaid predates the one at Zennor, but I do not know if that is true." Now she was prattling, and nervous, and if she did not turn the subject at once he would notice. "Sir Perran, I hope you are able to get your repairs under way soon. I know your grandmother and sister are pleased to have you so close at hand."

"I am pleased as well. But Miss Penrose, you have not answered me, and your reply is one I dearly wish."

He joined her before the empty hearth, as though to impress upon her how important her reply was to him. Her heart seemed to stop in her chest, and her eyes locked with his. His intensity seemed to burn away every thought in her head.

"My reply, sir?" She must not look at his lips. She must be … what? Oh, yes. *Polite. Ladylike. Civil.*

He bent his head so that she must see him, so that all the world contained was him alone. "Your acceptance of my most humble and sincere apology for my behavior, and its unlooked-for and most unfortunate consequences."

What had she presumed to think—that his dearest wish was her permission for a kiss? If she could not achieve *ladylike*, at least she might salvage her pride.

She lifted her chin. "My reply is this—if you can apologize so handsomely, then in time I may be able to forgive you."

"In time?"

"Perhaps." She crossed to the door and went out, conscious every moment that he turned his body to follow hers, as a sunflower turns with the passage of the sun.

CHAPTER 14

Perran and the Rogues returned to Gwennel Cottage bearing to the Admiral one message from Mr. Penrose and another from Lady Geoffrey.

The dinner waiting for them was simple but satisfying—stargazy pie made with local pilchards, boiled onions, and the first lettuces from the garden—and Perran ate with gusto as Griffin carried out his commissions.

"Lady Geoffrey wishes to call?" The Admiral paused with a fork halfway to his mouth. "But we are all at sixes and sevens here. I should not like her to see the place until we have settled in more. Much better I should wait upon her at Morvoren Manor."

"As you wish, sir," Griffin said. "Which brings me to the second of the messages to you. Miss Penrose and Lady Mainwaring together send their best regards and request the pleasure of your company at a small dinner on Tuesday next."

"Only my company?" the Admiral said, his fork resuming its journey. "What about yours?"

"Ours, too," Perran told him. "We will break it to Jago

tomorrow. There will be dancing, I understand, if one of the ladies can be prevailed upon to play the pianoforte."

"Capital." The Admiral's delight shone in his eyes. "Well, well … dinner and dancing at a house full of pretty young ladies. Tremayne ought to jump at it. So ought you, my lad." The fork pointed at Griffin. "Haven't you had enough of gadding about town, ruining reputations and betting too much on cards? Isn't it about time you hauled in your canvas and found a safe harbor in which to moor?"

"Sir!" Griffin looked offended. "I do not bet too much at cards."

His father sniffed at this poor excuse for a dodge. "Perhaps I did well to accompany you down here. It seems to me you need a nudge in the right direction."

"I pray you will not, sir," Griffin said with an uneasy glance at Perran. "There has been enough talk already."

"About whom? You? Serves you right."

Since the Admiral did not appear to know about Perran's involvement in the scandal at Almack's, Perran was not about to enlighten the older man. Time to change the subject.

"With Lord and Lady Mainwaring at Morvoren Manor, sir," Perran said, "it seems you will have no shortage of friends in the district."

"All the more reason for me to call—it will be downright shabby if both Lady Geoffrey and Lord Mainwaring know I am here and I have not made an early effort to visit."

"You are welcome at any time," Griffin said. "We, however, will be spending most of our days at Rosevear Court."

"After I hazard a visit to my banker," Perran reminded him. "It is rather hard of me to send men for lumber and slates without something with which to pay the reckoning. And until I have supplies on hand, there is nothing for you to do but sweep up sawdust."

"I wish you would let me lend you the money," the Admiral groused. Perran had spent half the journey down to Cornwall as determined not to take it as the older man had been to give it. "Better a loan from a friend than a drubbing from a userer."

"The Bank of Cornwall hardly engages in usury, sir," Griffin pointed out.

But the next day, it was almost as though the banker knew of his dire straits and had been waiting by the window of his office in Falmouth for Perran to turn up.

Mr. Beswetherick folded his hands upon the desk and looked apologetic. "I am very sorry, Sir Perran, but I cannot loan so much to you."

Perran had half expected this, but to hear the words set his teeth on edge. "I cannot complete the work with any less, sir. Would you have Lady Geoffrey sitting under a parasol within doors when it rains?"

"Certainly not." The banker looked uncomfortable, his folded hands gripping one another as though this conversation was as uncomfortable to him as it was to his guest. "But since we cannot attach a mortgage to the property, and you possess no collateral, my hands are tied. It is completely out of my power to lend you such a sum."

"Then what do you suggest I do?" Exasperated, Perran did not really expect an answer. And he did not get one. Only more apologies, and an offer of tea, which he declined.

Fighting an attack of the blue devils, he rode away on Kit, the horse he'd borrowed from Griffin, wondering what in heaven's name he ought to do next. He held Kit's bridle on the ferry across to St. Mawes, murmuring to him. Poor creature.

The traffic of the Mayfair streets held no fears for him, but braving the sea was a new experience. The ferry decanted them on the dock at St. Mawes, and Perran led the horse up the stone ramp to the street.

What were his choices now? He tied Kit outside a public house, and ducked inside to order some food. He must have a moment to think. Over his plate of fried fish, he considered his list of possibilities for the hundredth time.

He could accept the Admiral's generous offer of assistance. While to the outside observer this might seem the most reasonable course, it was to him the most abhorrent. The Admiral was well off, but Perran was honest. The amount that he required would make anyone blink. A sensible man would be better served to put that sum toward either of his own houses, where he might at least be certain of a return. For when could Perran repay the loan? How soon might his circumstances change? Why, they could be attending the Admiral's funeral before Perran had repaid even half the sum.

No, he would not choose that course. He took a fortifying bite of his lunch.

There was Constance. She had declined his offer; there was nothing but pride to prevent his trying again. Pride was poor comfort next to the image of Grand-mère sitting in her bedchamber under a dripping parasol. But Constance had been right to decline his suit. They had merely been fooling themselves. They did not love one another—at least, not in the way that Lord and Lady Mainwaring loved one another. While they enjoyed each other's company, and some of the same entertainments, it was rather a shock to realize that he wanted more from a marriage than entertainment. Now that he was back in Cornwall, where people listened to each other and were concerned for the well-being of their neighbors, the endless round of balls, theatre, and parties seemed shallow and unsatisfying.

Constance loved those things. Would he be happy to let her go out to enjoy them without him? And how would he fill his time in London once his obligations here were fulfilled?

He finished up his plate and pushed that option to one side, only to be confronted with one closer to hand.

Alwyn Penrose.

The opinions of his sister and Jago aside, he had to admit that there was something about the girl that had caught his attention and would not let go. It was more than her looks, for Constance was more beautiful in the classical sense. He could not define it, any more than he could define the cause of an itch that would not go away. Could he court her and make her his wife, after all that had happened in London despite his best efforts to prevent it? For if he did, then he must commit to a life here in Cornwall. He doubted very much that Alwyn would return to London to endure its favors and foibles again, though he was quite sure that as Lady Geoffrey, the doors of Almack's would be opened wide to her. Perran was quite certain that the innocent who had reformed the Rogue would be irresistible to the Lady Patronesses. Could he, then, return alone to his old life, now well funded and without a care in the world?

Despite his best efforts to see into such a future, it remained stubbornly clouded. The innkeeper whisked away his plate, while Perran drank deeply of his ale.

His gaze drifted out the window to patient Kit waiting at the rail, and beyond to the silver glitter of the sea plied by pleasure craft, coasters, and gaff-rigged fishing boats. Beyond that, far to the south, lay France.

And the last answer to his dilemma.

Accepting that answer meant risk, to be sure. What he contemplated was illegal, though by no means uncommon. It was woven so tightly into Cornish life that it was the largest, most invisible industry in the county. Even Admiral Teague took part, and one could not find a more upstanding man than he.

Perran paid for his lunch and collected Kit, who was glad to be moving out of the sun. Tucked into the back of St. Mawes harbor was a thatch-roofed pub said to be frequented by a relative of the famous Carter brothers of Prussia Cove.

The most successful smugglers in all Cornwall.

Perran turned Kit's head in that direction and in a few minutes had tied him in the shade and pushed open the door of the pub. He leaned on the wide beam that did service as the bar, and ordered a tankard of their finest. When he was served, he said to the tavern keeper, "I understand I might find Kenal Carter here. Is he on the premises today?"

The barkeep took in his clothes and the horse waiting outside in one all-encompassing glance. He nodded toward a table where three men sat watching him. "Kenal is facing us, sir. You'll find him tough but fair."

"Thank you." He laid a coin on the bar and took his ale into the back, where the man he sought nodded politely.

"Sir Perran Geoffrey," Carter said. "We'd be honored to have you join us."

"You know my name, Mr. Carter?" He dispensed with any thought of normal introductions and seated himself facing the man, which left his back exposed to the room. No doubt on purpose.

"I make it my business to know the names of all the property owners along the fairest stretch of coast in the world."

"I do not doubt it." Perran lowered his voice. "I wonder if you might like to know my property better still."

"I might." Carter gazed at him, his eyes uncompromising, his skin the ruddy, weathered leather of the seaman, his hands rough and callused with hauling rope. And yet his linen was fine and clean, his coat only five years out of date, and a tawny jewel rode the forefinger of his right hand. "What do you propose, Sir Perran?"

Perran had never negotiated with a smuggler before, but it could hardly be different from outfoxing the professional gamblers that frequented the gaming hells of London. The trick was a steady hand and an unflinching eye.

"I wish to assist the brave men of the free trade," he said. "But I am not certain of their needs at present. Perhaps you could enlighten me."

"Seems to me you might be the one in need, sir," Carter drawled. "Which places you in a less secure position to bargain, if you'll pardon my saying so. Roofs and walls come dear, as many of us know."

Perran did his best to conceal his shock that this well-dressed ruffian should not only know his property, but his business as well. But he was about to know even more of it, and as he had so aptly pointed out, Perran was in no position to quibble.

Not when he was still smarting from his visit to the bank.

"It is merely a temporary setback," he said. "I hope to be in funds soon. But in the meanwhile, the sum and substance is this: You are quite right. I need money now, and I am willing to allow certain liberties upon the property in order to obtain it."

"Is that so? And will ye take certain liberties with my men's lives, too? For we have never dealt together before now."

Perran did his best not to take this as an insult. "I assure you, your business is as valuable to me at the moment as my own."

For the first time, Carter's eyes crinkled in a smile. "Spoken like a true gentleman."

One of the other men growled, "Ought to sow a crop."

The third nodded. "The moon will be dark on Tuesday. An' with luck, the winds favorable from France."

"What does that mean, exactly?" Perran asked, looking from one to the other. "Sowing a crop?"

"Why, sir, when a ship runs afoul of the preventive men, sometimes there is no time to beach the goods," Kenal Carter explained. "So a crew ties the barrels of brandy together in a long line and dumps them into the sea."

What a horrifying picture. "Is the brandy not tainted by seawater?"

"French coopers are skilled," Carter said. "The barrels sink quietly to the bottom, and bide their time until it is safe and they are retrieved."

"The cove where Rosevear Creek empties is not yet known to the preventive men," Perran said thoughtfully. "At least, I have never seen any activity of that kind."

"I know some boys who will go a-creeping, then, so do not be alarmed if you should see a fishing boat or two."

Fishing boats did not work at night for legitimate reasons, to be sure. "Creeping?"

The men with Carter chuckled at Perran's ignorance. The second said, "Instead of lines and fishhooks, sir, the boys trawl the bottom with grappling hooks, until they hook the crop and pull it up."

What an education he was receiving.

"Fear not, Sir Perran." Carter eyed him closely. "We will save you a tribute of ten per cent, and sell your share for you, too, if that is agreeable to you. I know how you gentlemen disdain the thought of trade."

The less contact he had with his … crop … the better. "Twenty-five percent."

Carter's gaze lost its twinkle. "Would you beggar me, sir, when all the risk is mine? Fifteen."

"Twenty."

The man shook his head in sorrow. "I had thought you a man of honor, sir. Fifteen is all I am willing to risk with one who is all but a stranger to me."

Perran knew when he was beaten. "Very well. Fifteen. And in turn I will post a man on the cliffs to warn of an approaching cutter." Young Tregarrow had sharp eyes, and would relish such a task.

"That is proper neighborly of you, sir." Carter inclined his head. "If you will leave the door of your carriage house unlocked, we will leave the proceeds in one of your fine carriages."

Perran huffed a laugh. "In that case, you will search in the dark to no avail. I have only one coach, and it was built in my great-grandfather's time."

"It will do. You will have your house roofed and repaired in a pig's whisker."

And he reached across the table to shake Perran's hand.

CHAPTER 15

Somewhat to Perran's surprise, Kenal Carter was as good as his word. By the time the week was out, the old coach in the carriage house had seen a deposit of two leather bags of coins. And with the receipt of the second, Tregarrow and the Falmouth builder he had engaged could bring in their workmen and begin the repairs.

The only people he told of his new business dealings were Griffin and the Admiral. Neither had been shocked. All the Admiral had said was, "Fair weather brings good fortune," and the conversation had turned to other topics.

Cornishmen were a pragmatic lot. Smuggling had been a means of making a living here for generations. There was no dishonor in it. And heaven only knew that Perran needed those coins more than Prinny.

Once the old oak had been cleared away, Perran had been dismayed at the scope of the damage. The tree had fallen on the side of the house that formed the spine of the *E* near the top stroke, crushing the roof and two of the servants' rooms on the third floor, and piercing the floor through to the guest room that lay beside those of Isolde and his grandmother.

He could only thank a merciful Lord that the wind had not directed the massive trunk toward either of the ladies' rooms that night, or he would be paying for a funeral with smuggled liquor as well as for repairs. As it was, windows of both their rooms had been smashed in by branches, and it was only thanks to the heavy curtains on both ladies' beds that they had not been injured by flying glass.

The household staff had cleaned up the glass, leaves and branches in the rooms, and once the shutters had been repaired, Mrs. Tregarrow had closed them all to keep the weather out. So the workmen began with the roof.

"If the ladies of London could see the Rogues now!" Griffin said, hammer in hand as he straddled a beam in buckskin breeches, a disgraceful hat upon his blond head and his shirtsleeves rolled up to the elbow.

"Not that way, sir!" the harried builder called up before the blow fell. "I showed you—you must drive in the nails at an angle." They'd had a time of it convincing the builder to let them help at all, especially since he had to teach both Perran and Griffin first, as though they were boys who didn't know a plank from a slate. Which was probably a good estimation.

But the nine days' wonder of the three of them sullying their lily-white hands with labor hardly lasted as long as that, and by the end of the week the builder was verbally abusing them with as much gusto as he did any of his crew. Perran did not mind. For with every shout, a nail was pounded in and his home came back to life a little more.

The ugly truth was that the roof needed to be replaced in its entirety and new slates laid, but how long Kenal Carter might get away with continuing to sow his soggy crops in the sea was anyone's guess. How had Perran's father allowed the place to fall into such disrepair? And how had Perran been foolish enough to ignore it for so long?

He sat on the ridge of the roof, a safety line knotted about his waist. In the distance, he could see the chimney pots of Morvoren Manor, nestled in its sweep of land that led down to the cliffs. Much closer to, under his very knees, he could see the patches of the moss and a century's worth of lichen, busily lifting the slates and letting the weather in. The plaster and panelling inside needed repair, the piping had rusted through, and the window casements had warped so badly from moisture that it was no wonder they couldn't keep the place warm.

It was enough to make a man sit on his roof's ridge-cap, put his head in his hands, and weep.

Perhaps he was doomed to a life of crime in perpetuity— or at least until the house had been renewed from the inside out. Which could take years, at the rate of two bags of coins a week.

If he had it all to do again, though, what could he have changed? His father would still have gambled away everything but the land—and might have thrown the deed to that in the pot had he not died of an apoplectic fit before he thought of it. Grand-mère had kept the house going as best she could, but still the tenants' own roofs and cribs went begging, and the price of corn rose.

I am responsible for life and property. I cannot go on any longer, lurching from repair to repair, taking a hand in the free trade, and running to London to escape it all. I must stay and make what I can of my inheritance, for Grand-mère's and Isolde's dear sakes.

A low phaeton crested the hill, its two ponies moving at a smart pace. A woman was driving, but he could see nothing of her face because of her straw bonnet. However, a quick estimation of the ladies in the neighborhood and the likelihood that any of them would be driving themselves told him this must be one of the Penrose sisters. She pulled the horses up at the gates, but did not turn in. Instead, the reins lay in her lap as she gazed at the house, as though to take in the progress his crew was making.

Like a boy, he waved.

She pushed her bonnet back to see better, and he recognized the autumn color of her hair.

Alwyn.

Would she turn in at the drive and call upon him? If so, he must untie himself and scramble down from the roof immediately. He stood, balancing on the old slates and gripping a chimney with one hand, and waved again. In the stiffening of her body he knew that she had recognized his figure, in shirt sleeves and completely out of his normal sphere.

To his surprise, she tipped back her head and laughed, then waved back, with energy. She pointed in the direction of the village to indicate her errand, took up the reins once more, and shook them over the horses' backs. The little phaeton bowled on, leaving him smiling and with a peculiar warmth in his chest.

Was she learning to forgive him? Surely a woman could not laugh and wave with a man whom she despised. And there had been that moment in the mermaid's room, as they stood before the hearth. He had looked into her face, and her lips had parted, just as though she thought he might kiss her.

He nearly had—or would have, had she given him the

chance. For she had departed so swiftly he had been left looking after her, half of him yearning for the lost moment, half of him astonished that he could even think such a thing after what had passed between them.

Could there be hope for him?

She will think your only object is her forty thousand pounds.

Well, no man of sense could discount that. But Perran had learned to be honest with himself. This spark between them—this crackle in the air whenever the two of them were in the same room—what if—?

Could it be?

Could he go to Morvoren Manor tomorrow evening, dressed in his best, and court a woman who still had every reason to hate him? Could she forgive him? Could they regain the footing they had had as children so long ago?

And most important, did he have the courage to do what he had already half determined to do? To follow that road wherever it would lead … even if it meant the ruination of his former life?

ONCE THE HOUSEHOLD had come out of mourning after Mama's passing, Alwyn and her sisters had learned to do the honors of their home for Papa when he invited his neighbors for quiet dinners, for musical evenings, for cards. Alwyn was no stranger to arranging rooms and writing menus, and neither were Karensa and Rowena. That said, Alwyn had had so much on her mind since her return to Cornwall that when Lady Geoffrey and Lady Mainwaring both requested that they be allowed to assist her in preparing for Tuesday night, she acquiesced with gratitude.

"For I shall be on tenterhooks every moment," she told Lady Mainwaring in a low tone while they arranged the flowers Tuesday afternoon. "This is the first time we have had company since Papa's accident. I shall be watching closely to be sure he is not in pain."

"And we will watch everything else," Lady Mainwaring said in the calm tone that always caused the ache in Alwyn's heart where the memory of her mother lived to throb a little. Mama had been equal to everything ... except the wasting disease that had finally taken her life. "If you will allow me, his lordship and I will be happy to stand in your parents' places and receive with you."

"I should be delighted." Alwyn kissed her. "Papa cannot stand for so long, but he may receive in the drawing room. How wonderful it is to have you and my uncle here!"

"How clever your grandfather was to design two drawing rooms, separated by folding partitions." Lady Geoffrey came into the room to set a vase of flowers on the mantel over the second fireplace. "I had forgotten that the sea parlor is only half of what amounts to a ballroom. Yet with the partitions pulled back, they look as though they have always been one room. And I am happy to see my original suggestion of colors for the walls is still in use."

"It has been a long time since it has been made one room for dancing." Alwyn could not even remember the last time— though it was likely because she had been so young that the closest she had been allowed to the party was to peep through the stair railings as the guests arrived below.

"We may even have enough people for two sets." Rowena

came in with more roses, and Alwyn offered her a Royal Morvoren vase whose India Lily pattern was picked out in gold. She expected Rowena to put the flowers in it and turn away before Alwyn could speak, but to her surprise, her sister did not. "You must wear your pale green silk from London, Alwyn, as a compliment to our aunt."

"Yes, do, my dear," Lady Mainwaring said. "To my mind, that color becomes you above all others."

Alwyn felt a loosening in her chest. Had Rowena learned to forgive her for the disaster in London? And if so, might she not in turn forgive Perran for causing it?

For perhaps a tiny chance existed that she might have been at fault. Too eager to be thought the toast of the town. Too precipitate and headstrong in refusing to heed his caution.

The sight of him on his roof yesterday had surprised and delighted her so much that she had been forced to look into her stubborn heart and do a little housekeeping there herself. But first, she must start closer to home.

She gave her sister a quick kiss. "If it pleases you that I wear that gown, then I shall." She had never had a chance to wear it, so precipitous had been their departure from Town. And while she could not wear an evening dress to church, or while visiting, surely it would not be too top-lofty of her to wear it tonight, in her own home?

She was outside in the garden with her basket, cutting a little more fern for the arrangements and untangling her untidy thoughts about forgiveness, when her uncle found her.

"My dear, I have just received a letter, and I would like your opinion as to how I should answer it."

She turned from the fern, scissors in hand. "My opinion, sir?"

He heard the surprise in her tone, and smiled. "Indeed, your feelings are most relevant in this case. It is from Arthur Landry."

"Arthur Landry!"

"The very man. Listen—*Lord Mainwaring, et cetera, humble servant, applied to your man for the address.* No, not that bit. Ah, here we are.

"Having made the acquaintance of your nieces my cousins, and spent a little time in their company, I found myself wishing to know them better. You can imagine my astonishment when I heard they had returned home to Cornwall, leaving not so much as a note to reassure their friends as to the date of their return. Having learned that you and her ladyship have vouchsafed them your company as well, I find myself quite bereft.

"I earnestly apply to you then, sir, to tell me if I have offended in any way. If I have, I throw myself upon your goodwill and ask that I might present myself to you and my cousins to discover wherein I may have erred and to correct my misstep."

"Misstep?" Alwyn said blankly. "Mr. Landry has committed no error that I know of."

"Quite so, my dear," her uncle said. "An extraordinary sentiment, to be sure.

"I await your convenience at the White Swan in St. Just, where I have taken rooms."

"What?" Alwyn exclaimed.

"I will abide by your counsel, for I know full well that while the

name of Penrose is celebrated on every side, there are a few who would revile a branch of it. In fact, it is the most cherished wish of my heart that the rift between the elder be healed by the younger.

"I remain, sir, your servant, et cetera."

"Arthur Landry is here?" Alwyn's voice was pitched a little high. "In St. Just? He is not in London?"

"So it would seem."

"My goodness." She cast about her wildly, as though he might step through the hedges at any moment. "What can he mean by it? What if Papa should hear? What are we to do with him?"

"Why, nothing that I can see." Lord Mainwaring offered his arm, and Alwyn put down both scissors and basket and took it rather as one grasps at a beam of wood to stay afloat. They paced along the gravel terrace, then down the flagged steps to the lawns. "He has worked himself up to think that your departure is somehow his fault. He has either a great opinion of himself or a very small one."

"I think perhaps the latter, Uncle," she said, attempting to collect her thoughts. The wide space of the lawns and the imperturbable woolly faces of the sheep scattered under the trees were helping her to breathe normally again. "He seemed to me to be everything that is amiable, and not tending toward conceit or arrogance at all. He is the son of a clergy-man, and must have been taught humility. Perhaps his upbringing shows itself in that aspect of his character."

"Be that as it may, the question is, am I to bring these events to your father's attention? For I have long been aware of the rift, as Mr. Landry so neatly puts it, in your father's family."

Alwyn took several silent steps at his side. "What is your own opinion, sir?"

"If your father were as he once was, I would have no hesitation in laying it all before him. But in his present condition…"

"It may agitate him. Especially if he were to take it into his head to order the carriage and deal with the matter himself. What if he were to take a fall?"

"Precisely."

"On the other hand," Alwyn said thoughtfully, "if *you* were to call upon my cousin at the White Swan, and word got back to Papa that you had done so, his agitation would be augmented by the belief that you had somehow betrayed him by—by consorting with the enemy."

"You have an excellent grasp of the dilemma this young man has created for me, my dear," said his lordship with a frown. "And the young scamp need not imagine that I enjoy being put in such a position, either."

"Certainly not. What was he thinking, to come post haste over hundreds of miles, just because he thought he had caused some offense? A letter would have done perfectly well."

"I hesitate to dignify his presumption by riding over and asking that very question. I am sorely tempted to send him a note telling him not to be a simpleton, and to return to his family with nothing more said of the matter."

Alwyn thought quickly. "We cannot do anything about the letter now—our guests will be arriving soon, and neither of us are dressed to receive them. I believe that we should not leave Papa in the dark, however. It is for him to say whether or not we might receive my cousin here. Which is so unlikely as to be impossible. What you choose to do about writing to Mr. Landry in St. Just, of course, is your own affair, Uncle."

Her uncle nodded, and they turned back to the house. "I will confer with your father tomorrow, then, and own all the truth. I should not wish to appear underhand by communicating with a man for whom he holds so much dislike. Indeed, if he finds the idea repugnant, I shall reconsider the acquaintance altogether, and tell the young man so."

Alwyn squeezed his arm in thanks, and, satisfied, Lord Mainwaring set off for a walk along the cliffs while she returned to the garden to retrieve her basket of fern.

What a strange week it had been. Two months ago, there had been no young men in the neighborhood. Today, three estates had welcomed their heirs home again, and a cousin who had been lost had found them.

As a child, she had once thought that nothing ever changed here, and as a young girl, the idea of being buried in the pastoral quiet of St. Just for ever had sent her into fits of the dismals.

Now, Alwyn wondered if anything could be the same ever again.

CHAPTER 16

A festive party they made, Perran thought, rolling through the long summer gloaming in the Admiral's carriage, all of them dressed in their London finest. He devoutly hoped that there would be no one among the company so long in the tooth that they would recognize the fabric of his father's superfine coat, a green so dark it was nearly black, made over by the close-mouthed tailor in the very pink of modern fashion. His waistcoat was embroidered in silver and green (cut down from a court coat from the era when the mad king was young), its collar points open at a jaunty angle, and his linen was as snowy as any matron could wish, thanks to the excellent care of the Admiral's staff at the cottage.

Jago had chosen to be taken up in the carriage with the Rogues rather than to crush his parents and three siblings in the family coach. "For the boys are like a pair of puppies at the prospect of a frolic," he said in tones of exhaustion. "I had forgotten what it is like to be in their company."

"Says the old man of the sea at eight and twenty," scoffed

Griffin. "We ought to have sent for a sedan chair for you. Does such a thing still exist in this day and age?"

"I rather think it does here, but there is no one to carry it for miles over country roads," the Admiral pointed out with a smile. "Young men of strength are likely working at the china clay pit. Look, there is the Manor now. How brightly it is lit!"

If Perran had entertained a doubt as to his reception by the Penrose family, it soon vanished in the sheer impact of the picture made by the three daughters of the house, ranged in the hall at the foot of the staircase with their aunt to receive their guests.

The sight of Alwyn stole his breath from his lungs.

There was something about the pale green of her silk gown that brought out the russet tints in her hair and the bloom in her cheeks, and it was cut just low enough in the bosom to make a man fall into speculation about the perfect curves nestled there. Her hair was pulled up into a cascade of curls, with a bit of feathery fern twisted into the green ribbon twined through them.

It was all he could do to keep his jaw from sagging. Instead, he concentrated on bowing over Lady Mainwaring's hand.

"Sir Perran," she said with the warmth and calm he had been used to in London. Did she consider her chicks safer now, in the protection of their nest? "You are very welcome. You will find Mr. Penrose and Lord Mainwaring in the drawing room near the fire. They will be delighted to see you."

He murmured his compliments, and then moved to his left, where he bowed to Alwyn and her sisters. They returned the courtesy and he was finally able to speak a rational sentence.

"Miss Penrose."

"Sir Perran. Welcome." Despite her words, her smile trembled a little at the edges, not quite full-fledged.

"You look … very well this evening."

A slight flush of color stained her cheeks. "Thank you."

A rational man would be thinking of the forty thousand pounds, the smuggling, his own dire straits and need. But at this moment, all that faded into nothing beside the bloom upon her cheeks. If he could not make her smile properly here in company, as he had yesterday upon the roof, at least he had made her blush. It was a beginning.

Perran moved down to greet her sisters, both of whom smiled with civility, if they were not positively happy to see him. He felt a moment of dismay when Jago did more than simply bow to Rowena, but took her gloved hand in his.

"I hope you will save me the first waltz," the poor bufflehead blurted, as though there were not others waiting behind him.

"This is hardly the time to ask me," she hissed. "Go pay your respects to our father and uncle, sir, and stop being such a bumble."

This incivility brought him up short with a vengeance, and both Perran and Griffin bore him away in a direction that might promise a restorative drink.

"What has got into you?" Griffin murmured as they bowed to their acquaintance and navigated toward their host. "You will quite ruin your reputation—and mine."

"She looks like an angel," was all Jago could manage. "In a dress the color of the sky."

Perran rolled his eyes. This was most unlike Jago— not the boorish behavior, but the flights of fancy. Rowena was a tolerably pretty girl, but … an angel?

"Pull yourself together, man," he ordered his friend. "You are a gentleman, and must be a good example to your brothers, who, from the commotion I detect behind us, have just arrived."

They found Mr. Penrose standing by the fire, one hand on the back of a wing chair, receiving his guests with cheeks flushed with pleasure. Lord Mainwaring stood by, ready to assist if need be. Perran bowed first to Mainwaring, who knew of the evening at Almack's, and then to Mr. Penrose, who did not, and never would if Perran had anything to say about it.

"Sir Perran, may I say again how pleased I am at your return to the neighborhood?" Mr. Penrose's tone held a hint of his old bluff geniality. "And Captain Teague, Mr. Tremayne. You are all very welcome to the Manor once again. We hope to see more of you all."

"I am happy to witness your return to health, sir," Griffin said, his smile as easy as his manners. "St. Just is simply not the same without you bruising along the lanes on one horse or another."

Mr. Penrose smiled. "It will be some time before I can mount up again, Captain, but I am determined that at the very least, you will see me by Michaelmas, bruising along in a curricle with a rug over my legs."

"One step at a time," Perran cautioned him. "I have no doubt that a man of your character and determination will enjoy a return to full activity before the year is out."

Griffin and Jago bowed and moved off, either to find that

drink or to corral the twins before they overturned something.

But Perran leaned closer to his host. "Mr. Penrose, I wonder if I might have a private word with you at some time during the evening?"

Alwyn's father gazed at him curiously. "With me, sir? I have no objection, if I may know the subject?"

Perran could not help a glance toward the hall, where the young ladies had concluded the reception of their guests and were coming into the drawing rooms behind Lady Mainwaring.

"I would like to speak to you about … a matter close to both our hearts."

"Oh, you would, would you?" He glanced from Perran to his daughters. "Then there is no time like the present. Brother, would you greet the Tremaynes in my stead? Sir Perran and I will be in my study for a few minutes."

"Of course," Lord Mainwaring told him with a keen glance at Perran, and handed Mr. Penrose his cane.

Perran offered the older man his arm, thankful that his host had chosen to receive his guests at this end of the double room and not the far end overlooking the terrace. He did not want to pace the entire length of it with Alwyn staring at him in surprise for absconding with her father.

The door of Mr. Penrose's room closed behind them, shutting out the murmur of talk and laughter as neighbors old and new re-formed their acquaintance. He had understood from Isolde that this had been his study, and now it combined books and desk with a comfortable-looking bed, neatly made. He must not yet be able to manage the stairs, though it was clear it would not be long before he could.

Mr. Penrose released Perran's arm and indicated the decanters ranged on a side table by the bookcases. "Help yourself, sir, and I'll have one, too, if what you wish to discuss with me is what I believe it to be."

"Am I so transparent?" Perran filled two cut crystal glasses with brandy that may well have come from Sunday night's wet harvest. He handed one to his host, who had seated himself not behind the desk, but in one of a pair of chairs before the fire.

Mr. Penrose accepted the brandy, but did not lift his glass in a salute of any kind. "Transparent? Far from it. If the information I have is correct, you are painted as the very blackest of blackguards."

Perran nearly dropped the glass. Did Alwyn's father know about his involvement with Kenal Carter? Did she?

To recover his countenance, he lowered himself into the chair facing Mr. Penrose. "Sir?"

"A report of an alarming nature was provided to me by my sister in law some weeks ago, explaining the sudden reappearance of my daughters at home when they were supposed to have been enjoying their Season in London."

Never in his wildest dreams would Perran have imagined that Lady Mainwaring would have told Alwyn's father what had happened. But at least his most recent secret seemed still to be secure. He focused on this most pressing matter of all. For if Mr. Penrose had already set his mind against him, then all was lost.

"I am sure Lady Mainwaring's account was scrupulous in its accuracy, sir. Do you wish to rescind your welcome, and ask me to leave your house?"

Mr. Penrose frowned. "Certainly not. I wish you to tell me

your version of the events that led to my daughter's public humiliation."

"Has she told you her version?"

"She has."

Perran took a fortifying gulp of his brandy—it was both excellent and French—and began to speak. Of the moment between himself and Alwyn in the Blessings' library. Of the drive home in the rain where they had been seen by Arthur Landry—

Mr. Penrose snorted, but did not interrupt.

Of the snide hints in the columns of An Observant Gentleman that had resulted in the sentence of impropriety being leveled upon Alwyn, and by association, upon her sisters.

"I have apologized to Miss Penrose for my involvement in the entire painful affair, sir," he said in conclusion, "but as yet I have had no indication that she has forgiven me."

He waited for his sentence to be passed upon him. The brandy, instead of settling his stomach, seemed to be forming a tossing sea.

"Nor have I," Mr. Penrose said at last, "save for an invitation sent out with your direction upon it."

"I must be grateful, then." Perran's tone held no irony. "You and your family have every right to cut me from your acquaintance. I would not blame you in the least—I would only ask that you do not include my sister and grandmother in any such interdiction."

Mr. Penrose eyed him. "Certainly I will not. Such a thing never occurred to me or anyone here. But tell me, is your character so bad that these brief moments—one accidental, one no less than kind—could be so construed as to ruin a young lady's reputation?"

This man could give Jago a lesson or two in plain speaking. But Perran did not dare to feel relief as yet.

"I have always sought to be civil and gentlemanlike to everyone, sir. But it is all too true that I am, like many others, fond of a woman's company, of driving too fast, of sport and cards. But so are many men. The *ton* thrive on gossip when there is no truth to hand, and small actions can blow up into thunderstorms of speculation and discussion. I and Jago and Griffin avoid the company of young ladies in their first Season for that reason."

"But you did not avoid my daughters."

"No, for our families are acquainted, as I tried to explain to Countess Lieven on that night at Almack's. To no avail. The sentence had already been passed, and no appeal was permitted."

Mr. Penrose considered him much as a lion might consider an antelope.

"What do you know of this Landry fellow?" he asked, rather unexpectedly.

Perran could not help feeling slightly relieved that there might be another antelope within range of his host's ire.

"Why, nothing. He came to Town some weeks before your family did. Received an introduction to your brother Mainwaring, and upon discovery of the connection, was subsequently received by him. I know nothing more."

"Nothing of his character, his prospects?"

"No."

"Hm." The golden gaze flashed up, and Perran braced

himself. "Well, then. What was it you wished to speak to me about?"

Perran took a deep breath, both to steady himself and to gather his resolution. "Despite all that has just passed between us, I wish to ask your permission to pay my addresses to your eldest daughter."

He raised his gaze to find Mr. Penrose staring at him with something akin to anger. "My daughter? You wish to court Alwyn?"

"I do, sir."

"After you were instrumental in bringing about her public disgrace? Were your actions then in support of this end, sir?"

It took a moment for Perran to recover from this blow. Which he fully deserved.

"No indeed. My actions were all designed to preserve her reputation, not sully it. While I must acknowledge the friendship between our families, I dared not show her any but the most expected civilities in public. Which, as it turned out, was still too much. And so here we are."

"Indeed."

"But let us be under no misapprehension, sir. I am not trying to make up for past mistakes. My thoughts are all of the future. I believe Miss Penrose to be a young lady of spirit and fine character. We grew up together, and I hazard to say a house here in the country, so close to her family, would suit her more than the London life."

"Do you plan to return to—as you say—the London life?"

"To be as blunt as yourself, sir, I cannot afford it. I must complete the repairs to Rosevear Court as soon as may be, so that my family might not trespass any longer than necessary upon your kind hospitality."

Mr. Penrose waved this off. "Nonsense. Happy to be of help. But to the main point—do you care for my girl?"

Did he care for Alwyn the way he had cared for Constance? The answer to that had to be no. Not yet. He did not know her nearly so well. But in recent days he had learned he was not nearly so disinterested as he had fooled himself into believing. Those moments—those sparks—even something as simple as a smile and a wave … oh, yes, they were all working together to prove the truth. And now he must offer some of these truths to her father before he wondered at his silence.

"I care for her happiness, and for her well-being. I believe that her character and mine would suit each other. We share an upbringing and a similar outlook on what constitutes a useful life." He met Mr. Penrose's intent gaze. "In short, sir, I believe I could make her happy if she would let me."

"And you need her marriage portion to make your home a place to which you could bring her as a bride. So that you will no longer need to throw in your lot with the gentlemen of the free trade."

The truth could feel like a punch to the gut. He rallied enough to say, "Those things are also true, sir."

Mr. Penrose looked as though he was enjoying Perran's discomfiture. "Young Tregarrow told us, on one of his visits. There is no shame in it. I would do the same, in your position. But to return to the more important matter, I will be honest with you, Sir Perran." He leaned forward in his chair. "Even if I were the gambler your father was, I would not bet on your chances with my daughter."

Another punch to the gut, which he absorbed with a deep

breath. Perran's sensibilities were taking quite the beating, but he did not allow himself to flinch.

"That said, it was my late wife's dearest wish that one of her daughters should bear a title, and if you are the only prospect that will make that wish come true, then I will not refuse my permission."

Even Gentleman Jackson could not deliver a backhand with such finesse. For this man made no bones about the fact that it was Perran's title he approved for his daughter, not Perran himself.

Why should that be a surprise? Perran thought bitterly. Did it not confirm he had been right to despair of ever making a match? For it seemed even now that finding a woman who could love him for himself was as much a distant dream as it had ever been.

Mr. Penrose was not finished. "But if during your courtship your actions—or a single word you utter—cause my Alwyn's name to be bandied about in St. Just the way I understand it has been in London, you will answer to me. I may be lame, but it will not be forever. I am not without resources that can bring your ability to rebuild your home or your tenancies to a sudden and permanent end."

He meant the preventive men. Perran's lungs constricted, and he was forced to breathe slowly. "You have my word, sir."

"See to it that you keep it. And now, if you would be so kind as to let my brother Mainwaring know, I think I would like to retire. They may all go in to dinner without me."

Perran managed to get himself out of the study without his knees buckling. But it was a near thing.

After delivering the message to Lord Mainwaring, he crossed the hall. The butler bowed him out the front door, where he strolled around to the side of the house that afforded a view of the sea.

He stood there in the moonshadow of the laurel hedge, head up, absorbing the stunning truth that he had been given permission to court Alwyn Penrose.

Heaven help him.

He wondered how fast the news would travel to London, and if Constance Eaton would have even a moment's regret on his account.

CHAPTER 17

Tonight's task, Alwyn decided—aside from seeing to the comfort and entertainment of their guests—was to stay out of Perran Geoffrey's way until she could face him without blushing.

She had not been able to help herself yesterday, as soon as she had spotted him on the roof. Before she could remember her dignity or the fact that she had not yet forgiven him, she had waved with all the delight of a small child.

And he had waved back. He had been too far away for her to see his face, but his entire form had expressed recognition and even welcome.

She should hate him for the wreck he had made of her hopes and prospects in her first London Season. But she was nothing if not honest, though not in the way Karensa was honest. She could look into her own heart and acknowledge that he had done his best to keep his reputation from casting a shadow over hers. The fact that their good intentions had led to ruin despite his efforts was, she saw now, not his fault.

After his arrival with his friends, he seemed to disappear until it was time to take his sister in to dinner. He would, she suspected, have offered his grandmother his arm, had he not been rendered superfluous by Admiral Teague, who had bowed gallantly and won that lady as his dinner partner. How kind of the Admiral to treat Lady Geoffrey as the first lady of the company, Alwyn thought with a smile. How fortunate they were that he was back in the neighborhood again!

Alwyn herself was seated at her uncle's right hand, since Papa had been fatigued by the long day, and had taken a tray in his room. She kept an eye on the courses and their timing, and by the time Lady Mainwaring rose at the other end of the table to indicate the ladies should leave the gentlemen to their port and conversation, Alwyn dared to be pleased that dinner had gone off rather well.

While they had been at table, Mrs. Menabilly and her staff had seen the carpets rolled up and chairs placed around the perimeter of the double drawing room, with the pianoforte at the top and the second fireplace at the bottom.

Rowena sat down to play a few light melodies while the ladies conversed.

"Surely she does not intend to play for the dancing," Lady Mainwaring said in a low tone to Alwyn. "That would not send a suitable message to the young men at all."

"Not Rowena," Alwyn assured her. "I hope you still intend to give us the pleasure of hearing you?"

"Oh yes. I will keep my word, my dear, if you will arrange for someone to spell me long enough to dance with his lordship before he finds himself some cronies for cards. I cannot trust your dear uncle not to disappear before I have secured his promise for two dances."

Alwyn never ceased to be delighted at her aunt's love for her husband—and for dancing. "We will be on watch, dear Aunt, to make certain he does not."

The sense of anticipation in the room increased some time later as the gentlemen came in. How long it had been since there had been dancing at Morvoren Manor!

And now here were their neighbors—the Geoffreys, the Tremaynes, the two Teagues, Mr. Pengowan, who was one of the trustees at the pit, and his lady; the vicar Mr. Birch and his wife; and Lord and Lady Tregothnan and their relations, who were proving rather difficult to know. The young man and his two sisters could not have been more different. He was as quiet and as soberly dressed as a parson, while the young ladies fluttered about the room in their simple white muslins, exclaiming over this arrangement of flowers and that painted vase. Their parents, in the meanwhile, made conversation when they were spoken to, but Alwyn could not tell whether or not they enjoyed their company. They seemed rather in awe of their noble connections.

Rowena's prediction that there would be enough dancers for two sets was happily borne out. In fact they were in a fair way to having eight in each set, which as far as Alwyn was concerned, made the evening a success, even if it were not what the London hostesses might call *a sad crush*.

But who would be her partner? As the eldest daughter of the house, it was her honor to lead off the top set. She was rather on tenterhooks waiting for a gentleman to ask her, though Lord Mainwaring would do so if she wished it. The Tregothnan relation? Oh dear, no. They had been introduced, but since she could not even remember the young man's name, he would by no means do. Had he ever had a lesson from a dancing master in the whole of his life?

Mr. Jago Tremayne? Perhaps she had better attempt to smile at him, or he would ask Rowena and make a cake of himself. As for one of his twin brothers, goodness, no—it would be like dancing with a grasshopper.

Captain Teague? A fine choice. At least he could be depended on to—

"Miss Penrose," said a deep, musical voice behind her that sent a ripple along her nerves, as though he had plucked them. "May I enquire whether you are engaged for the first dance?"

Turning, Alwyn found herself so close to Perran Geoffrey she could easily have stepped into his arms. He moved back just enough to bow politely.

At that moment, Aunt Celia seated herself at the pianoforte and played a few preliminary chords to gain the room's attention.

What should she do? Alwyn wondered wildly. She had forgiven him—but not completely enough for him to know it. He would certainly see her blood beating in her very veins, to say nothing of the heat in her cheeks. If only she could dance with somebody else, somebody who did not have such an effect upon her!

But she could not. If she refused him, she would be forced to refuse every prospective partner thereafter, and that would never do at the first evening for which she had ever acted as hostess.

There was nothing for it but to control her rioting emotions, curtsey, and accept his hand.

He squeezed her fingers as though offering encourage-ment at this important moment, and led her to the top of the set. Couples stepped into position as though they had been waiting for them, and Aunt Celia launched into the opening chords of *Mr. Beveridge's Magot*, which she knew was Alwyn's favorite.

"You look particularly well this evening," was her partner's first remark. He kept perfect time, his gaze upon her with—could that be pleasure?—even as he handed her through the opening figures without appearing to so much as think about them.

"As do you," came out of her mouth without benefit of thought beforehand. "But you said so before."

"The truth bears repeating." Color appeared on his cheekbones … no, Alwyn would not look at his cheekbones, for certainly they were a fine example of their kind and far too distracting.

"I do not believe I saw this frock in London."

"No, you would not have. We were obliged to come away before I had a chance to wear it." Her tone was airy, but all the same, his eyes darkened.

"Have you forgiven me yet, Miss Penrose?"

"I have not decided."

"Will you do so within my lifetime?"

"I do not know."

"What may I do to induce you to soften your heart?"

Did she dare tell him that her heart had softened already? For what London rogue lacking in conscience would be up on a roof, hammer in hand, sacrificing his own pride and consequence for the sake of his responsibility to his ladies? Not one man in a thousand. She could not make him out. Why put on such a character in London, as one might put on a mask for a fancy dress ball, when at home in Cornwall he was so different? If she had stayed in Town, would such a change also have come over her?

Now, there was a sobering thought.

Two figures passed. Two figures in which she had time to reflect upon that man and this one. But one thing was clear—she could not dodge the fact that even had he been wearing the mask of a rogue, he had done his best to consider her prospects before his own. That reflected well upon his character. That was the character he displayed here, to his neighbors and family.

Perhaps a reputation stayed with the set of people among whom it was first formed. Somewhere along the road to the West Country, might it not have detached itself and a new one begun?

She smiled at her own fancy.

"A smile, Miss Penrose? Dare I hope that the softening I spoke of might be occurring even now?"

Was he watching her so carefully? A kind of hum thrummed along her veins at the thought of a man like this giving her such attention, as though she were the only woman in the room.

"Oh, do be quiet, sir. I was about to apologize for my ungraciousness and you have spoiled it."

"I am all ears." But he could not keep a smile from his own lips, and it transformed his face. Rather than the saturnine, knowing, even shuttered expression she had grown used to, this was a real smile. One that made him look almost boyish. That gave him the face of a man who had no reputation but that of a gentleman. Of a friend she might once have known.

"Very well, then. I am sorry I was ungracious. You are

sorry for what happened in London. Leaving out degrees of calamity in both cases, I suppose we must now begin again."

"That would make me very happy, Miss Penrose. Might I have the second waltz, later this evening?"

She nearly lost her footing and turned to the right—toward the door—rather than the left. He rescued her smoothly and they flowed into the final figure.

"The second, sir?"

"Why, yes. Since the company does not number itself in the hundreds this evening, if one wishes to dance a man must ask for more than one with each lady."

"But will that not be thought fast?"

"In some circles, perhaps. But we are among friends and family here." His knowledge of society was much greater than hers, but even she knew that in St. Just, two dances meant something.

Perhaps more than she wanted to convey.

Then again, she wanted to be friends. Wanted to see that smile once more—the one that was a reminder like a distant echo of the boy who had laughed as they raced their ponies across the fields.

"Very well," she said at last. "The second waltz."

When he escorted her off the floor, she expected him to stalk away and take refuge with the gentlemen playing cards. Instead, he bowed. "May I fetch you some punch?"

Goodness me. "How very kind of you, Sir Perran, but truly, there is no need—"

"I will return in a moment."

She was still standing there, slack-jawed with astonishment, when Karensa joined her. The latter curtseyed to her uncle, who had danced the first with her at the top of the second set, and turned to her sister.

"What has you looking positively calf-witted?"

Alwyn closed her mouth with a snap, then permitted herself to speak. "Sir Perran Geoffrey is behaving like a gentleman."

"He *is* a gentleman."

"Yes, but he is not the same sort of gentleman here as he is in London."

"One would hope not."

"Karensa, whichever gentleman he is this evening, he has asked me for the second waltz."

"Of course he asked. That is what gentlemen do. To the main point—did you accept?"

"I rather think I did … and now he has gone to fetch me some punch. It feels very strange."

"It feels rather like he may be courting you."

Alwyn made a rude noise that caused Mrs. Birch to glance over at her as though she could not believe what she had just heard. Alwyn gave her a hasty smile.

"He is not courting me," she told her sister through the smile. "You are all about in the head even to imagine such a thing." He was behaving like a gentleman to elicit her forgiveness, and she had given it. Anything more was—was foolish imagining. She would do well to control the unruly gallop of her mind … to say nothing of that peculiar hum in her blood whenever she caught sight of him.

Her sister was prevented from making the reply a-tiptoe on her tongue by the reappearance of the subject under consideration.

He handed Alwyn a cup of punch, and then offered his

own to Karensa, who could clearly see no reason why she should not accept it. "Thank you, Sir Perran. How kind."

"You will have to open the French doors soon," he said. "It is becoming warm—surely the sign of an excellent party. Miss Karensa, may I secure you for the quadrille?"

"You may, sir. And do ask Rowena for the third waltz, for Mr. Tremayne will make a fool of himself by asking for all of them, and that we must prevent."

"I quite agree." Clearly Jago's buffleheaded behavior upon their arrival and Rowena's tart response had not escaped him. "If you wish it, I will suggest he dance that one with Isolde."

"Thank you. He has not seen Rowena in a ball gown very often, I suspect. Perhaps only once or twice," Karensa said, clearly aiming to make allowances. "He is not the only one to lose his head over her. But we do not wish him to draw too much attention to her, all the same. Not in front of Lord and Lady Tregothnan. They are the foremost family in the district."

"Are you a high stickler, Miss Karensa?" he asked with a gravity that made Alwyn suspect he was trying not to laugh.

"No indeed, no more than anyone here," she responded calmly. "But this is the first time the Tregothnans have ever accepted an invitation to Morvoren Manor. I would not wish anything *else* to cloud their view of us."

He absorbed the pointed reference to London with silent grace. "Nor would I," he said at last.

"I suspect it is the presence of your grandmother in the house that has lent us the gloss of acceptability in that quarter," Alwyn said to him. "To say nothing of our dinner being in honor of Lord and Lady Mainwaring, which I was careful to note on the invitations."

"We are fortunate in our relatives, then," he said. "I am happy to lend mine in a good cause." He bowed. "Until later, then, Miss Karensa, Miss Penrose."

Alwyn watched his tall form move from group to group, conversing with that one and bowing to this one. "So affable," she mused aloud. "Such fine manners. One would never suspect he was laughing at you, sister."

"Not *at* me," Karensa replied. *"With* me. I am glad he has a sense of humor as well as a sense of propriety."

"Neither of which he has displayed in the whole of our acquaintance, until this evening. He is up to something," Alwyn finished darkly. "I know it."

But what it was she could not winkle out of him during the second waltz, no matter how discreetly she approached the matter. His conversation was without fault, his smile reappearing just often enough to disarm her. For every time she saw it, something melted inside her. And yet, conversely, snowflakes seemed to be tingling all along her veins. How could a smile have such an effect upon her? It was almost a relief to see him dance the cotillion with Karensa and the third waltz with Rowena, exactly as promised.

Really, for a man whose reputation as a rogue was the talk of London, he was an exemplary guest. Alwyn could not make him out. She must simply leave him to his own devices and enjoy her own party.

Alwyn danced with Captain Teague with great pleasure, with Mr. Jago Tremayne with great civility, and with his twin brothers with great economy. At least they did not step on her, or cause her to trip over their feet. She even accepted a country dance with the Tregothnan relative, who performed it in complete silence. She felt rather sorry for the poor young man, who was bathed in sweat by the end of the proceedings. It was clear that he had not been much in company, for making conversation while dancing was utterly out of his power.

The last waltz was to be just before a cold collation and dessert were served at midnight. Not for St. Just was the city custom of dancing until dawn. No, the dancing would cease before the lunch, so that Lady Mainwaring and the other ladies who had taken turns at the pianoforte might enjoy dessert and visit a little before the carriages were summoned.

When Perran Geoffrey reappeared at Alwyn's elbow, then, she felt a tingle of shock. She had thought him well and truly ensconced in the study with her uncle and the other card-playing gentlemen.

"Miss Penrose, is your supper waltz spoken for?"

"Why, no. I am afraid I have been seeing to the table and have not been in the room."

"Then I beg you will allow me to partner you."

She eyed him. "Sir Perran, it cannot have escaped your attention that we have already danced two together."

"It has not. And a great pleasure they were. I should like to experience the same pleasure again."

And there was that delicious tingle once more. A man should not say *pleasure* like that in public. It was indecent.

But how marvelous it would be if we were alone.

Dear me, no, she must not think such things when he was bending his hazel gaze upon her as though, once again, she were the only woman present.

"Certainly not," she had the presence of mind to say, though it came out in a husky whisper.

"I assure you I would," he murmured.

"Would what?" She had entirely lost the thread of the conversation.

"Would you?" He took her hand and led her out on the floor for the third time that evening, dazed and humming in a way she had never felt before in her life.

CHAPTER 18

By dancing three with Alwyn, Perran made a statement of his intentions to the entire neighborhood. His grandmother looked scandalized, Lady Mainwaring worried, as the two of them spun gracefully about the room. It was quite likely that such a statement carried more impact here than it did even in London, despite what he had so blithely said about friends and family, for the company was much smaller and every married lady, he was sure, had been counting dances since the music had first begun.

He did his best not to smile with satisfaction, but it was difficult.

"Sir Perran, I am fairly sure that we are causing a scandal." He heard uncertainty in Alwyn's tone. "Again."

"You may be right," he murmured into her ear. "Does it cause you concern?" He held her very properly, and so far her body showed no resistance to his guidance. But that could change in a twinkling. For now, he allowed himself to enjoy the sensation, feeling the movement of her muscles under his gloved hand at her waist, his thighs brushing hers in the turns.

Even the way her hair curled upon her forehead and temples, the way her lips parted with the rush of their movement, heated his blood. He was familiar with the signs of attraction, but he had never experienced this before—this fascination with the tiny details. It drew him closer, in case he might miss some little gift, some soft word, some speaking glance, she might give him.

She met his gaze. "It is just that if I am not received in St. Just, I will have no bolt-holes left in which to hide."

Such lovely eyes she had, starred with long lashes. But he must stop this, and speak. "Then allow me to act as your bolt-hole. Should any whisper leave this room, I will deal with it."

"I am sorry to say that this does not comfort me as much as you think it ought."

He did not give her a reassuring squeeze, but it was a near thing. Nor could he squeeze her hand, for it lay properly upon the back of his as they dipped and spun. If he turned his hand over so that he held hers palm to palm—but no, much as he wanted to, he must not. There was enough speculation wafting about the room already, like a fine mist in an early morning field.

So he gazed into her upturned face. "I suppose this would be the wrong time to ask if you would go in to supper with me?"

"And risk the censure of every body in the room? You will take another lady in to supper and I'll hear no more about it."

"But Miss Penrose, it is customary for one to take one's partner in after the supper dance."

"I am perfectly aware of that. But this is my house," she reminded him. "I am sure there is something that will unexpectedly need my attention in the kitchen." A tiny pleat was beginning to form between her brows. Compunction assailed him and he relented.

"Very well. I will make myself useful to the Tregothnan connection and see if I might buff my reputation there."

"I can think of nothing I would like more." Her tone would have been dismissive had it not been quite so breathless. He allowed himself some satisfaction in that, too.

Two more turns about the room, and the music would end soon. He did not have much time left.

"You are a talented dancer, Miss Penrose."

"As are you, sir."

"It is like dancing with a wave upon the ocean."

"Consider yourself lucky it is not like being slapped by one."

He chuckled at his success in getting a rise out of her. "So you remember our first kiss, do you?" Was it his imagination, or had her back stiffened under his hand? He did not, however, imagine the color suffusing her face, nor the gentle increase in the heat of her body.

"I remember the behavior of the wave was much more appropriate than the behavior of the boy."

"Have you indulged in sea-bathing since you have been home?"

Her color did not decrease. Sea-bathing, an activity that was never enjoyed in mixed company, was evidently not to be a subject of conversation, either. But Alwyn did not let his teasing cow her. She rose to the occasion and spoke as though he had been quite serious.

"Karensa is fond of it, so I accompany her from time to time. The beach in the cove changes depending on the heaviness of the winter seas. At the moment it is fairly wide and lends itself well to such entertainments."

"You are not so fond of diving from the rocks as you once were?"

"I … no."

Before he could inquire further, the music came to an end and he released her, bowing in thanks.

And as promised, she vanished, though whether she really meant to supervise the laying out of supper, he could not tell. Mrs. Menabilly and her staff seemed to have the process well in hand. For himself, he was satisfied with this evening's work. A proposal of marriage would surprise no one … except possibly Alwyn herself.

Griffin found him out on the terrace thoughtfully consuming a plate of comestibles and a glass of wine, not necessarily in that order. His friend set his own plate on the stone rail and chose a strawberry tart. "I hear you have been behaving scandalously again, old man. Clearly I should not have been enjoying myself so much, and paid more attention to acting as your chaperone."

"What tittle-tattle have you been listening to?"

"I have not had to converse at all—I merely saunter about and hear your name on everyone's lips. Along with that of Miss Penrose, of course." Griffin's tone lost its lightness. "What are you thinking of, Perran? Why are you setting out to ruin the poor girl?"

"I am doing no such thing."

"In that I think you would be contradicted by every guest

in the house, save possibly Mr. Penrose, who will likely hear of it before morning."

"It is Mr. Penrose's opinion that matters most to me," Perran said with the casual air of a cat about to spring. "Which is why I spoke to him in private when we arrived, and asked his permission to pay my addresses to his eldest daughter."

Griffin clutched wildly at his wineglass, and managed not to lose it in the box hedge below the balustrade. "Jupiter aloft, man, are you serious?"

"I am. This is but the first salvo in a very intense, and hopefully very brief, campaign."

"Do you mean to say Mr. Penrose gave his permission? To you?"

Perran frowned. "You needn't sound so surprised."

"Surprise is the least of it. I am quite off my stride. If she accepts you, I will lose five guineas at White's."

This was so unexpected—yet so very Griffin—that Perran lost his frown in a bark of laughter. "Who was your front runner?"

"Why, Lady Eaton, of course. She whom you have been squiring about so assiduously that we all thought it a sure thing."

His smile faded. "Griff, let us be serious."

"I am always serious about five guineas."

"As am I, of late. I cannot afford to live in London any longer, and there is an end to it. My responsibilities lie here, and it is only the greatest of good fortune that there is a well-dowered woman of the right age and temper here, too."

How mercenary he sounded! It did Alwyn an injustice to

sound like the man he had been even three months ago. But there was no taking the words back now.

"You speak as though you had nothing whatever to do with her being back here again." Griffin glanced over his shoulder through the French doors. "Those cannot be her only attractions."

His friend was no fool. "I think you know the answer to that."

"She is not made of the same stuff as Constance."

"That I grant you."

"Do you care for her?"

"As I replied when her father asked me the same question, I care that she should be happy. I do not think she would be in London. She has been brought up to a country life, and I will resign myself to it in time, for Grand-mère's and Isolde's sakes."

Liar. You are putting on a show. Can you not be honest?

"Very noble of you," Griffin said dryly. "I am sure she will appreciate your sense of resignation above all things."

"What would you have me do?" Perran's stomach tightened in frustration, both with himself and with his situation. "I must set the Court to rights. Two women must have a place to live, or we will all be living on charity. I cannot depend on enabling the local smugglers for my livelihood. I have no choice in the matter. Marriage is the only solution."

Griffin had opened his mouth to reply, when a sound like a sharp intake of breath came from behind them. Perran turned, glass in hand, to see Alwyn framed in the doorway, the light from behind her turning her gown a degree more transparent than propriety might dictate.

Without a word, she whirled and vanished into the chattering crowd.

He was to be married?

Alwyn could not catch her breath. Absence certainly had made the heart grow fonder, if his intended was the beautiful Dowager Countess Eaton. But why on earth would he trifle with her, Alwyn, if he planned to marry someone else? Why put her reputation to the test? And more important, why on earth had she let him?

Shame showered through her body in a prickling tide. Shame, and disappointment, and the never-silent voice in the back of her mind: *Not enough. Never good enough.*

She must never indulge her silly imaginings about Sir Perran Geoffrey again, for the sake of her family … and for her own sanity. Should he come to visit his ladies, she would be busy elsewhere in the house. Should he be seated next to her at dinner in the home of their mutual acquaintance, she would offer replies so brief and so cool that frost would form upon the wine glasses. And in the unlikely event that—

"Miss Penrose?" Menabilly, dressed in his best bib and tucker, and roped into helping with moving furniture, assisting people to their carriages, and generally making their guests feel comfortable, appeared at her side as she stood, utterly distracted, in the doorway between drawing room and hall.

"Yes? Am I needed?" She devoutly hoped so, for facing Perran Geoffrey in her present state would never do.

"You are, miss. Your father asked me to come find you."

Alwyn's heartbeat sped up in sudden alarm. "Is he in pain? Has something happened?"

"Oh no, miss, he is quite comfortable, and had a good dinner. You are not to worry. He wishes to speak with you upon a certain matter, that is all."

"At this moment? While we have guests?"

"Yes, miss. I was to tell you he would not keep you long."

Alwyn found her father sitting up in the wing chair by the fire, a banyan wrapped about him. "You wished to see me, Papa?"

"I do, daughter. Come, sit by me."

She sank on to the tuffet next to him, her pale green silk rustling. "Menabilly assures me you are quite all right—you are, are you not?"

"I am. But I have something to say to you, and did not want to let it go until tomorrow."

Alwyn waited. There was no rushing her father; he would say what needed to be said and further anxious questions would only make him cross.

"I had an interview earlier this evening with Sir Perran Geoffrey."

This was the last thing she had expected. Orders for china, yes. The name of the new brigantine, yes. They often discussed such matters, after she was sent for with equal urgency, though not usually during a house party.

But Perran Geoffrey?

"I noticed he was not among the company for some time after he arrived, Papa." She hoped he would not ask why that particular gentleman or his absence had drawn her notice.

"In point of fact, he came to me asking my permission to pay his addresses to you."

Alwyn leaped from the stool and gaped at him. *"To me?"* Her very blood was running cold in her veins—no, hot—no, it was receding from her head. She was about to swoon.

She sat abruptly upon the tuffet again and gripped it on either side with both hands, as though it might toss her to the floor. Her heart was truly pounding in her chest, quite as if she had received the worst kind of fright.

"I must say, I did not think this would come as a surprise to you, after the events in London." Her father was observing her closely, clearly concerned.

"No one could possibly be more surprised."

"And is the surprise an unpleasant one?"

"I—I do not—I thought he was in—" In love with the countess.

I have no choice in the matter. Marriage is the only solution.

The countess must have refused him. So he had applied to Papa for permission to court her. His second choice.

Second best.

Not good enough.

Alwyn swayed, gripping the stool, feeling perspiration prickle out on her temples in the heat from the fire.

"Daughter? Alwyn, are you quite well?"

She took a deep breath and willed herself into some semblance of composure. "Yes, Papa." She cleared her throat so that her next words would not come out as a croak. "I am quite well. Am I to understand, then, that you approve his suit?"

"Did his behavior this evening communicate otherwise?"

There was an understatement. "He asked me to stand up for three dances. The entire parish will be talking of it over their toast tomorrow morning."

"Ah. Then he is making his intentions known."

"Is that what I am to call it? Rather, it is another example of his ability to ruin a woman simply by being in her general neighborhood." She jumped up once more, and began to pace the rug.

"I think you exaggerate just a little, my dear," her father said, watching her. "He seems a good man, and of course we are well acquainted with his family. You would bring him a very generous portion, and he will make you Lady Geoffrey, as your mother always dreamed."

"Is this … is this what you wish for me, Papa?" she asked, hardly daring to apprehend the answer.

"He simply requested my permission, not my blessing. But after what happened in London, if this is no longer what you want, then I will put my own wishes aside. You have every right to refuse his addresses … though I would ask you to consider very carefully before you do."

Was he what she wanted?

Alwyn hardly knew. Oh, there was no getting around the fact that Perran had a scandalous effect upon her. Those eyes … that smile … they were a match to the fire of a dozen girlish dreams. But a woman could not stake her life on dreams. Especially after they had already been dashed.

Marriage is the only solution.

She had known him as a child, had longed for the return of that friendship and regard. But she was not a child any more. She was a woman grown, and what woman of her consequence and ability wanted to go through life with the niggling question biting at the edges of her mind: *Why am I only second best?*

Would it not be better to wait until she was another gentleman's first choice?

Or should she accept Perran's addresses and show him once and for all that she would make him a far better choice than any number of countesses? Perhaps even ruin him for any other woman?

Now, there was a prospect as fair as any she had seen yet. He had made a whirligig of her life and emotions. Had any woman ever done the same for him? Could she, with all her inexperience and self-doubt?

And if she could … what then?

"Alwyn? Have I been mistaken in allowing him to address you? Do you wish me to put a stop to it?"

Alwyn had the curious sensation that she was standing on the edge of a cliff, looking down at the heaving surf. One choice would take her over into the unknown. One would allow her to step back to safety.

She took a deep breath, and leaped.

CHAPTER 19

Do let us stop in at Rosevear Court and ask Perran to come with us." Isolde wriggled with excitement in the barouche, causing her grandmother to frown.

"Stop bouncing, dear," Lady Geoffrey said. "You will make me seasick."

"I am sorry, Grand-mère. But I am just so excited to see the ship! I know Perran would be interested, too."

"Your brother is likely very much occupied with the rebuilding," Alwyn offered. She hardly knew which would offer more relief—for Perran Geoffrey to accompany them while being thoroughly chaperoned by his ladies, or for Broome the coachman to pass the lane to Rosevear at a fast gallop.

"The rebuilding will go on for weeks," Isolde said. "But the ship will only sail on her maiden voyage once."

"I have no objection to his coming with us," Alwyn said at last. He might be up on the roof or performing some urgent task, and be unable to come. Best to give the appearance of graciousness, and hope that no one noticed the pounding of her heart under her embroidered linen spencer at the mention of his name.

They waved the second carriage on, and Lord and Lady Mainwaring, Karensa, and Rowena waved back in acknowledgment as they passed. When they reached the Court, they found Sir Perran inspecting the stonework in progress and very much interested in accompanying the party.

It would have been almost flattering … if Alwyn had not heard those words out on the terrace.

I have no choice in the matter. Marriage is the only solution.

The plan she had hatched to ruin him for anyone else, which had seemed so daring and perfect, was still daring. But now, in the light of day, it did not seem so perfect. It seemed terrifying. Who was she to make him forget his countess and ruin him for any other woman? No man save her father had ever put her first among women, and even Papa had brushed aside her desire to design glazes instead of considering it seriously. Why should Perran be different?

Stop behaving like a mopish spinster and grow a bit of spine, Alwyn Penrose.

It was not quite her mother's voice in her head, but it was close. She must not stray from her course. The point of making up one's mind was to stick to it, no matter the obstacles. She did straighten her spine, at least, as Perran climbed into the barouche, its top down on such a fine day.

Oh my … she could not prevent the jumping in her stomach at the strength in his tall form and the quiet elegance of his dress.

Isolde, the minx, would have clung to her seat next to her grandmother, forcing him to sit beside Alwyn. But Lady Geoffrey was having none of that. She elbowed her granddaughter so mercilessly that the girl had no choice, and flopped into the rear-facing seat.

"This is an unexpected pleasure." Perran patted his grandmother's hand as the vehicle lurched forward, but his gaze took in Alwyn from head to foot, leaving tingles in its wake. "I must thank you for including me in the party. Isolde says you are christening a ship?"

"Yes," Alwyn said a little breathlessly, then commanded herself not to be such a ninny. "She is a fine brigantine of one hundred fourteen tons. She was built for us by Mr. Thompson in Mevagissey. I will name her today and we will all see her off to France on her maiden voyage."

"I must say it will be an experience new to me," he said. But his gaze had not left her. In its quiet intensity it almost seemed to convey something else. *An outing with you, sanctioned by my grandmother, is also new to me. What luck.*

"And to me," his grandmother agreed as the barouche clattered down the lane and out to the main road.

"I am filled with admiration," Isolde said with anticipation. "Imagine having a ship named after one."

Alwyn smiled. "Mama would have been in her element. I understand from Papa that the next will be named for me, and any others after my sisters."

"Is he planning to build a fleet?" Perran said, surprise evident in his tone.

"It depends upon the cost of shipping versus the risk of building ships ourselves," Alwyn told him, trying to speak as calmly as though they were discussing the merits of hiring a hackney versus buying a carriage. "It is Papa's belief that if the company is to send its china to France, the Lowlands, and even the kingdom of the Tsar or to America, it would be wise to own its ships. Royal Morvoren would bear the risk, true, but it would also keep the lion's share of the profit."

"How businesslike you sound," Isolde said.

"And how unfeminine." Lady Geoffrey's eyes, which had been bright with interest over the excursion, narrowed a little. "Your father has done you no favors in allowing your education to extend so far, my dear. You must be careful that no one overhears you, or you will be accused of too great an interest in trade."

"Grand-mère," Perran said, his tone tinged with reproof.

"The only people in the neighborhood who might consider us still to be in trade are the Tregothnans, your ladyship," Alwyn said as respectfully as she could. "But the truth is that while Papa has the oversight of pit, pottery, and piers, he has never worked them. If a gentleman is known by his property and his manners, then surely he fits the definition?"

"I am not talking about your father, miss," the old lady said. "I am talking about you, and your knowledge of business that no young lady ought to possess."

"But it does interest me."

"An interest in china might be shared by any woman," her ladyship conceded. "But in the means by which it is made? Certainly not. Your interests ought to encompass your home and family, and charitable works, and engagements with friends and neighbors. Sewing. Millinery. That kind of thing."

"They do, your ladyship." Alwyn smarted under the criticism, given in front of her grandchildren to boot. But she must speak for herself, or no one else would. "I am much occupied with all those things, as are my sisters. I particularly enjoy painting in watercolors the designs that might be suitable for dinner services, or vases, or soup tureens."

"You are evading the point, young lady."

"Grand-mère, while I agree with you in principle—" Perran began.

"I should hope so."

"—I, too, might be accused of dabbling in trade, since I am up on a ladder half the day, hammer in hand."

Goodness, Alwyn thought. Was he coming to her defense?

"That is different. You are the lord of the manor, and no one will question what you choose to do. And as for those rapscallion friends of yours, they are helping you out of friendship and boredom, not because you are paying them a wage."

"But Jago possesses knowledge of hammers and saws that no gentleman ought to possess."

"Until a tree falls on *his* roof."

"If a woman exercises her mind with thoughts of ships and china, I see no difference."

"Yes, you do," his grandmother told him sternly. "You are simply arguing the losing side to vex me."

He lifted her gloved hand and kissed it. "Forgive me. I will cease my prattle, then, and talk of something more agreeable. How fortunate that the weather is fine for the christening of Mrs. Penrose's ship."

His grandmother rapped his knee with one gloved hand, and he subsided.

But not before he caught Alwyn's eye and winked.

The heat bloomed in her face and she looked away, down the patchwork of the fields to the sea. It was all she could do not to smile.

~

OF COURSE his grandmother was right and a young lady should not be indulging herself in the details, as Alwyn put it, of pit, pottery, and piers. Perran would have to make it up to his grandmother later, but for now, risking Lady Geoffrey's censure had been worth it to see Alwyn blush.

That she could talk so knowledgeably about shipping routes and blush like a schoolgirl a moment later intrigued him in spite of himself. While no man of fashion would admit to wishing for a bluestocking across the breakfast table pouring his tea, the fact was that conversing on subjects more meaningful than bonnets or the weather over one's dinner might be a mark on the positive side of the domestic ledger.

As though she had heard his thoughts, her lashes lifted and their eyes met. He smiled—not the roguish smile that made girls in white dresses flee to their chaperones, but a smile meant to be shared.

And her lips turned up at the corners, producing a pair of enchanting dimples, as she turned to look at the landscape through which they passed. He sat back, feeling far more satisfaction than such a tiny moment justified. He made up his mind to find another, and soon.

The road took them down the Morvoren River valley, which widened into a harbor deep enough to accept ocean-going ships, but protected enough by cliffs and rocks to keep them safe from storms while they loaded and unloaded. The ever-present white clay dust lay on some of the buildings downwind of the docks, but Perran could tell that some effort had been made to wash it off for this festive day. Bunting in the national colors hung from the eaves of the warehouses, and the pier itself had been swept clean. Riding gently beside it was the new ship, smelling sweetly of tar and fresh wood, the canvas rolled on the yards ready to be released at the urging of the tide.

The coachman stopped at the landward end of the pier, behind the Mainwaring carriage, and Perran and the ladies alighted. He offered his arm to his grandmother.

Ever aware that she was beholden to the Penrose family at present, she said, "Give your other arm to Miss Penrose, Perran. This is her day, and I would not diminish her consequence."

How like Grand-mère to remonstrate with Alwyn one moment and give her precedence in the next! He must certainly do his best to live up to two such ladies. They paraded up the pier to where the other half of the Morvoren party already stood, bowing and nodding to the cheering crowd of men, women, and children. These people were obviously employed by the Morvoren China Clay Company in some capacity or other, but he was impressed by the honest regard in which the daughter of the principal shareholder was held.

At the gangway to the ship, two men waited. Both bowed from the waist, one clearly the captain with his tricorne under his arm and his brass buttons polished to a gleam. The other, a young man of about Perran's own age, was dressed plainly but in a coat of good quality.

Alwyn released his arm, and at once he missed the warmth of her hand. "Lady Geoffrey, Sir Perran, may I present to you Captain Ennis Dyer, who has the command of our new ship, and Mr. Jory Boscawen, the Royal Morvoren pit manager."

Perran and his grandmother inclined their heads, politely acknowledging the introduction.

"We would be honored to welcome you aboard, your ladyship, Sir Perran," Captain Dyer said. "If you will follow me, the gangplank is not steep, but it may be slippery." He offered his arm to Alwyn.

Grand-mère took Perran's arm and held it tightly, while Mr. Boscawen escorted Isolde, agog with excitement, up the planks. The other members of their party followed.

On deck, a little girl curtseyed and presented Alwyn with a bouquet of flowers, which she accepted with a smile and a kiss. Then the captain handed her up a small set of temporary steps before the mainmast.

The people crowded the pier to hear her, while the sailors stood in their ranks on deck. Even Perran was impressed by the importance and festivity of it all. This would certainly never come into his sphere of experience in London.

And how feminine and solemn she looked amid the soaring lines of the masts, her tawny gown snapping about her ankles in the breeze, the feathers on her hat waving in celebration. From her reticule Alwyn took a small Bible, and turned to a place marked with a bit of ribbon.

Her hands shook, and Perran could not help but wish there had been some way for him to lend her courage.

But then she raised her chin.

"From the one hundred and seventh Psalm," she said, her clear voice ringing across deck and water.

> "They that go down to the sea in ships,
> that do business in great waters;
> These see the works of the Lord,
> and his wonders in the deep.
> For he commandeth, and raiseth the stormy
>   wind,

which lifteth up the waves thereof.
They mount up to the heaven,
they go down again to the depths:
their soul is melted because of trouble.
They reel to and fro, and stagger like a drunken
    man,
and are at their wits' end.
Then they cry unto the Lord in their trouble,
and he bringeth them out of their distresses.
He maketh the storm a calm,
so that the waves thereof are still.
Then are they glad because they be quiet;
so he bringeth them unto their desired haven.
Oh that men would praise the Lord for his
    goodness,
and for his wonderful works to the children of
    men!"

The sailors broke out into cheers and clapping as she closed the little Bible and returned it to her reticule. Mr. Boscawen handed Alwyn a porcelain teacup with a grey-blue band about the rim, filled with wine. "Here you are, Miss Penrose—one of your own."

Alwyn held it up for all to see. Her smile as bright as the sun upon the water, she cried, "I name this ship the *Morvoren Anne*. May God bless her and all who sail in her!" With a flourish, she splashed the wine on mast and deck to christen the ship.

The sailors cheered again, and a tumult of clapping rose on the pier. Tots of rum went from hand to hand, and from somewhere in the stern someone played a sea-shanty on a pipe.

Perran stepped forward to hand her down from the makeshift steps, which were whisked away, and Mr. Boscawen took the cup. "Well done," Perran said to her in a low tone. "I find myself possessed of an unaccountable urge to become a sailor, if it means such a sendoff."

Again there was that lift of the chin, as though she thought he might be chaffing her. "Then you would have to begin as a lowly midshipman, sir. For Captain Dyer would agree with me that you are sadly inexperienced."

"Only when it comes to ships," he said for her ears alone, and was rewarded with such a blush as any man could hope for.

"Experience of *that* kind will hardly be useful on a ship," she said.

"Will it suffice on land, then?"

"Perhaps for some." Color burned in her cheeks, but she did not crumble and flee, as he might have expected. The brave feathers danced upon her hat as she stood her ground.

"You wound me, Miss Penrose," he said with a theatrical sigh.

The dimples flashed. "As a pinprick wounds a balloon, sir, when deflation is necessary."

He laughed and let her go to accept the felicitations of the captain and his officers. Alwyn and her party bade them farewell after half an hour of celebrations, and then one of the sailors called, "Tide, ho! Anchor aweigh!"

From the pier, Perran watched the sailors lower canvas and cast off, and then the ship made her way out of the harbor as gracefully as an Arabian mare. The outgoing tide caught her in the deeper channel. The foretopsail canvas was lowered with a snap, and the *Morvoren Anne* put her shoulder to the wind.

"There she goes!" cried Rowena, clapping in delight. "Is she not a sight to be seen?"

Alwyn stood as if entranced, her hands clasped to her chest, holding the bouquet. She watched the beautiful ship named for her mother gain way, until even the foresail caught the breeze and she sailed into the English Channel like a cloud scudding before the wind.

The *Morvoren Anne* was beautiful. But nothing was more beautiful than Alwyn, a-tiptoe as though she would fly before the wind, too, her lips parted in joy.

Here was a woman who could attach a man for life even without her money or prospects. Here was a woman who could hold her own in the world—who, in fact, had the courage to look outside her own sphere, even if society did not allow her to step outside of it. The will and intelligence were still there. Here was a woman whom any man would be glad to have at his side.

Not for the sake of her marriage portion. Not for the sake of her family, or any past history as children, dim with memory.

But for herself—body, soul, mind, and heart.

Perran felt the planks of the pier tilt beneath his feet, as though they had come unmoored.

Or maybe it was not the pier at all, but his conception of the world and the people in it, tilting off its axis and spinning in a very different direction.

A direction that, until this moment, he had neither known of nor intended.

CHAPTER 20

*A*lwyn felt as exhilarated as though she herself had sailed away before the wind, so when Lord Mainwaring suggested they prolong their outing with tea at the White Swan, she assented readily.

"An excellent plan," Lady Geoffrey said. "A glass of lemonade and some cake will bring us all back to earth."

Alwyn had completely forgotten that her cousin Arthur Landry was staying at the principal inn in St. Just—so completely that the sight of him rising from his table in the common room and bowing as they came in was rather a shock.

"Mr. Landry," Lord Mainwaring greeted him. "How do you do?"

"Sir," that gentleman said, bowing a second time. "This is an unexpected pleasure. Lady Mainwaring—Sir Perran. I am pleased to see you again."

"Lady Geoffrey," Perran said rather stiffly to his grandmother, "may I introduce Mr. Arthur Landry, a familial connection of Mr. Alexander Penrose."

Her ladyship inclined her head as the young man bowed once more. "Miss Penrose's great-grandfather and mine were brothers," the latter offered. "I am in the neighborhood hoping for a glimpse of my cousins, and my patience has been amply rewarded. Good afternoon, Miss Penrose, Miss Karensa, Miss Rowena. You are all looking very well, if a little windblown. Have you been driving?"

"We have been down to Morvoren harbor," Karensa said, curtseying. "Alwyn has christened our newest ship, the *Morvoren Anne*, which is bound for France today."

Mr. Landry's eyes widened. "How extraordinary. I wish I had known—I should have enjoyed such a sight very much."

This guileless speech had an effect opposite to the one he probably intended. For he was not an accepted member of the family as yet. Papa knew he was in the neighborhood, but no invitation to Morvoren Manor or to any family outing had been issued. Therefore Alwyn was powerless to remedy the situation.

"Will you join us, sir?" Lord Mainwaring said politely, exercising the prerogative he did possess in the acquaintance. Mr. Tomgallon, the innkeeper and brother-in-law of the Widow Tomgallon who loved her turkeys so, made haste to join two tables for their large party.

When lemonade had come for the ladies and a tawny port for the gentlemen, and a platter of fruitcake and thick wedges of cheese, Lord Mainwaring said, "There are no secrets among us, Mr. Landry. I will speak plainly. Mr. Penrose is aware of your being in the neighborhood, but his feelings on that subject I cannot tell you."

Mr. Landry brightened. "I am hopeful, then, that if prox-imity does not incline him to allow me to visit, then perhaps curiosity might." He glanced at Alwyn. "Your esteemed father will not object to an already established friendship, I hope?"

"He has not objected in my hearing," Alwyn said. "But I confess I am not entirely comfortable with the situation. I had rather we met with his approval than without it."

"I will shoulder the blame for today's meeting, niece," Lord Mainwaring said with a smile. "For it was I who needed sustenance, and of course we did not know Mr. Landry would be in the public room."

"I would not wish to be the cause of any blame." Mr. Landry's fine brow creased with anxiety. "Indeed not. The olive branch cannot flourish in such soil. I will leave you to your lemonade, then, and be about my business."

"But sir, I did not mean—" Alwyn began.

He bowed gracefully to the company, then made his way through the tables to the door and departed.

"What a peculiar performance," Lady Geoffrey remarked after an astonished pause.

"He is a very sensitive young man, finding fault with himself at every turn," Lord Mainwaring said in a tone he might have used to marvel at an exotic creature. "What are we to make of him?"

"It's deuced peculiar," Perran said in tones that mixed puzzlement with impatience. "Pardon me, Grand-mère, Lady Mainwaring. Why on earth does he not simply go to the house and call upon Mr. Penrose? How long has he been skulking about the countryside?"

"Since Tuesday—the day of our dinner party," Alwyn said. "Though I would not exactly call it *skulking*. He has been very open about his presence here."

"He sent me a note telling me he had arrived and was

staying here," Lord Mainwaring said. "I told Mr. Penrose of it and that was that. We have been too much occupied to think of it further. Which perhaps was rude of me. I ought to have brought it up again with your father, Alwyn, and ascertained his feelings on the matter."

"I do not see why you should," Perran said. "If Landry wishes to be acknowledged by this branch of the family, he does not need to employ you for that purpose, sir. He may act for himself."

"Perhaps delicacy prevents him," Rowena ventured. "For Papa has been fearsome in his dislike of any family of his grandfather's brother." She turned to Lady Geoffrey. "Papa fears that Mr. Landry may lay claim to the Morvoren property, you see, upon his death. Should none of us marry before then, we would be left unprotected."

"Does he indeed?" Her ladyship's keen blue gaze turned upon Alwyn. "And what is this *business* the gentleman speaks of, pray?"

"I—I do not know," Alwyn stammered, since the question appeared to be directed at her. She had been watching Perran's expression, which was darkening every moment like a thunderstorm coming ashore.

"It is as plain as the nose on your face, young lady. If he possesses a claim in the event of your father's death, and he has never been to St. Just before, *and* he made your acquaintance in London, then I suspect his business is *you*."

"I? La, ma'am—surely not—"

"Preposterous!" Perran exclaimed. "Presumption! The pup deserves a thrashing."

But it was not preposterous. Had she not thought that very thing herself, when they were all in Town? For there could be nothing else so far from either London or his own home that would bring a young man here. Nothing but the prospect of a wife, and a wealthy one at that, who could bring him his heart's desire without having to wait to fill a dead man's shoes —or a lawyer's pockets.

But it was all utterly impossible, now that Perran had spoken to Papa.

Two men could not state their intentions to one's father at the same time, could they? Papa would tell Mr. Landry, surely? Oh, if only Mama were alive to help her navigate this maze! Perhaps she had better closet herself with Aunt Celia at the first opportunity, to find out how best to behave before the situation became untenable.

"Well, that certainly puts a different complexion on the matter," Lord Mainwaring said genially, as though the intentions of the young man under discussion had honestly never occurred to him before.

"My dear, this is hardly the time or the place," his lady said in a low tone.

"All the same, hadn't you better bring Mr. Penrose into the picture?" Perran drawled, leaning back on one arm of his chair, having evidently mastered his ill temper. "And that right sharply? He might wish to run him off rather than acknowledge the connection."

"Why would he do that?" Karensa wanted to know. "Mr. Landry is harmless, as far as we can see. Though I do agree that if he wishes to court Alwyn, he ought to see Papa first, and waste no more time."

Alwyn could keep silent no longer. "I am sitting right here. Pray do not discuss my affairs—or what you imagine them to be—as though I am out of the room."

"Of course not, dear." Aunt Celia gave her husband a speaking glance. "We will say no more about it."

Even Karensa dared not disobey her aunt, so the remainder of the repast was spent in discussions of the *Morvoren Anne* and her destination, the prospect of good weather, and the general health of the gardens at the manor.

On the journey home, Sir Perran seemed abstracted, as though he were considering a complicated problem. When he did speak, it was half a beat behind, or he answered a question that had been asked moments before.

When they arrived at Rosevear Court, he thanked Alwyn for including him in the day's party, but he did not go into the house with his grandmother and Isolde, who wished to inspect the progress of the repairs. Instead, he rested an arm on the still-open door of the landau.

"Miss Penrose, may I have a word?"

It seemed she was about to find out what had been weighing on his mind. "Of course, sir. Broome, would you wait here for Lady Geoffrey and Miss Isolde? Sir Perran and I will walk up the drive."

When the landau was out of earshot, Perran offered her his arm. His sleeve was warm under her hand, his arm steady and … well, not comforting, exactly. Being so close to him was far from comfortable, if the butterflies rioting in her stomach were any indication.

"Is it safe to assume that your father has told you of my desire to pay my addresses to you, Miss Penrose?"

Thank goodness for her bonnet, that hid the sudden heat in her cheeks. "He has, sir. And in light of that, perhaps you might call me Alwyn, as you once did."

"Alwyn." How his baritone caressed her name! The butterflies turned somersaults. "Is it also safe to assume that the rest of your family is for the time being ignorant of the matter?"

"Yes, though your behavior last Tuesday at the ball has left them in no doubt. It seems I had better inform them, or we may have a repeat of the awkward scene at the White Swan." She glanced up into his face. "You have not told your family, either?"

"No. An error that I must rectify." Now it was his turn to gaze into her face—no, more than that. He stopped in the middle of the gravel drive to take both her hands. "You do not object?"

"I—I—no, I—" *Good heavens, Alwyn. Do not be such a goose!* "Despite what passed between us in Town, your behavior here in Cornwall has been nothing but exemplary." Far from being a goose, now she sounded like the very starchiest of sticklers. She met his gaze. "I do not know which Sir Perran to trust, or even to believe, of the two I have seen. Perhaps you had better help me."

A smile glowed in his eyes, and spread to the rest of his face. The butterflies in her stomach gave a great sigh of longing and half of them fainted.

"I should be very happy to, if you will give me your assurance that Mr. Arthur Landry has not taken up residence in even the smallest part of your heart."

So this was the reason for his distraction! He thought Mr. Landry had taken the field against him! Would wonders never cease. She may not have ruined him yet for any other woman, but here was a promising beginning.

"I can assure you, sir, that Mr. Landry does not reside anywhere near my heart. He does not take up so much as a caned chair, or even a cushion."

They could hear the carriage now, coming up the lane. Perran lifted her gloved hand and kissed it.

"Then I look forward to the day when I may become its sole occupant." Those hazel eyes did not let her go. Nor did she want them to. "I hope to see you very soon."

"Yes," she said. It was all she could do to form the word.

When Broome pulled up beside them, he handed her back into the landau and closed the door firmly, as though he wanted to be certain she would be safe inside. "Until then, Alwyn."

"Good-bye," she said, unable to keep the smile from her face.

He bowed to his ladies, and the carriage was off.

It took great powers of concentration to listen to Isolde's excited report of the workmen's progress. For there were no longer butterflies dancing and bubbling inside her. It was something very like a tremble of happiness.

A BRISK WALK on the cliffs would restore her to herself and make her feel as though she had not left her heart behind as well as her composure. And then she would go to her aunt and sisters and tell them that Perran had asked Papa for permission to court her. That would end all discussion of Mr. Landry, in public or otherwise.

The path along the cliffs was a public right of way, mostly for sheep but often for those who used it as an alternate route to reach the Morvoren harbor from one of the fishing villages along the coast. If one turned to the west, so that the sea was on one's left, one eventually came to the bustling seaside town of St. Mawes, and the Carrick Roads shipping channel that led inland to Truro.

Alwyn would not go nearly so far. Only to the ancient Celtic cross that marked the border between the Morvoren lands and those of their neighbors.

"Alwyn, wait!"

She turned to see Karensa coming along the path, the wide blue ribbons of her bonnet snapping behind her in the wind.

"I thought to find you with your poultry," Karensa said breathlessly, "and when I did not, I had to guess where you might have gone."

"I trust it was not a difficult guess?" Alwyn smiled and linked her arm with that of her sister. "I felt the need of some solitude after such a full and busy day."

Karensa slowed. "Would you rather I left you?"

"No indeed. In fact, I have something to tell you."

"Something to do with Sir Perran?"

Alwyn peered around the brim of her sister's bonnet to see her face. "Did Papa inform you?"

"No, but I wish you would. I wish to be clear on why Sir Perran accompanied us today—"

"Because his grandmother and sister thought he would enjoy it."

"—and why he got all *blawed up like a wilkie*, as Mrs. Menabilly might say, at the mention of Mr. Landry."

Alwyn had a brief vision of Perran puffed up like said toad, and giggled, at that and at Karensa's perfect imitation of Mrs. Menabilly's broad country accents. "You must not talk that way. For he has asked Papa's permission to pay his addresses to me."

Now her sister stopped altogether, her brown eyes wide,

her pale muslin skirts blowing against her legs while the waves thundered and crashed far below. "He never did."

"It is true. During the ball. Papa told me himself."

"Sir Perran Geoffrey, who has naught but his name to recommend him?"

It did not sit well with Alwyn that her sister should have such a low opinion of him. "He has much more than that. He has apologized for what happened in London, and moreover, has made me see that he did all he could to prevent the scene at Almack's."

"Sir Perran Geoffrey." Karensa walked on as though she had forgotten Alwyn was there, forcing the latter to skip to catch up and take her arm again.

"Do you have any objections, Karensa?"

"No indeed, if you do not."

"I do not know yet," Alwyn confessed. "I am betwixt and between on the matter. At some moments, there is something between us. I can feel it." That was putting it mildly. "And at others, I wonder who the real Perran Geoffrey is."

Marriage is the only solution. Oh, why did that have to intrude now, after such a delightful day?

"You would certainly be better for him than the Dowager Countess," Karensa said. "But with a man of his reputation … it is said he and Lady Eaton were seen much together while she was still in black."

Alwyn gasped. "Karensa Penrose, you are an unmarried woman! How do you hear such things, never mind speak of them?"

"I spend most of my time listening and not speaking."

"What a confabulation!"

"When we are in company," Karensa amended.

"I should hope so, if such things are going to come out of your mouth."

"I allow that I should not listen to gossip," Karensa said, but she sounded almost regretful.

Thanks to her sister's unbridled tongue, here was another unwelcome thought to plague her. For if he had been so anxious to court the countess that he could hardly wait until it was decent, perhaps he truly loved her, whether she had rejected him or not. It seemed a proof undeniable. And upon being refused, he had taken his wounded heart down to Cornwall and … there was Alwyn, a means to soothe his pride. Alwyn felt a plunge in her stomach so severe it nearly made her ill.

She brought herself back to the here and now with an effort. "I must ask you to keep this just in the family, sister. I do not want it generally known."

"Your three dances together the other night put paid to that, I am afraid. If in the end you refuse him, it will make you look like the most heartless flirt that ever lived."

"Thank you, dear."

Karensa's face crumpled in distress, and she clutched the bonnet on either side of her own head. "Oh, Alwyn, I am so sorry. I am doing it again, amn't I?"

"Yes, dear."

"Please forgive me. I so often speak aloud to myself, that it is difficult not to do so when I am with you. And now I have hurt your feelings."

Alwyn hugged her. "My feelings will recover. Though truly, you must not repeat gossip. It is not fair to Sir Perran to speculate about him that way, and it is certainly not fair to me."

"I am so sorry."

"Apology accepted. Come, here is the cross. Let us go down to the cove, out of the wind."

Karensa gripped her arm a little more tightly. "I believe we have company. What do you suppose Mr. Landry is doing all the way out here so soon after our meeting?"

Before Alwyn could stop her, she waved cheerfully, and the gentleman coming along the path on the neighbors' side waved back. In a few moments he had joined them.

"I say, we are well met a second time," he said cheerfully. The wind had blown his hair out of its orderly Titus arrangement, and he carried his hat, so that it might not be blown out to sea. "I have been walking the cliffs. How fortunate that you enjoy the same activity."

"You are a fast walker, sir," Alwyn said. "We have barely been home an hour."

"Why did you leave us so abruptly at the inn?" Karensa asked. "There was no reason to do so. Our uncle was quite surprised, to say nothing of Lady Geoffrey."

The animation in his face was replaced by concern. "I did not cause offense, did I? Oh, I should be distressed indeed if, in attempting to do as I ought, I caused his lordship or her ladyship a moment's irritation."

Alwyn seized the bull by the proverbial horns. "What you ought to do, Mr. Landry, is call upon our father as soon as may be, and make yourself known to him. Then there need be no awkwardness among us, and we may meet as friends as well as relations."

"Do you honestly think so?"

"We do," Karensa said firmly. "In fact, there is no time like the present. If you are not comfortable coming in state to see him alone, then come in with us. He may huff and puff, but he will not bite off your head if we are there."

For a moment he gazed at her in sheer horror. Then his face relaxed in a smile. "You are bamming me, to be sure. Do you really believe that to be the proper course? I should not wait for Lord Mainwaring to smooth the waters and tell me if I will be received?"

"It is high time that the two sides of the family are reconciled," Alwyn told him. "It is for you alone to extend the olive branch you mentioned earlier. Come. We will protect you, if nothing else."

He laughed, and would have offered each an arm, except that the cliff path was too narrow and too deeply cut between hillocks to allow for three. So Karensa obligingly dropped back and Alwyn took his arm.

He was not as tall as Perran, and his arm felt less substantial. But that was not his fault. Two men from different families, brought up in different circumstances, could hardly be expected to share any similarities at all. But Alwyn had to admit that Perran's greater substance did make her feel safe and protected.

With Mr. Landry at this moment, it was almost as though she were the protector, and not he. Especially since he clearly did not know that the gentleman, not the lady, was supposed to walk on the outside of the path, closer to the cliff edge.

Another proof that he had never been to Cornwall. She smiled as they reached the bottom of the spreading lawns and saw the manor's creamy white pillars in the distance.

CHAPTER 21

*A*lwyn went into her father's study first, to smooth the way. For if Papa refused to receive Mr. Landry, then it would be much better if she were to inform the younger man. Karensa would probably deliver the message verbatim, complete with unsuitable language.

Papa looked up from the newspaper with pleasure, his eyes twinkling. "Good afternoon, my dear. How was the christening of our new vessel?"

"It was wonderful, Papa." She could not help her smile in return as she bent to kiss him. "I read the passage you suggested, and how the sailors cheered! Everyone wished you could have been there, and I bring particular salutations from Mr. Boscawen and Captain Dyer, who escorted us aboard. And then, after the *Morvoren Anne* went out on the tide, we all took tea at the White Swan."

"Yes, your uncle has been in to tell me all about it."

Alwyn braced herself. "Then you know that Mr. Arthur Landry was there also."

"I do."

"What you may not know, Papa, is that Karensa and I met him on the cliffs just now. He is enjoying the view from our lawn at the moment, but our ability to receive him depends, of course, upon you."

The twinkle faded from his eyes. "He is here, on the property? Why, that presumptuous young puppy!"

Presumption! she heard Perran say in her memory.

"No, no indeed, Papa, he is as far from presumptuous as anyone could be," Alwyn said earnestly. "We could barely convince him to step past the cross. He was terribly worried about causing offense."

"So he ought to be. What is he doing here, pray?"

"He wishes to mend the breach in the family. To call upon you and begin an acquaintance on his own merits, not those of earlier generations. Will you come out and receive him?"

Her father leaned back in his leather chair and gazed at her. "What difference does it make to you, maidey, whether I receive him or not? For when you marry and have a son, that gentleman's interest in the Morvoren property is ended."

"There is more to family than interests in property, Papa."

"Is there, now?"

"He seems a harmless young man. Studious. Of good character," she said. "He plans to write a book about the ruins and *menhirs* in the neighborhood. In that event, it would be so much more comfortable if we were all on good terms, would it not?"

Her father snorted. "With any luck, one of the Lorn Ladies at Minear Park will fall over on him. Oh, very well. If you will fetch the importunate wild-de-go, I will receive him in the sea parlor."

Alwyn smothered a smile at the anxiously proper Arthur

Landry described as a *wild-de-go*—a Cornish term for the rash and reckless. She would call him brave, rather. She could barely keep herself to a sedate pace as she left the house and crossed the terrace to the bench near the garden hedge where Karensa and Mr. Landry were talking.

The latter leaped up when he saw her. "Oh, Cousin, put me out of my misery at once! Will he see me?"

"He will. Come in, do, and for pity's sake calm yourself. Our father is a plain-spoken man, and appreciates a settled and sensible mien in others."

"Settled. Sensible." He recited the words like a charm, brushing his hair into place with his fingers. "Yes. I must be calm."

When they entered the sea parlor, it was to find Mr. Penrose seated in a wing chair near the French doors, at an angle to the sofa.

"Papa," Alwyn said, "may I introduce our cousin Mr. Arthur Landry, presently of London, but whose mother and sisters live near York."

Mr. Landry bowed nearly in half. "I am honored to make your acquaintance, sir."

"I see you have made the acquaintance of my daughters," Papa said. "In London, I believe, through my brother in law Lord Mainwaring."

"Yes, sir."

"Do sit down," Alwyn and Karensa said together, then laughed.

Mr. Landry sat between them, on the sofa facing their father, where Alwyn was aware the light fell on their faces and her father might examine his guest's bearing and countenance at his leisure.

"Mr. Penrose," their cousin said, "allow me to say what a very great pleasure it is to make myself known to you and your family. It has long been the desire of my heart to do so, and to mend the breach between us."

Papa inclined his head. "What has your father told you of Morvoren Manor?"

Mr. Landry looked about him, clearly impressed with what he saw. "He was never fortunate enough to visit, of course, or even to pass by it. But he was a man who appreciated both man-made and natural beauties. He would have been as bowled over as I am were he still living."

"My condolences. And your visit here, to St. Just? Was it solely to, as you say, mend the breach?"

"I would never have dared to make the first overture, had I not met your family in London. I am afraid that your daughters' company has made me anxious to peep over the hedges that my ancestors set in place, and in fact to see if I might find a stile to climb upon."

"And so you have. Well, Mr. Landry, the first meeting is over, with no bloodshed. Perhaps you might come to dinner some evening this week? Would Sunday suit?"

The smile that broke over Mr. Landry's face seemed to make all his prior anxiety fade away. "Nothing in this world would make me happier, sir."

"Very well." Papa rose to his feet with the help of his cane. "I shall repair to my study. Alwyn, you may show our guest the gardens, and have a look about for Rowena while you are at it. She was to experiment upon me with a new salve. If Mr. Landry has an affinity for chickens, his character is assured."

In her earlier haste, Alwyn had not yet taken off her spencer, so it was only the work of a moment to fetch her bonnet and Mr. Landry's beaver hat, and lead him through the kitchen passage and out into the garden.

"The kitchen garden is my sister Rowena's particular kingdom," she said, noting that her sister was not there, weeding or gathering herbs. "I wonder where she is? She will be so pleased to know that you are here and Papa has received you."

"I will see her Sunday, if nothing else. How good it smells in here."

The scent of the lemon balm, rosemary, and the elder trees against the tawny stone of the enclosing wall was indeed sweet in the warmth of the summer afternoon.

"Are you fond of poultry?" she asked, her hand on the gate into the hens' yard.

"Very fond," he said with a smile. "From duck to turkey to a nice young cockerel, I enjoy them roasted to a turn. I have not tried swan or peacock, but I understand they are very fine as well."

Alwyn's hand fell away from the gate, and she turned to lead him rather more quickly than they had come, through the south gate and back out to the rose and flower gardens, which were sheltered from the wind off the sea by their laurel hedges.

"This is one of the loveliest places I have ever seen," he said, gazing about him with happiness. Then his eyes fell on her. "I wonder if you are aware that— But no. I will not speak of it."

"That you may believe you have a claim to Morvoren Manor?" With a prickle of prescience, she finished his sentence as calmly as she was able.

"I had not—" His tone was hushed, but even so, he stopped himself.

"Such a belief is partly why Papa has not until now pursued the acquaintance." A little apologetically, she said, "I am afraid that he might have ascribed the character of his grandfather's brother rather unfairly to you and your own grandparent."

"Is that the reason?" Mr. Landry nodded slowly. "I have always wondered. I never knew the old rascal, my great-grandfather. All I ever knew was that there was a branch of the family down here, and a tendency for there to be more girls in every generation than boys. This would seem to be borne out, for I have two sisters and so do you."

"True, sir," Alwyn agreed. Then she said, "The estate has been in the family since the fourteen hundreds."

It would not be delicate for her to tell him that the estate did not include pit, pottery, or piers, for that was Papa's to say if he wished. Papa might will as he would the wealth provided by the latter, which was the reason she and her sisters were so well dowered. The estate on its own could never have provided such generous portions. Even if Mr. Landry did attempt to claim the estate, it would do him no good if a fortune was his aim. Only a small portion of their wealth and all of their gentility came from the land.

Mr. Landry invited her to sit on the same bench on which he and Karensa had been conversing. "I confess this is not the most comfortable topic to engage in with you. But I thank you for your candor, at least."

"Why should it be uncomfortable?" she asked curiously. "It is best if everyone concerned should know the facts. Do you plan to contest my father's will, which leaves the estate to the heirs of his body, not heirs male?"

"If that thought ever entered my head, it has flown away

now, like a gull out to sea." He chuckled, in a way that made Alwyn straighten and grip her hands in her lap. "Now that I have met the woman most nearly concerned."

"Nearly concerned with what, Cousin?"

As though he had just now noticed her hands, he took both of them in his. Sheer surprise rendered her immobile, and in that moment, he raised his gaze to her own.

"Yes. For my concerns might well be yours, Cousin Alwyn —dear Alwyn. Surely you must have speculated just the smallest bit about my presence in the neighborhood?"

"Yes," she managed to get out. "But that is now resolved. Papa has received you, and—Cousin, please—"

"But it was not only your esteemed father for whom I made an eight days' journey. It was you."

Good heavens, both she and Lady Geoffrey had been right!

"From the moment we first saw one another I have been unable to think of any other woman. Your face has haunted my dreams. Your voice is the one I most want in my ear, your—"

"When did we first see one another?" she asked, cutting through his nonsense and finally freeing her hands.

"Why, in London."

"Yes, but specifically. Was it that evening at my aunt and uncle's?"

"Each moment is etched in your memory, too, I see. But please give me leave to correct you. The first time I saw you was before that."

"Were you at the Summer Exhibition? Viewing the watercolors?" Surely this could not be An Observant Gentleman?

"No indeed. My tastes need more substantial meat. I prefer

oils. No, you were in a phaeton, driven by Sir Perran Geoffrey, when I was out exercising the horses of a friend."

Right again. "In a high flyer. I remember. You nearly ran us down."

He laughed. "I recollect no such thing. Though they were a spirited pair of cattle and I did not drive them again. But enough of the past. My concern is with the present—and the future."

Had he been the one to tattle to An Observant Gentleman? "Sir, there is no talking of the future when my father may live many years yet."

He stared at her as though she had suddenly begun speaking Italian. Then his face cleared and he laughed. "You are a practical woman, and I believe you share a habit of plain speaking with your father. But it is not his future that concerns me at this moment. It is yours. Ours. Oh, wonderful word!"

He rose, then knelt upon the grass at her feet, capturing one hand again as he did so. She managed to keep the other out of his reach. "Dear Cousin Alwyn, as I was saying, you have enchanted me. I see a future filled with naught but happiness if you are by my side. Will you do me the honor of becoming my wife?"

In Alwyn, astonishment and dismay and the urge to laugh flapped madly about, as though a stranger had run through a flock of gulls upon the beach. A careless, insensitive stranger.

But she must say something, for he was still down on one knee, gazing up at her raptly. He looked exactly the way the hens did when she had a treat in her hand.

Oh dear, she must not giggle. What were the conventional

phrases a young lady was taught to have on the tip of her tongue for moments like this?

"Sir," she began, hoping such phrases would come to her, "I am fully aware of the honor of your proposals." Why on earth had he made them without first seeing Papa? For surely he would have told Mr. Landry that someone else had already spoken. "But it is rather extraordinary that you should speak to me before speaking to my father."

As though his position was becoming uncomfortable, he rose and seated himself once again beside her. Sure enough, the knee of his pantaloons was damp. She took the opportunity to repossess her hand—to no avail, for now he captured both of them.

She was beginning to dislike the sensation. Would he hold her down if she were to try to rise?

"That is such an old-fashioned convention. The strength of my passion is such that I could not restrain myself. Say yes, do, and then I will go in to your father."

"We are rather old-fashioned down here." Firmly, she removed her hands from his grip. "You do me great honor, but if you had spoken to Papa as you ought, you would have been informed that my affections lie elsewhere."

It was not exactly the truth. The thrill along the nerves that she felt whenever she thought of Perran—her perpetual watchfulness for a horse and rider with the straight set of the shoulders he alone seemed to possess—the melting of her insides when she heard his voice … Were these affections, or something more?

Surely affection was a more tender feeling. Such as when he had taken her up in the phaeton that rainy day of the balloon ascension, to shelter her from the storm. When he had written to her following that dreadful night at Almack's. What had the note said? She would give anything to know, now. What a fool she had been to burn it unread.

But Mr. Landry was speaking again, and with an effort, she prevented her thoughts from winging their way across the fields to Rosevear Court.

"Do you mean to tell me that someone else has asked your father's permission to marry you?"

Truthfulness obliged her to say, "To pay his addresses to me. As you ought to have done."

"Would your father have given permission for two men to address you?" He looked astounded at this catastrophic breach of etiquette.

"Of course not." How irritating that he could even ask! "But at least you would have known that I am not free to accept yours, and spared both of us this embarrassment."

This reproof, which would have made any other man bow in acquiescence and take himself off, only served to intensify his attention. "Who is this man who has so captured you, Cousin?"

"That is no concern of yours."

"But if not for him, would you have considered me?"

How could she put this without offending him and tearing open the family breach once more? Without resurrecting his resolve to put forward his claim?

At one time she *had* considered him. Considered, and concluded that the match would be a good one. But believing a match was suitable and actually being a party to it were two different things. That day in the rain, she and Perran had looked at one another and something she had never experienced before had caused her to change between one moment and the next. To become deeply aware of him in a way she had never experienced with any other man.

But even if that moment had not happened, she could not say in all honesty that Mr. Arthur Landry was improving on further acquaintance. Yes, he was a sensible match. But must a woman spend the next forty years with *sensible* when she could have … butterflies, and heat, and a smile that could melt a statue? To say nothing of respect, and humor, and a willingness to admit when he was wrong … those must surely count in this reckoning as well.

Again, Mr. Landry was waiting and again she must say something. "I cannot say. It does no good to think of the might-have-beens."

"But things may change," he persisted. "For all I know, you could refuse him."

There was no civil answer to this. She turned her face away.

"You have not refuted it," he exclaimed. "I will continue to hope. For in time, another man's disappointment may be my most cherished opportunity."

"I would not pin my hopes on that, sir." Then, like a beacon on the cliffs, she spotted Rowena's slender form coming along the path from the opposite direction. "I will see you out, Cousin, and fetch my sister to my father, as he requested." She rose, and stood expectantly on the gravel walk.

"But—"

But she was having no more of this interview, and he had no choice but to tag along after her. And since he had come on foot, she had no compunction about seeing him off up the drive with a wave, and plunging through a gap in the garden hedge with a sob of relief.

Which was where Rowena found her a few minutes later, sitting on the bench, rocking back and forth in a paroxysm of laughter and tears.

CHAPTER 22

"Sir Perran, welcome." Mr. Menabilly took his hat and gloves from him on Sunday evening when he arrived at Morvoren Manor for dinner. "You will find Lady Geoffrey and Miss Isolde on the terrace with the other ladies."

"Thank you, Menabilly. I trust you have recovered after Tuesday's ball?"

"Plum as bun dough, sir, and Mrs. Menabilly, too."

Perran laughed. "And glad I am to hear it. Will Mr. Penrose be joining us for dinner?"

"Aye, sir. He, Mr. Landry, and Lord Mainwaring are in the study, fortifying themselves, if I may say so."

Mr. Landry? Well, well, it seemed changes were afoot in the few days since he had been here last. "I will look in on my ladies first, then."

"As you will, sir."

The early evening air was soft and scented as the breeze caressed the roses blooming in the garden. He stepped through the French doors on to the terrace, pausing before any of the ladies caught sight of him. His gaze went directly to

Alwyn, who this evening was wearing the embroidered cream gown in which he had seen her at Lord Blessing's house—the evening when she had surprised him with poetry in the library and he had so precipitately fled.

He was not fleeing now. Quite the opposite, for he could not take his eyes from her as the sun settled into the ocean and threw the last of its golden light upon her skin. Had any woman ever possessed such tints of chestnut, tawny and rose? His hands itched to touch her, to caress that soft skin, for here, at dinner *en famille*, she did not wear gloves.

"Perran!" His sister broke in on his reverie, and he wrenched his gaze from Alwyn before she looked up and caught it.

"Isolde." He kissed her, then his grandmother. "Grand-mère. You are looking well. It seems life here on the other side of Morvoren vale suits you."

"Comfortable as we are, I shall be better suited when I can sleep in my own bed," she retorted.

He bowed to his hostesses and Lady Mainwaring, whose face was lifted to the last of the sun as though it were confer-ring a blessing. Perhaps it was, for surely Lord Mainwaring was blessed in his wife.

"How are the repairs coming, Perran?" Isolde asked, settling on a footstool next to Grand-mère while he leaned a hip against the stone balustrade. Karensa leaned upon it, too, her attention wandering to the sparrows flitting through the hedge below.

"The work is going well," he reported. "We have a roof with new slates, and the stone-masons have been busy on the walls. A bricklayer will come to replace the bricks that fell from the chimney. Jago has not relinquished his hammer and saw, however. In fact, he tells me that if the guest room floor is not repaired by this time next week, I may call him a turbot and sack him."

"Dear me," Lady Mainwaring said faintly. "What on earth is a turbot?"

Laughing, Rowena said, "A kind of flat fish, like a flounder, Aunt Celia. It is rather an insult in these parts."

"I see." Her ladyship was smiling now. "Fish notwithstanding, it all sounds very exciting."

"What is exciting, my dear?" Lord Mainwaring stepped through the French doors, Mr. Landry behind him. Karensa had been perched on the balustrade near Perran. Then, by some sisterly alchemy, as Mr. Landry emerged on to the terrace, it was suddenly Karensa who occupied one of the empty chairs and Alwyn who leaned upon the balustrade, and rather closer to Perran than her sister had been.

"This is unexpected," he murmured, leaning slightly toward her. "What, pray, have I done to merit this?"

"You had the very good sense not to be a turbot."

He laughed, and noted with interest that while her words might be saucy, she had made herself blush. He took the opportunity to move a fraction of an inch closer, expecting her to do as the sparrows did, and flit away. But she merely lifted her chin and smiled in welcome at the additions to their number.

He would much rather soak in that smile than acknowledge someone like Landry, with whom he was barely acquainted, but that would be rude to his hosts.

Landry took in the pair of them, then stared at Alwyn as though she had betrayed him in some awful way. And suddenly Perran understood. Even as he had made a statement by asking her for three dances, she was making one now in situating herself beside him instead of in the chair whose neighbor was empty.

Landry settled into it and began to make conversation with Karensa as though nothing had happened.

But something had. A line had been drawn. A choice made, perhaps, or a competition announced.

Perran fought down the rise in his blood at the whiff of any such competition, and amused himself instead by watching Landry ignore Alwyn in a dozen subtle ways, none of which seemed to bother her at all. When she excused herself to check on the dinner, she glanced over her shoulder at Perran. His gaze locked with hers for a mere second longer than propriety might dictate, and for the length of that second, he forgot where he was. There was only Alwyn, in the doorway with one hand on the frame, half turned in the last of the sunlight.

Landry caught that moment, too. His face darkened. And Perran came back to himself.

The silly trout! Would Landry call him out next, to serve him grass for breakfast? Perran would set him to rights with a few choice words, and there would be no more of this nonsense.

Perhaps it was beneath him, but at dinner he could not help being pleased at being seated across from Alwyn, on Lady Mainwaring's right at the foot of the table, while Mr. Landry was on Mr. Penrose's left at the other end. He was able to enjoy a spirited conversation with both ladies while Landry was interrogated with relentless courtesy by Mr. Penrose about his life history.

Perran was struck more than once by Alwyn's humor,

which was never pointed or snide, but was leavened with compassion. And aside from her familiarity with the family business, her interests ranged from poetry and painting, which he knew of, to poultry and philosophy, which he did not. She held a subscription to the lending library in Truro, and the family took a newspaper, which it was clear she read from first page to last.

"So much for the competition," his grandmother murmured on his other hand as the main course came in and Alwyn was distracted. When he glanced at her in surprise, she said, "Mr. Penrose informed me of your intentions last Wednesday at breakfast. Since you did not favor me with your confidence, I have not shared it with other members of our family, but the news is out regardless. There is no keeping a secret in a house full of young ladies."

"It was not meant to be a secret. I am sorry, Grand-mère. I should have told you myself."

She allowed him to help her to the pigeon pie. "I approve your choice heartily."

"She has not accepted me yet."

"She would be a fool if she did not." Her voice was so low he could barely hear her, which was fortunate, because Alwyn, having satisfied herself about the roast, looked across to him as though she had heard her name.

"The people in the village are still talking about the *Morvoren Anne*," she said. "I hear the *Cumberland* is moored in Falmouth harbor, but newly arrived from France."

"I hear the same," he said with imperturbable calm that hid his surprise. So much for secrets—clearly none were harbored in the family bosom, discreet as they might be in public. If she knew about the *Cumberland*, she clearly knew the whole. "She made a stop before she moored, but she was still tied up by dawn."

For the first time, it occurred to him that, while the *Morvoren Anne* might have porcelain and china clay in her hold on her outbound voyage, she might be laden with something significantly different on her way home. Perhaps he was not so alone in his support of the gentlemen of the free trade as he'd thought. What were the odds that the *Morvoren Anne* would return with a cargo of brandy, laces, and tea on which taxes had likewise not been paid? He must remember to place a bet with Griffin on odds like that.

"This is hardly a fitting subject for the dinner table, missy," Lady Geoffrey said. She was no fool, either.

"I beg your pardon, your ladyship," called Mr. Landry from all the way at the other end of the table. "But I do agree with you. While I was not invited to the event, I understand my cousin honored the crew of the *Morvoren Anne* by her presence t'other day. Still, it is quite out of the question that any of the young ladies be seen near the docks of Falmouth. Imagine if they should be accosted by sailors."

Lady Geoffrey looked as though being accosted by an acquaintance so newly met was worse.

"My daughters are very familiar with Falmouth, sir," said Mr. Penrose. "As for Morvoren harbor, it does, after all, lie on our land. Every person there knows and respects them."

"But why should the presence or absence of the *Cumberland* have any importance to a young lady?"

"Every ship safely returned to harbor has importance to someone," Isolde ventured. "As we have seen, even in summer a storm can blow up unexpectedly, and cause loss of life and property."

"But why should Cousin Alwyn care one way or another about the *Cumb—*"

"Do you enjoy music, Mr. Landry?" Lord Mainwaring asked, interrupting him so firmly that Perran had to admire him. And the young man, distracted by the necessity of answering his lordship satisfactorily, was at last detached from the subject of ships.

Perran wondered what Mainwaring's position might be on the subject of smuggling. Or was Landry's querulous inability to mind his own business his lordship's only motive in giving him something else to talk about?

After dinner, Perran had the pleasure of hearing Alwyn play the pianoforte for the first time. She did not sing, but her hands ran lightly upon the keys of what was clearly a fairly new instrument. Rowena, to whom the graceful arts seemed to come naturally, gave them several pieces, her voice clear and mobile as that of a lark.

Perran had a moment to be thankful that Jago was nowhere about, for then they would all be forced to listen to panegyrics upon the extent of the young lady's accomplishments. Perran had no fault to find with them—it was the admirer's repetition afterward he objected to, like an echo that would not stop.

Karensa did not play or sing. Instead, she brought in a small porcelain sculpture, delicate and in places even translucent. It was a peacock, his plumage and tail painted in swirls like those of the paisley shawls from Persia and India that were so fashionable among the ladies. The edges of his beak and his feet were picked out in gold.

She presented it with humility to Lady Mainwaring. "It

would please me very much, Aunt Celia, if you would accept this as a memento of your stay with us."

Lady Mainwaring's eyes filled with tears, and she blinked to keep them from falling. "Why, Karensa, my dear girl. It is the most beautiful thing I have ever seen. Did you sculpt it?"

"I did. If you like him, then perhaps I might make him a mate, too?"

"Of all things I could imagine, I would like that most. They must be a pair. You see that I am a hopeless romantic." Lady Mainwaring hugged her niece, then took the peacock, which fit neatly in both her hands. "He is lovely—so regal, and yet with this tilt of his head, he seems to be listening to us. Thank you so much, my dear."

Perran helped his grandmother to her feet as the recital came to a close. "Are the Mainwarings leaving?" he asked in a low tone.

"Yes, day after tomorrow," she replied. "They have been here a number of weeks, though it hardly seems so. The girls will miss them—Lady Mainwaring is so much like Anne Langford Penrose in character, that Alwyn tells me it is almost like having their mother back again."

He bade the Mainwarings farewell and wished them an uneventful journey back to London. Then Alwyn walked slowly with him down the front steps. It seemed a miracle that the entire company had tacitly agreed that they might be alone together. Or perhaps it was merely that they were occupied elsewhere.

"Surely you did not walk this evening?" she asked, her face a dim oval in the light of the rising moon. "It is every bit of five miles."

"No, I rode. Menabilly has let them know in the stables,

but I find I am in no hurry for Kit to be brought round. Griffin has lent him to me while we are here, you know. I find we are fast becoming friends."

"I am glad." He could hear the smile in her voice—the pleasure of a woman who also found soothing companionship with God's creatures, even if it was in as unlikely a place as the hen-yard. "But why should you be in no hurry to see your new friend?"

"Because by some great oversight—or some immense mercy—I find myself alone with you."

Alwyn stepped away into the waving shadows of a tree, as though facing him even in such dim light might make her guilty of some *faux pas*. "We are in plain view in front of the house, sir. We have nothing to be ashamed of."

"Perran."

She turned back to him. "I beg your pardon?"

It was the work of only a few steps to close the distance between them, and move deeper into shadow. "My name is Perran, not 'sir.'"

"What, call you by your Christian name, as we used to do as children?"

"We are children no longer." His voice had become husky. "You have grown into a beautiful woman. I thought you pretty in London, but in Cornwall, it is as though you come into your own. You look very different here. Richer, somehow. More … luscious."

She had no answer for him. Only an indrawn breath as he ran his hands up her arms.

"I want very much to kiss you," he breathed.

"Perran…" His name came out as a whisper as he leaned

closer—tilted his head—his lips met hers and his knees nearly went weak at the softness of her mouth—

A clatter of hooves coming around the corner of the house made her jump back out of his reach with a gasp. At the same time, Arthur Landry bounded down the front steps and spotted the movement of her light dress.

"How now, Cousin, I am just leaving. Will you say good night?"

As she stepped forward, Perran did so with her.

Landry stopped short. "I beg your pardon, Cousin. I would never have spoken so informally. I believed you were alone."

Perran patted Kit's neck and took the reins from the groom with a nod of thanks. "In the dark? Hardly. She is with me."

He might as well have said, *I was ravishing her behind the laurel hedge* for all the good his civility did.

"How dare you, sir? She is a gentlewoman, and not meant to be out here cavorting in the shadows with the likes of you."

Cavorting? He had half a mind to make the insufferable pup eat gravel.

"Once again," Alwyn said with an edge to her voice, "I am right here. Please do not discuss me as though I were not. I am perfectly capable of walking about alone at night in my own drive, or my own garden, or on the cliffs, if I choose to. And, I might add, in the company of anyone I choose."

Landry was silenced, but only for a moment. "And you choose this gentleman, if I may use that term?"

"That is none of your affair, Cousin."

Perran recognized the danger in her tone, if Landry did not. *Better cast off your rope and get under way, my lad.*

"Is this the man?" Landry demanded. "Is this he of whom we were talking earlier?"

"Talking of me?" Perran drawled. "How very diverting. Do I hold some kind of fascination for you, Landry?"

"No, but you certainly hold enough for half the females in London," the other man snapped.

"Arthur!" Alwyn exclaimed, turned her back upon him, and stalked up the front steps.

"That is enough," Perran growled, and Kit sidestepped nervously. He swung himself into the saddle and touched the brim of his hat. "Good night, Miss Penrose. Thank you for a most enjoyable evening."

He nudged Kit into motion, and had the satisfaction of hearing the front door close firmly behind her, leaving Arthur Landry standing deserted in the drive.

Served him right, the fool.

Though he was rather interested in what would cause his name to come up in the course of conversation between Landry and Alwyn. If his intentions were for now known only to members of her immediate family, it was not likely she was telling the news to just any visitor, no matter their familial connections.

She had assured him that Landry possessed no part of her heart, no matter what the impudent buffoon thought. He must hold to that … and to the fact that she had waited breathlessly for his kiss. And allowed it, brief as it had been before they were interrupted.

He would return tomorrow. The thought of exchanging confidences—and possibly even kisses—on a cliff walk with Alwyn kept him warm enough to appreciate the wind of Kit's going along the road, eating up the five miles with effortless ease. When he arrived at Gwennel Cottage, he gave Kit some extra oats and a rubdown before he left him to the care of the Admiral's grooms.

In the house, he found the Admiral already gone up to bed, but Griffin lay upon the drawing room sofa reading, his boots toed off and on the floor.

"You look very comfortable," Perran remarked, shrugging out of his own coat and pouring himself a glass of brandy.

"I am, thank you. How was your evening?"

"Delightful in some ways and fraught in others. Did you know that the Mainwarings are leaving day after tomorrow?"

"No, I did not. That is a shame. The pater will have one less excuse to call now."

"I do not think he needs anything but friendship as an excuse, do you?"

But Griffin only chuckled. "A note came for you from the Court. I left it on the tray in the hall. You had best prepare yourself, my friend."

Frowning, Perran fetched it, and as he brought it into the light of the drawing room, his steps slowed to a halt. The direction was not written in Tregarrow's hand, conveying a report or a list of needed supplies.

This was Constance's hand.

It had been sent to him at Rosevear Court, not here at the cottage. It was not franked or otherwise marked by the postal service, so it had been delivered by a messenger. But that was impossible. Had she given it to an acquaintance or a courier to carry all the way to Cornwall, instead of sending it by the much more efficient post?

Griffin looked up. "I do not know the contents, but I am reliably informed that it was left at the house by a lady. In

London, this would not cause a blink. But we are not in London, and it is already causing significantly more than a blink."

Constance indeed.

Perran sank into a chair and broke the seal.

Dearest Perran,

By now you will have gathered that I am not in London, but here in your beautiful St. Just taking in all of its delights. I am staying with Lord and Lady Tregothnan, who were friends of my late husband and have been kind enough to insist that I remain as their guest.

Can you guess why I have come, dear Perran?

I have had several weeks in which to reconsider my answer to your proposals, and have concluded that I have been a very foolish girl. So I have come down hotfoot to claim you before some mermaid does so. In short, darling, I am very much honored to accept your offer of marriage. I know you will still feel as you did in June, for contrary to all appearances, your heart is loyal and, unlike that of some, does not faint with time and distance.

I believe I could come to love this country as much as I love you. I even like your house. The housekeeper was kind enough to take me over it today when I introduced myself as your intended.

I look forward to seeing you as soon as ever may be. Do call upon me at Tregothnan. Shall I wait at the window like an ingenue, I wonder?

Your own
Constance

O nly you, Geoffrey, could find yourself engaged to two women at once." Shaking his head, Jago Tremayne pulled his horse to a halt at the top of the hill.

Spread out before them were the trees and streams, pastures and fields of the Tregothnan estate. In the distance, grey and imposing under the bright sky, rose the turrets and towers of the house—quite a fanciful place, as though eight generations had tried in turn to cover up the guilty fact of its once having been a monastery.

"I am *not* engaged to two women." Perran was becoming quite testy on the subject, but only because his two best friends had been chaffing him about it for nearly eight miles. "I am not even engaged to one. For the last time, Constance refused me and I have not yet proposed to Alwyn."

"I doubt that either one sees it that way, old man," Griffin told him. "Nor do your staff. The lovely Constance caused quite the stir yesterday, from all accounts. When young Tregarrow brought the note, it was all he could do to keep his countenance. He told me that if his mother had not taken to her bed with the vapors after the countess departed, it was only because she had to keep everyone else from doing so."

"Thank you for repeating the tale for Jago's benefit," Perran said grimly. "I will deal with the staff after I have taken a sword to this Gordian knot."

"Better sooner than later." Jago kicked his horse into motion and set off down the hill.

"Easy for you to say," Perran grumbled.

"At least you have us with you." Griffin rode easily at his side, nodding pleasantly to any they passed, whether tradesman, gentleman, or workers from the fields. "We shall launch a triangulation maneuver and distract the Tregothnans while you have it out with Constance in private."

Perran did not trust that Constance would allow him that privacy. His entire household now believed that she was to be their new mistress. How long would it take for word of this sensation to travel across country and break upon Morvoren Manor like the seventh wave, larger than any that had gone before?

Such a thing was so terrible he could not make his imagination contemplate it. Instead, he must plan what he would do and say in the here and now. He would not put it past Constance to keep them both in company so that he could not put things right. Why, she might even introduce him as her fiancé, when the Tregothnans had seen him dance three with Alwyn only a few days ago!

The house was every bit as gloomy and imposing as the first family in the parish might wish, had they been of the sort that read novels like *The Mysteries of Udolpho*. Constance had probably felt a quiver in her nerves at her first sight of it, she being a regular subscriber to a lending library that offered such books.

The parlor into which they were shown was very pleasant, however, with a sweeping view that allowed a glimpse of the silver doorstep of the sea. Perran and his friends bowed first to her ladyship, who had been embroidering a screen, then to Constance, who had been reading, then to two girls about the same age as Isolde. The girls at the round table were much more plainly dressed than the other ladies, and had been doing something complicated and silvery with mesh and needles.

Lady Tregothnan put her work aside and rose. "Sir Perran, Captain Teague, Mr. Tremayne—do be seated over here near the windows, where it is more comfortable," she said.

Perran tried to ignore the whispered comments and giggles of the young ladies at their unexpected appearance. While Constance contained herself for the requisite quarter hour of their visit, the moment it was completed she took his arm. He would be forced by civility to abandon his friends to the other ladies' tender mercies—but it was urgent that he speak to Constance alone.

"Dear Lady Tregothnan, forgive me," Constance said, "but I simply must show Sir Perran what his lordship has done with the Italian knot garden. In walking those gravel paths, one might almost believe oneself to be on one's wedding tour in Italy."

"He would be delighted to know you think so, Lady Eaton," her ladyship said with a stiff smile. "He will be sorry to have missed such distinguished callers, but he has his duties to perform at the assizes in Truro."

A young man, also plainly dressed, appeared in the

doorway and was waved over. "Gentlemen, you will remember my great-nephew? He attended the party at Morvoren Manor with us."

Constance took the opportunity while her ladyship was instructing the young man where to sit to lead Perran from the room, down a dark paneled corridor, and into another, where a door decanted them into the garden.

"This place is worse than a maze," she said, taking his arm and strolling down a narrow avenue between perfectly aligned squares of box hedge filled with flowers and herbs. "No matter where you wish to go, you must be prepared to take at least two corridors to get there."

The orderly garden did seem to be a kind of rebuke to the house. "It was kind of them to invite you to stay," Perran said. "What was your other option?"

She fluttered her lashes at him. "Well, since Rosevear Court is not open to visitors just now, I defaulted to the White Swan."

"Good heavens. You?"

She laughed, a merry tinkle like a silver bell. "Thankfully, only for a night. I sent my card to the Tregothnans with a note, and their invitation came back with the most gratifying promptness."

"You might have sent a letter from London and told me, Constance, before you came all this way."

"But that would have spoiled the surprise." She pulled him down next to her on a carved bench that might have come from a Medici palace. "I did leave you a letter."

"As a consequence of which I am here." He took a deep breath. "Constance, this will not do."

"What will not? I have realized that despite what I said, I

love you, and do not wish to go on without you. I believe I can make you happy." Her lovely eyes caressed him. "I know you were cautious about saying you loved me, but I know you. I know that you conceal much when you feel the most. Under that sardonic exterior is a passionate man with a loyal heart." When he said nothing, she went on, "You have proposed, and I have now accepted. All the rest is merely sound and fury, signifying nothing."

He frowned. All the rest of what? "What do you mean? Did space constrain you to leave a detail or two out of your letter?"

"No, no. Lady Tregothnan did, however, make a point of telling me about a dinner party she recently attended, at which your conduct seems to have made a *particular* impression." She tapped his arm coyly. "Perran, Perran. What will I do with a man who cannot help his attentions to the ladies?"

"I do not know, if you will be so vague," he said with his best attempt at a pleasant tone. "The only house party to which I and the Tregothnans were both invited was at Morvoren Manor Tuesday last. And as I recall, my attentions, as you so aptly put it, were fairly evenly divided among all the ladies there. I even stood up with my grandmother, much to her astonishment."

Constance gazed up at him through her lashes. "Not three dances, though, I'll wager."

Lady Tregothnan's report had been detailed indeed, given that they had not been guests in the Penrose house above the once, and they could not be as well acquainted with Constance as they had been with the late earl. But Constance could coax a secret out of a stone statue. It would have taken her no effort at all to learn all the news of the neighborhood—

and of his behavior in particular. Anxiety and regret may have brought her down to Cornwall, but jealousy had taken her over to Rosevear Court to impose upon his staff and misrepresent herself as its future mistress.

"I see I shall have to keep you on a short rein, my darling," she said now, with a merry laugh. "Though men seem less inclined to dance once the marriage contracts are signed, I find. Perhaps, despite all previous experience, you will be the exception."

"Constance, enough," he said. Here was where he must make his stand. "If you will recall, you refused me when I made you my offer."

"And if *you* recall, I have already explained how much I regret my foolishness." She rubbed her cheek upon his shoulder. "I regretted it at once, in fact, but my pride got in the way."

"Your pride?"

"Yes, at the gossip all over Town about you and that Penrose girl. The things Silence and dear Dorothea said to me! But that is all behind us now. Come, if you must observe the proprieties, offer me your hand again and I will accept. And then let us talk about the future."

"The offer of one's hand is usually made only once," he said steadily. "Since you refused me, I feel I have the right to bestow my affections elsewhere."

"Your affections?" Again the trilling laugh. "You make it sound as though they are merely a knot of ribbons, to be fastened to someone else's sleeve. But we are more to each other than that, Perran." She tucked her hand into his elbow, leaning upon his shoulder. "You know as well as I do that in many ways, we are very well suited."

"You are missing the point." He rose, and she had perforce to straighten her posture.

"And what is that?"

"The point is that I *have* bestowed my affections elsewhere, and I must tell you that in honor, all relations between us except those of civility and acquaintance must end. This will be the last time we are alone together."

She gazed at him, her smile unwavering, as though he had made a joke and she was waiting for its meaning to become clear.

"Nonsense," she said at last. "I will be alone with whomever I please. Tell me, who could you possibly have fallen in love with so quickly?" Her gaze became reproachful. "Oh dear, surely there are no actresses or opera singers of the quality you tend to appreciate so deep in the country?"

He would not be baited. "I have applied to the lady's father for permission to address her, and the matter is closed."

"What lady?" Rapid calculations flashed behind her eyes. "Good heavens. Not the Penrose chit. Not after what happened at Almack's. La! What will Dorothea Lieven say? What merry hay she will make of this!"

"Please do not discuss her in those terms." His hands balled into fists, and it was only with an effort of will that he remembered her rapier-like skill with words, how easily she could wound and disarm.

"Perran, she is hardly out of the schoolroom." Pent-up laughter colored her voice.

He did not dignify this with a reply. Nor did she wait for one.

She waved a beringed hand as though conceding him this one point, and the diamonds flashed in the sun. "Oh very well.

Have your virginal bride. But I know you. I will wager a golden guinea that you will be dancing attendance upon me within six months—if, that is, I have not tired of waiting and found someone else whose attentions please me better."

His stomach clenched. Did Constance really think he would dishonor Alwyn in such a way? In fact, this entire distasteful conversation dishonored her. He must conclude it swiftly and ride to Morvoren Manor before the damage became worse.

"You may keep your guinea, Constance, for I will not be doing any such thing in six months' time, or at any other. I have found a worthy partner with whom to share my life, and I plan to honor the vows we will make. If she will have me, that is."

"Honor your vows?" Her tone was still silky, but that word *worthy* had clearly caused it to fray at the edges. "What of your vows to me? What of your declarations? What of the hours we spent together, at the risk of my own reputation? Do you hold those so cheaply?"

"My declarations, as you put it, became moot the moment you declined them."

"So this is all, then?" She rose, too. "I am to take myself back to London and never think of you again?"

"In a word, yes."

Two crimson flags of warning flew in her cheeks. "I daresay I will cease thinking of you long before you cease thinking of me, darling Perran. For I may go back to London, but you must stay here to deal with a neighborhood that believes you already engaged."

"It is a mistake soon mended."

"Oh, I do not think so." She smiled, her eyes narrowed

with a kind of spiteful anticipation. "If anyone knows the habits of that wily beast called gossip, it is I. And I have a feeling it is already too late."

"Be that as it may, I will leave you now." He bowed, with every ounce of the deference due her rank. "Good-bye, Lady Eaton. I wish you good health and happiness in the future."

"Get out of my sight."

The only thing he could give her now was the last word. So he turned and left, and silently wished her joy of it.

The two corridors that would take him back to his hostess seemed to stretch into infinity, growing longer with every urgent step. He must go to Alwyn at once. He must tell her what had happened—not with Constance, though he would tell her of this unpleasant visit—but in his heart.

For ever since Constance's letter had exploded in his mind, it was as though it had cleared the dense forest of his feelings, the past, all his mistakes—leaving behind the open air of certainty at last. He had finally come to understand himself. No matter the state of his title or property, he was not going to marry Alwyn for her money. No matter his feelings of unworthiness, he would not marry her for pleasant company. What a fool he'd been to have told himself those things—to pretend to be so disinterested, so cavalier about her future and his own!

No, he would marry Alwyn because to do anything else would be unthinkable. To live another day, to take a single breath without the knowledge that she was his and he was hers was more than he could bear.

He pushed through a door, found it led to a closet, reversed his course, and slammed through the next one into a corridor that looked familiar.

His very life depended on the outcome of the next hour. He must hurry.

He burst into the hall and abandoned all thought of taking leave of Lady Tregothnan. Instead, he plunged through the doorway, down the front steps, and shouted for his horse.

CHAPTER 24

*A*lwyn handed her father a plate of sandwiches and cake, and cut him a healthy slice of cheese to go with it. Karensa poured his tea and he took it with a smile.

"Ah, my pretty maidens, always coming up with something new to entertain me. Though I have to say that eating nuncheon out of doors is more comfortable and to my taste than some of your past schemes."

"At least one does not have to worry about spilling anything," Karensa sank gracefully to the rug they had spread upon the ground, and adjusted her parasol. "As for crumbs, we may be as untidy as we like and the birds will thank us."

"If you spill your tea on your pretty sprigged muslin, my dear, you may have cause to regret it." Lady Geoffrey and Lady Mainwaring occupied a small table brought out from the sea parlor—for no one could persuade them to sit upon the ground, rug or no. A canvas canopy lent them shade.

The little party had not gone far from the house; in fact they were still upon the lawn. Wrens and robins flitted through the hedges and shrubs behind them, and beyond the mowed grass, the sheep munched upon the wild tussocks. Under the canopy, Papa and Lord Mainwaring sat in the low, folding canvas chairs the family normally used down on the beach, while Alwyn, her sisters, and Isolde were grouped like a pretty bouquet upon the rug.

Isolde shaded her eyes with one hand. "Look, Grand-mère, is that not young Tregarrow? Perhaps he is come with a message from the Court."

"If you wore your bonnet upon your head, my girl, instead of letting it hang down your back, you would not have to do that. Nor would you risk your complexion in this sun."

"Yes, Grand-mère." Obediently, Isolde pulled the bonnet up and tied its ribbons under her chin, but its lacy brim only succeeded in making her look even prettier while doing hardly anything at all to preserve her complexion.

The young man walking with purpose across the grass was indeed young Tregarrow. "Good day, your lordship, your ladyships, Mr. Penrose, sir. Young ladies." He pulled off his hat and bowed.

"Good morning, Mr. Tregarrow," Lady Geoffrey said. "Have you news for us from home?"

"I do, ma'am," he said. "I would have come before, but we are all of a dither at the house, and I had to stay to help 'un."

"I do beg your pardon?" said Lady Mainwaring.

"He means there has been an upset of some kind," Isolde whispered. "What has happened, Mr. Tregarrow? Is all well with the building?"

"As well as may be, miss. The guest room now has a floor, and we're waitin' only on the glaziers, so it won't be long now before you and her ladyship can be back with us again. But that ent why I come." His gaze found that of Lady Geoffrey.

"Is the master here? For have you p'raps heard his intended bride have arrived from London Town last evening? My mother received 'er and showed her about the place. But she —my mother, that is—would be easier if you or Sir Perran were to come along home, ma'am, in case the lady returns today. She—my mother—is not accustomed to entertaining quality alone and beseeches you to receive her ladyship properly."

A resounding silence met this earnest petition.

Alwyn's mouth hung open. She could not have heard correctly.

Lady Geoffrey frowned in a way that made the young man begin a step backward, then reconsider and hold his ground. Clearly he knew his mistress well.

"I do not understand you, Lucas Tregarrow. *Whom* did your mother receive at Rosevear Court yesterday?"

"Her ladyship, ma'am. Countess Eaton, who is to marry the master."

Now Alwyn gasped, for she had forgotten to breathe.

She clapped a hand over her mouth.

But not soon enough. Every pair of eyes in the little group fixed themselves upon her for the space of five seconds. Then everyone recovered their manners, and swung back to the messenger.

Everyone save Lady Geoffrey, whose perplexed gaze had never left his ruddy, tanned face. "Mr. Tregarrow, you and your mother must be mistaken. Sir Perran is not engaged to be married."

"Begging your pardon, your ladyship, I wouldn't ever want to contradict you. But there the lady was at the door, silks and velvets and all, and a ruddy great crested carriage wi' four fine horses standing in the sweep. She come just before we was to sit down to our tea. My mother is sideways as a crab goin' to a christening even yet, ma'am."

"Young Tregarrow, this cannot be so." Mr. Penrose rose to his feet, declining Lord Mainwaring's help and leaning on his cane. He glanced at Alwyn, but she could not respond. She was frozen—motionless—staring at the young man while horror chilled her to her very bones.

"I am that sorry to have to say, Mr. Penrose, sir, but she were quite clear on the matter. I heard her myself. 'What a lovely place,' she said. 'When your master and I are wed, I shall be pleased to call it home.'"

"She said that?" Karensa blurted. "In front of the staff? Hasn't she got brass enough for a teakettle!"

"Sir Perran is going to marry Alwyn," Rowena told him with bald assurance.

"Girls!" thundered their father. "That is enough."

"Is the master not here?" Tregarrow clung to his duty no matter the gale raging around him.

"No, he is not," Mr. Penrose said. "But when you find him I should very much like a word with him."

"He is probably at Gwennel Cottage, sir," Isolde said—the first sensible thing anyone had said in minutes, Alwyn thought, dazed.

"I called there, miss, but he and Captain Teague had already gone. To Tregothnan, Mrs. Trewe says."

"Tregothnan?" repeated Lady Geoffrey. "Why on earth has he gone all the way to Tregothnan?"

"I cannot tell you, your ladyship. Will you come, ma'am, in case the lady comes back, and set my mother's mind at rest?"

"For pity's sake, I suppose I must." Lady Geoffrey rose. "I

had hoped to spend a little more time with you, Celia, before you leave tomorrow, but it seems it is not to be."

"But we have not been to the Court at all, dear Ghislaine. Perhaps his lordship and I might accompany you? For we are acquainted with the countess and may be able to get to the bottom of this confusion if she does call. In the meanwhile, I should like to see the work being done myself."

"I would consider it a great favor," Lady Geoffrey said with relief. "Mr. Penrose, may we borrow your barouche for this errand, since the Mainwaring carriage is being packed?"

"You may indeed. Young Tregarrow, go round to the stable, would you, and let them know? You may go home on the box with Broome."

"I will, sir. Thank you, sir. Your ladyships. Your lordship. Ladies." He bowed and in a moment was gone around the corner of the house.

Feeling as though she were in a heavy fog, her skin as clammy as though its mists embraced her already, Alwyn set her cup and saucer carefully on the rug.

Rose to her feet, a little unsteadily. And walked away across the lawn. The voices of her family calling her back had as little meaning as the cries of the gulls.

Not good enough.

The familiar refrain sang in Alwyn's head, but if it had been only one voice before, it was now a full choir in four-part harmony, with cherubs singing descant.

Not good enough to marry, but good enough to trifle with.

Clearly, she had utterly, tragically mistaken the matter. Perran had already been engaged before he left London. Why had she allowed herself to gaze into his eyes, to glow in the warmth of his smile, to sigh at the thought of one day capturing his heart?

Why had he asked her father if he might pay his addresses to her? So he could take advantage of her, treat her like a plaything, and ride back to Town with his fiancée, having ruined that simpleton of a country girl at Morvoren Manor all the more thoroughly this time, that was why.

How could she have thought for a moment she could ruin him for any other woman? That he would see her as his first choice after all? How he must have laughed at her gauche attempts at flirtation, at fascination! She was the worst idiot who had ever lived. As recently as yesterday evening, she had played right into his hands yet again, standing in the shadows, waiting for him, all but inviting him to join her.

To touch her.

To kiss her.

What man wouldn't take such an invitation, so freely and even wantonly given? Of course he had kissed her, never knowing that the sweetness of it had practically drawn the soul out of her body. For she had known then that it was not he who was ruined for any other woman.

Oh, no. She had ruined herself for any other man.

Like a fool, like any of his conquests in London, she had fallen in love with him. Given him her heart, when he already had that of Lady Eaton in his keeping. And now he would ride away, leaving her with nothing.

Was this how they behaved in London? Did gentlemen routinely ask a young lady's father for his permission to court her, all the while keeping his preference for someone else a secret? Alwyn had never felt like a country mouse before this, but she certainly did now. The rules must be different in

London. Breaking hearts—taking hearts—was a game, a gamble, and she had lost.

Not good enough to court, but good enough to kiss.

He was engaged to a countess. A woman of fortune and breeding. Alwyn possessed a fortune, too, but apparently that was not enough to tip the scales in her favor. For breeding was everything. Perran was the son of a baronet, and Alwyn was the great-granddaughter of a pitman. No matter how many years had passed since her great-grandfather had dug clay, society would not forget.

Still, he had owned the land on which the Manor sat. Ownership made a man a gentleman. There had been Penroses here for centuries. Farmers making the best of their reduced circumstances, helping their tenants where they could.

Not good enough.

Because Great-Grandfather's far-sightedness had spurred him to do what no one had thought of: to buy cheap land that he knew was hiding a treasure.

China clay.

In another world, another time perhaps, her great-grandfather would have been celebrated as a visionary. But here and now, no matter the size and comfort of the manor he had built, no matter the enlargement and improvement of the property, the clay dust still clung.

For the daughters and granddaughters of tradesmen were fair game for gentlemen, weren't they? Even she and her sisters had heard distasteful stories, and they had been protected and cosseted almost every moment.

Now, thought Alwyn bleakly, she was going to be a story herself, for the second time in as many months. A whisper behind a gloved hand. A glance, and the cut direct. A cautionary tale of how one ought not to behave, even when circumstances looked perfectly acceptable on the outside.

He had asked Papa's permission!

Her heart cried the words. That was the sticking point. The thing she simply did not understand.

Alwyn had reached the edge of the cliff, where the breeze off the sea fanned her hot face, cooling the tears on her cheeks.

Then she stepped off.

Her feet were sure on the zigzag path down its rocky face, softened with grass and bushes reduced to half their normal size by the wind. She had intended to go all the way down to the beach, but she had come away without her bonnet and the summer sun was hot. So she followed the path along the cliff face to where it broke in a point of land that thrust a little way into the sea.

Here was the ruined chapel, cool and quiet, still vigilant after many centuries. Still inviting prayers for sailors … and others who were lost.

She would take refuge and think awhile.

When she reached it, panting a little with the climb, she let herself inside. It was a tiny place, only big enough for one or two supplicants and the priest who had once lived in the room behind the altar. The room had crumbled away into the sea, and parts of the vaulted roof were missing, but the altar still stood—two steps up to a simple Cornish cross that some long-dead stone mason had carved and hauled up here on his back as an act of worship.

She knelt on the stone step that formed a *pre-dieu* and bowed her head.

In this place, before God, she was good enough.

Penrose women, fishermen's wives, the wives of sailors and smugglers alike—they had all been coming here for generations to pray for those they loved. Prayer seemed to have soaked the walls inside just as much as the storms of winter soaked the stones outside, leaving peace once they had passed.

She had come with her mind in turmoil, the voices of self-doubt that had so long attacked and assailed her shrieking so loudly it was a wonder she had not gone mad. But as she knelt … as the peace of the place began to soak into her, too … that sticking point became clearer than it had some minutes before.

He had asked Papa's permission.

In London they called him a rogue, but not a rake. There was a difference. Regardless of what others named him, Perran had never been anything but kind to her, never made her feel as though she were less than he. On the contrary, he had gone out of his way to protect her, if not from himself, then certainly from his reputation.

She had made herself feel less than he.

She had listened to the voice of self-doubt, given credence to the whispers, allowed gossip to take her self-respect from her.

That boy who had trusted her to know her way through the sea swells—trusted her to take the reins and not overturn the pony cart—trusted her to use her skills to ride as well as he—would not break the trust she had given him when he had kissed her. No matter the trappings he had gathered about himself in London, that core of honor and respect in him that she had recognized even as a child was still there.

It had to be.

She did not know what Lady Eaton thought she was doing, but until Perran stood before her and told her otherwise himself, Alwyn would believe in him.

She must. Her own core of honor and her own need to respect herself demanded it.

And if she turned out to have been fooled in truth, then she could not be faulted. For since his return to Cornwall, he had behaved as an honorable man would. With her father, and with her. She must cling to that, even as the women who had prayed here clung to the last memory they had of their menfolk before they sailed away.

There was a sound behind her—a scratch upon the stone. Perhaps a gull had landed on the doorstep, curious about this unexpected intrusion into its domain.

Still kneeling, Alwyn turned and looked over her shoulder.

CHAPTER 25

The mazes and traps of Tregothnan may not have sheltered a Minotaur at their heart, but Perran had escaped with his life nonetheless. He had abandoned his friends to the tender mercies of her ladyship's drawing room, and ridden like the wind across field and pasture, jumping stone walls and stiles like a madman.

Fortunately, Kit enjoyed a challenge, and they covered the few miles to Morvoren Manor in record time, arriving before the front door in a clatter of hooves and a spray of gravel. He tossed Kit's reins to the groom and before he could even demand to know where Miss Penrose was, the boy said, "They're all out on the lawn, sir, eating a picnic nuncheon."

When he let himself into the garden, he saw that the family were all on their feet, gazing down the lawn toward the sea in what appeared to be a mild state of distress. In the distance, on the edge of the cliff, was a slender figure in a pale dress.

She stepped off the edge.

Perran let out a cry of agony that brought all the family swinging around in astonishment.

"Perran!" his grandmother cried.

"I say, sir—!" Mr. Penrose roared.

"Go to her, *this instant.*" Karensa's was the only voice he heeded. He vaulted the box hedge, losing his top hat in the process, and sprinted for the cliffs, leaving dignity and pride in tatters behind him.

"Come back here at once, you rogue!" Mr. Penrose shouted. "I want a word with you!"

But there was only one person with whom he wanted a word. One word that would secure his heart … or destroy it.

He took the cliff path at a pace just this side of suicidal, losing his footing and regaining it, sliding and running down the steep cut in the cliff. Had she gone to the beach? Panting, he surveyed the rocks. He caught a glimpse of her pale skirt, and he changed direction to climb the promontory.

And here she was, kneeling in the ruins of the chapel where they had once huddled as children, taking shelter in a storm, telling secrets and ghost stories.

She turned as his boots scraped the ancient stone threshold.

"I did not mean to intrude," he said, breathing as though he had run and not ridden all the way from Tregothnan. "Would you like me to leave?"

"Perran." Nothing had ever sounded so sweet as his name on her lips. "How did you find me?" She rose and turned to face him, before the ancient cross.

His breathing was calming now. Strange that she had that effect on him. "I will always find you. Alwyn, there is something I must tell you."

"I already know." She looked up at him as he joined her

before the old cross and took her hands in his. "Lady Eaton is here in St. Just."

"She is, heaven help me, and making quite an impression. But whatever you have heard, it is not true. You must believe me."

She gazed at him. "She says you are engaged to be married. Your household is all in a proper boil, sir."

He could not help it—he laughed at the sound of the country expression and her tone of reproof.

"Young Tregarrow came to ask your grandmother to come home," she went on, "in case Lady Eaton comes back, and told us the whole."

"Your father wants my head on a pike."

"That would rather defeat the purpose, wouldn't it?" She tried to remove her hands from his, but he only gripped them more tightly.

"Alwyn, please be serious, and listen. What she told my household—it is not true. There is only one woman whom I wish to bring home as mistress of Rosevear Court, and that is you."

"I … and my forty thousand pounds?"

The question rocked him in the same way her father's bluntness had, and he settled his feet more firmly. He would answer with the honesty she deserved. "I would marry you if you had nothing to your name but the clothes you stood up in to say your vows, my darling."

She took a surprised breath at the endearment, searching his face as though asking him if he meant it.

Oh, yes, he meant every word. The truth settled into his heart once and for all. Even if she were penniless, this was the woman with whom he wanted to spend the next fifty years, if the good Lord granted them both that many.

"The poor Court would be in a fine pickle if you took me with so little, would it not?" Clearly, she was trying to regain her footing with gentle humor.

"No, for I would simply become much better friends with the free tradesmen plying the waters between here and France," he said, amazed at his own frankness in the face of hers. "My share of a wet harvest or two was enough to put a roof on. Imagine what I could do with regular visits on moonless nights."

Her lips twitched, until she could no longer control her smile. "The *ton* in London may call you a rogue, but I know the truth. You are a pirate and a smuggler, sir. What will I have to do to keep you on the right side of the preventive men, I wonder?" Her eyes held a universe of beauty, and he struggled to say the words he must, and not kiss her.

"You must accept me at once, to save me from a life of crime," he said. "Though why you would want the son of a drunkard and a gambler, who consorts with smugglers simply to pay the bills, is beyond me."

"Is that how you see yourself?" she asked softly, all seriousness now.

"It is the truth." He took a breath to steady himself. "I was only good enough for Lady Eaton when I was an amusement. She never considered me as a husband. Not really."

"So you did propose."

"I did," he said, the honest words scratching in his throat. "I must thank her some day for refusing me. For when she came to Cornwall to tell me she had changed her mind, my eyes were opened. I never loved her. My company was convenient for her, and hers for me, but that is no foundation upon which to build a marriage."

"And yet she came all this way to make an engagement public."

He released one hand to touch her jaw with his finger, marveling at the softness of her skin. "I think she might have heard a whisper about you."

"Poor lady. How humiliating to have lost to the great-granddaughter of a pitman. I wonder at your coming to find me, sir. You will not be received in Town once everyone hears you have been blinded by clay dust."

"I care not one whit for what anyone thinks," he said, for her bitter, self-deprecating tone wounded his tender heart. "You are a gentleman's daughter. Your family's investment in pit, pottery, and piers was inspired. You have done more to employ the men in this parish than ever occurred to most of the *ton*, I'll be bound." He tapped her chin, and it turned into a caress. "I'll have no more nonsense about who is less worthy than whom, Miss Penrose. For if we are satisfied with each other, than everyone else may simply go to—" He stopped himself. "—Helston."

"Perran! We are in chapel." But her smile held no censure now, her eyes no dismay.

"Had this chapel a room with an anchorite still in residence, I would make sure of you this moment," he said.

"You have not proposed, sir," she said a little breathlessly, the color blooming in her cheeks. "You are putting the cart quite before the horse."

"Then let me rectify that oversight now." He dropped to

one knee, capturing her hands in his once again. Neither of them wore gloves, and the feel of her skin was a revelation. For those fine, strong hands did not lie in his palms lifelessly, coldly. Oh, no. She entwined her fingers in his with a sensual determination every bit as marked as his own.

He hauled his thoughts back from the direction they were tending. "Alwyn Penrose, will you make me the happiest man in Cornwall by becoming my wife?"

"I will."

He dipped his head to kiss her knuckles. "Despite the public censure I have heaped upon you, because I did not know my own heart?"

"I did not know my own heart either," she admitted softly. "With a reputation and a future in ruins, all I could feel was anger and grief. And then you returned and—and even a glimpse of you made my heart race. When you gave me your apology … that was when I realized that the man I knew in London was not the man everyone else there seemed to know."

"You are one of the few," he said. "What then? When did your heart begin to change toward me?"

"I hardly know," she said softly. "I think it has been yours since we were children, and it has taken me all this time to see it. Oh, do get up, Perran. The stone floor is cold."

He did so, but only to take her in his arms, there before the altar. "No matter how long it has taken, you have surely ruined me for any other woman. And I would have it no other way."

She made a tiny sound into the front of his coat.

"My dear … what have I said that was funny?"

She lifted her face, filled with joy, her eyes sparkling with laughter even as they swam with tears. "On our first anniversary, I will tell you."

"Once again we are putting the cart before the horse," he said, kissing her eyelids, her nose, her cheeks. "We must climb the cliff and tell your family before anything else happens to complicate what should be perfectly simple. What *will* be."

She hugged him. "In a little while. Come. Sit with me on the rocks and let us watch for the *morvoronyon*."

"There are no mermaids in this modern age, you minx. Though I used to wonder if you had a little *morvoren* in your blood, you were so fond of the water."

He let her pull him out of the little chapel and down to the flat, golden rocks where they had played in the sea as children. He spread his handkerchief on the stone for her to sit upon, and their feet dangled over the edge.

"The memories I made here with you are some of the best of my life." He could not help slipping his arm around her, now that he had the right to do so. She leaned her head upon his shoulder as though it was the most natural thing in the world. They fit together like two pieces of a puzzle. "Life at Rosevear Court was not happy in those early years. You and your family were all that kept a young boy from despair."

She looked at up him, love shining in her eyes. "We will make new memories there. The Court is being rebuilt, and we will fill it with a family of our own. The rooms will ring with music and laughter, for our doors will always be open to our friends."

"I can hear it now."

"Perhaps you hear the mermaids singing," she teased.

"Perhaps it is my heart singing."

And he took her mouth in a kiss that rocked him to his

core. They fell into the warmth and the delight of each other as they sealed their promises with kisses, the sun warm upon them and the sea murmuring at their feet, in this place whose enchantment had at last brought them back to the beginning.

In this place where they belonged. Together.

Forever and always.

EPILOGUE

After Perran made his hasty and unequivocal departure, it took Jago a full half hour to extract Griffin from the clutches of Lady Tregothnan and the two young ladies. The elder seemed to be demonstrating an alarming set of notions about their staying to lunch, and Jago was having none of it. That would set expectations where expectations had no right to be, and he had had enough of those to last a lifetime.

"You don't suppose Lady Eaton has gone somewhere with Perran, do you?" Griffin's tone held doubt as he rode at Jago's side. "The road is empty."

"Of course it is empty," Jago said with impatience. "He has had a head start on us. But no, I do not. He left on Kit at a dead gallop. I could hear the hooves on the gravel. And it is rather difficult to believe that he would have taken Lady Eaton up behind him. She is not that sort of woman."

"Good point." Griffin cheered up. "Let us ride to Morvoren Manor, then, shall we? Whether he is there or not, we will see if the news of his impending nuptials has arrived."

When they finally reached the Manor, they handed off their horses to the groom, and then on his direction made their way through the garden with all haste.

"—to tell you that Alwyn has made me the happiest man alive by accepting my proposal of marriage," Jago heard Perran say as they passed through the gate to find the family upon the lawn.

"Jupiter aloft, he's really done it," Griffin muttered, his face bright with a comical combination of disbelief and warmth.

Isolde flew into her brother's arms and gave him a smacking kiss. "Oh, I'm so happy!" She did the same to Alwyn with slightly more restraint. "I have been hoping for this moment. I cannot wait to call you sister!"

Mr. Penrose seemed to be less enthused and more cautious, which was odd, for Jago was certain Perran had done the expected thing and asked his permission to court Alwyn. Mr. Penrose glared at Perran like a lion about to pounce, and turned to his daughter. "Is it so, maidey? You have accepted this man despite this news of an extra fiancée bowling about the countryside?"

Ah. The news had reached the Manor faster than Perran had. How had he managed to dodge that cannon ball so efficiently that he was now safely engaged to the right woman?

Alwyn laughed and hugged her father. "Lady Eaton has been laboring under a delusion, which has now been cleared up, and I expect she will depart as quickly as she came. Sir Perran is to be your son, and I hope you will welcome him."

Perran stood at attention, resembling nothing so much as a man steadying himself for a blow. Perhaps there were more balls to be dodged.

"He has been honorable in his dealings with me," Mr.

Penrose said. "I will believe that he is honorable now. Shake hands, then, sir, and welcome to the family."

Perran did so, a smile that Jago had never seen before breaking like dawn on his face. That word—*family*—had always had a strange effect on Perran. Perhaps that blackness like a bruise on his friend's heart left by his father could now begin to heal.

Jago hung back as the family converged on the newly engaged couple, hugging and expressing their delight. Even Lady Geoffrey unbent long enough to kiss Miss Penrose upon the cheek. "I am very happy that my grandson has made such a fine choice, my dear. I wish you every happiness."

"Thank you, your ladyship," Alwyn said softly.

"When is the happy event to be?"

"I—we—have not seen quite that far into the future," Alwyn stammered, "but for my part, I should like to be able to walk down the aisle on Papa's arm without his needing to use his cane."

Her father clapped Lord Mainwaring on the back and turned to her. "Then I will make every effort to do as my brother in law here tells me, maidey, and take exercise every day."

"And do as your daughter tells you," Rowena said firmly, "by using the salve I gave you, morning and night."

"With such a goal in view, my dear, I will put up with your salve." He touched Rowena's cheek and smiled into her eyes. "I vow I will walk your sister down the aisle in St. Just church on Twelfth Night. What say you, Sir Perran?"

"I say I could not have chosen better, sir," Perran told him. "The Court will be ready for its mistress by then, or I will know the reason why." Slipping an arm around Alwyn's waist, he looked down into his fiancée's face with an expression Jago had never seen before.

It was love, to be sure. But not the kind that had to be hidden in furtive glances or behind closed doors. It was the kind of love that could be celebrated openly. Talked of among family and friends with joy and anticipation. And lived in public between the two people whom it concerned the most.

Jago gazed at Rowena, who was taking in her sister and future brother in law with a kind of rapture, her hands clasped in pure happiness under her chin.

What wouldn't he give to have her look at him in that way?

But it was impossible. He was nearly ten years older than she. He was hopeless with women, always saying the wrong thing, always offending when he meant to compliment. He had a reputation as a droll flirt that neither he nor his friends could understand in the slightest. Worst of all, Rowena herself had made it plain that she was emphatically not interested in him, treating him like a sort of awkward older brother who must be shushed into silence before he embarrassed the family.

Family. That word again.

Jago scrubbed his face and dragged his gaze away from her. What would his own family think if he acted on his desires and pursued Rowena? His father in particular, who was set on a match with some ward or other he hardly remembered. Relations between them had become positively strained since he had returned to St. Just.

No matter how he looked at it, his hopeless *tendre* for Rowena had no future.

And yet … and yet … His gaze returned to her as though it

were a compass needle and she true north. Jago's heart seemed to swell ... and break ... all at the same time.

And not once did she look at him, or return his regard...

WILL Jago lay his heart at Rowena's feet? Who is this mysterious ward? And is Arthur Landry still lurking in St. Just? For answers to all these questions, watch for Jago's story, The Rogue Not Taken, coming in September 2019!

Dear reader,

I hope you enjoy watching the Rogues of St. Just fall in love as much as I do. You might leave a review on your favorite retailer's site to tell others about the books. And you can find both digital and print editions of the series online. I hope you might visit my website, www.charlotte-henry.com, where you can, in true Regency style, subscribe to my newsletter and be the first to know of new releases, special promotions, and the progress of the next Regency gown or patchwork quilt on my sewing table.

I used a number of research sources to write these books. If this interests you, I invite you to turn the page.

Under the name Shelley Adina, I write steampunk adventures set in the Victorian era, with heroines of compassion and spirit. If you'd like to learn more, do visit me at www.shelleyadina.com.

With affection,

Charlotte

ACKNOWLEDGMENTS

Anyone who has been so fortunate as to travel to Cornwall will have realized that the parish of St. Just is fictional. There is a town called St. Just-in-Penwith, and there is another called St. Just-in-Roseland, but that is as close as the sticklers among us may come.

However, one might imagine the landscape that the Rogues call home to bear certain similarities to the Roseland Heritage Coast, one of the loveliest places in the world. And if one were to imagine Morvoren Manor as being rather strikingly like Trelissick in appearance and location, one would not be very far off the mark.

IN PRINT

Fogg, Roger and Brown, Adrian, *Cornwall's China Clay Country: Exploring the Land of the White Pyramid* (Halsgrove, 2011)

Hawke, Kathleen, *Cornish Sayings, Superstitions and Remedies* (St Agnes: Truran, Goonance, 2009)

Hendrickson, Emily, *The Regency Reference Book* (unpublished photocopy, 1999)

Nicolson, Nigel, *The World of Jane Austen* (London: Orion, 1997)

Quayle, Eric and Foreman, Michael, *Cornish Tales*, (Plymouth: Mabecron Books, 1986)

Quennell, Peter, ed., *The Private Letters of Princess Lieven to Price Metternich 1820–1826* (New York: E.P. Dutton & Co., 1938)

White, Paul, *The Cornish Smuggling Industry* (Redruth: Tor Mark, 2010)

Wilson, Kim, *At Home with Jane Austen* (New York: Abbeville Press, 2014)

Worsley, Lucy, *Jane Austen at Home: A Biography* (New York: St. Martin's Press, 2017)

ONLINE

- Jane Austen's World
- The Cornish Dictionary
- *King's Cutters and Smugglers 1700-1855* by E. Keble Chatterton
- Regency Dances

ORGANIZATIONS

- Bay Area English Regency Society
- Jane Austen Society of North America
- Romance Writers of America

Gwynn Place (novella)

The Mysterious Devices series
The Bride Wore Constant White
The Dancer Wore Opera Rose
The Matchmaker Wore Mars Yellow
The Engineer Wore Venetian Red
The Judge Wore Lamp Black
The Professor Wore Prussian Blue

ABOUT THE AUTHOR

Charlotte Henry is the author of 24 novels published by Harlequin, Warner, and Hachette, and a dozen more published by Moonshell Books, Inc., her own independent press. As Charlotte, she writes the Rogues of St. Just series of classic Regency romances. As Shelley Adina, she writes steampunk adventure, and as Adina Senft, writes Amish women's fiction. She holds an MFA in Writing Popular Fiction, and is currently at work on a PhD in Creative Writing at Lancaster University in the UK. She won the Romance Writers of America RITA Award® for Best Inspirational Novel in 2005, and was a finalist in 2006. When she's not writing, you can find Charlotte sewing historical dresses, traveling for research, reading, or enjoying the garden with her flock of rescued chickens.

www.charlotte-henry.com
www.shelleyadina.com

www.ingramcontent.com/pod-product-compliance
Lightning Source LLC
Chambersburg PA
CBHW060905190726
48286CB00002B/385